American Boy

By: Kevin Brown

Dedicated to Mary Brown. Thank you for everything. I love you.

Chapter 1

I'm willing to bet anything in the world that if my family had to describe me in one word as a child, adorable, intelligent, courteous and polite would all come to mind. But every single one of those words would be overshadowed by a five letter word that I can't deny ... **NOSEY.**

Even as an infant it's said that I would stare in the faces of anyone who spoke around me as if I could fully understand every word coming out of their mouth. And while 'DaDa or MaMa' are usually the first words heard from most babies, mine were instead a full sentence, 'What you say?'

As a toddler I'd bombard anyone I came across with random questions. I know that really doesn't seem like too much of a stretch from the average toddler but I'm told I went overboard. I wanted to know what their name was. Did their Mother name them? Where is their Mother? Did they like their Mother? Was their Mother fat? I'm told the 'fat' question was one of my favorites.

They say I had some type of weird fascination with overweight people. Anytime I came in contact with an obesed person, I immediately began quizzing them on their life as a fat person.

How long have you been fat? Do you like being fat? Are your kid's fat? Do you sit on people? Can you tie your own shoe? Have you ever broken anything when you sat down? Can you put on a seatbelt? What's your favorite food? etc, etc,.

My Mom would try to stop me. But, when you're next in line at the grocery store and the fat guys standing behind you, there's really not much you can do. It wasn't like she could beat the shit out of a two year old or something. So she'd be forced to stand there with the look of shame as some chubby white guy stares her down with the 'Can't you control your own damn baby look'.

By the time I got to pre-school my gift of nosiness had reached an all time high. I had mastered the art of learning my ABC's while still managing to keep tabs on exactly what everyone else in the class was doing. It hurts my heart to say this but I was known as 'Pete the Snitch'. No kid could escape me. But it sort of evened out because at recess, I couldn't escape them. If my memory serves me correct, I caught more than my fair share of baby beat downs.

At night when I was supposed to be tucked in bed asleep, I'd stay up all night listening to the adults in my family engage in 'Grown Folks Business'. Sometimes they'd be talking too low for me to hear everything they'd be saying, so I'd creep over to the door to hear as much as my little ears would allow. There were even times when my Mom would come to my room to wake me up for school and my little ass would be laid out on the floor next to the door.

So, when I turned five and my Mom and Dad finally got Married and got a place together, I was thrilled that it would be the first time, my Mom, my Pops,my baby bro and me would be living under one roof. But what was even better was the fact that my second floor bedroom window had a top notch view of the entire neighborhood.

Looking out my window, I had a clear view of everything. We lived in Wellington Oaks right in the heart of Norfolk, Virginia. It wasn't the worst hood in Norfolk but it for damn sure wasn't the best.

Staring out my window I saw everything. I saw the pre-teen boys playing all types of games, football, basketball, and wrestling; occasionally they'd even pick up a gang of rocks and have rock wars.

I'd see all the neighborhood pre teen girls playing hop scotch and jumping rope. Mostly they just stood around watching the guys play around. Some would even join in with the boys. But when things would get too rough I'd always see some girl crying, storming down the street to tell her Mom that some boy had tackled her too hard or that she'd gotten hit with a rock upside her head.

The late teen crowd was pretty boring. All the guys did was sit around drinking, smoking, talking loud, and shooting dice while the girls just stood around watching. Occasionally the females would get into arguments with each other and they'd have a quick tussle before one of the guys broke it up. But the fights couldn't have been that important because in a couple day's I'd see those same girls back together doing nothing, watching the guys all over again.

Directly across the street from me lived Mrs. Red and her husband Big Tim. If you didn't know them you'd think they were the perfect couple. Every Friday and Saturday they'd get all dressed up and hit the town. I'd be passed out by the time they came home but I'd see them all cleaned up on Sunday morning to hit the 10:00 service for church.

4

I guess too much quality time isn't always a good thing. Those two used to throw down. And when I say throw down, I'm talking about THROW DOWN!

Actually, let me take that back; Big Tim used to throw down. Mrs. Red was usually busy running for cover.

There's one particular instance that really sticks out in my mind. I guess Mrs. Red forgot to tell Big Tim that there wasn't any soap left in the bathroom or something because she came running, screaming to the top of her lungs out the house with him trailing behind in nothing but a towel, body still soaking wet. Mind you, Mrs. Red was a tad bit on the hefty side and Big Tim was about 6 feet tall and athletically built, so it kind of goes without saying that it didn't take him long to capture his prey. Now usually she goes hard for a few seconds and Big Tim would always get the best in the end.

But things were different that day. As Big Tim grabbed her, spinning her around so that they were face to face, instead of swinging recklessly like she usually did, she did the unexpected. In the blink of an eye Mrs. Red grabbed the towel from around Tim's waist and hauled tail down the street.

Did I mention it was a beautiful day outside? The older kids were out, the younger kids were out, ladies were sitting on their porches, men were washing cars and barbequing. Everyone was there to witness Big Tim standing in the middle of the street butt ass naked.

Still that didn't stop him. Nope, he chased Mrs. Red down the street screaming 'I'ma kill you bitch!' When he finally caught her, it wasn't pretty. He pounded her face in like a man. It was beyond sad.

5

Usually when they fought some guy always comes over and breaks it up. But not that day. It seems as if no man was willing to break up a fight with a guy whose balls were swinging all over the place. I can't really remember how that fight got broken up. Big Tim's crazy ass probably just got tired and walked away. I don't know, but up until then, that was the craziest thing I'd ever seen staring out my window. That all changed on May 3rd 2000.

It was about 3 a.m. and I was awoken out of my sleep by the sudden urge to take a piss. I hopped up out of bed and headed for the door, as usual my curiosity (nosiness) got the best of me and I was unable to leave the room without checking out what was going on in the hood. So I walked over to my window and took a glance out into the world. I scanned the block and like most streets at 3 a.m., it was completely empty. I proceeded to make my way to the bathroom before I heard a strange voice seeming to come from the front lawn.

I took another peek and almost jumped out of my socks. There were two goons dressed in all black attempting to break into my Dad's 1997 Nissan Maxima.

"Hurry up, you gon get us knocked," whispered one of the goons.

"Shut up bitch, I don't see your ass doing shit to help" said the other as he stuck what looked like a hanger through a crack in the driver side window.

My little heart was racing. I knew I couldn't just stand there and let them nigga's take my families only means of transportation. But as soon as I was about to make a run for my parent's room, I saw my Dad flying out the house in nothing but his drawers, clutching a wooden baseball bat, prepared to wreck shop on those clowns. "Get the fuck away from my house,' said my Dad, as he cocked back his bat.

"Oh shit," both cowards screamed as they attempted to make their way away from the whip.

They were too slow, my Dad smacked one of the bastard's dead in the shoulder, knocking him to the ground screaming in pain.

"Yall think you can steal from me?" shouted my Dad as he cranked back the bat once more, aiming for the other thug.

I was waiting for my Pops to lay the other thug down flat when I heard a sound that will stick with me for the rest of my life. **BAM!** My Father was shot point blank in the middle of the eyes, dropping him to the ground instantly.

My body transformed into a statue as piss rolled down my leg and I stared at the lifeless body of my Dad lying motionlessly on the ground.

The shooter than picked his accomplice up and took one last look at my Father. "Bitch," bellowed the shooter staring down at my Dad as the other spit on his blood covered face before escaping into the night.

Seconds later my Mom rushed out of the house screaming at the sight of the only man she'd ever loved spread out on the front lawn. "Oh my God …Help … Help," she shouted with tears streaming down her face. She dropped down onto her knees cradling my Dad's bloody head. At that moment there's no question that she wanted to go with him.

Neighbors from all over rushed to the scene. I still hadn't blinked nor moved as Mrs. Red fell to the ground next to my Mom. "Who did this?, Who did this?" she asked my Mom failing to realize that my Mother's body had just went limp leaving her and my Father both laying flat on the ground.

"Mommy," screamed my baby brother Korbin as he ran out of the house before a neighbor grabbed him and shielded him from the horror scene.

"Oh my God," screamed Mrs. Red, finally noticing that my Mother was out cold. "Call the Ambulance, call the fucking Ambulance," she screamed as more neighbors gathered around talking amongst themselves.

I had just witnessed my Father killed right before my eyes. And even though I loved him, I had no emotions. It's like as soon as that bullet hit him, his soul rose from his body to mine and at that very moment I became a man. Sadly his soul didn't come with his wisdom, I was gonna have to learn that the best way I knew how.

Chapter 2

"50 dollars," shouted Trell holding a fifty dollar bill up to the sky. "Feels good to be a working man. I think I might take Tinka to the movies tonight."

"In your dreams," said Josh wiping the sweat off of his face. It was the first day of summer and it was blazing hot. I think the birds were even sweating. It definitely didn't make it any better that we were all hauling lawn mowers and weed whackers down the street.

"You crazy," said Trell. "I was on the phone with her for 3 hours last night."

"Well while she was on the phone with you she was texting me, telling me how she wanted a little cream in her coffee," said Josh.

"Stop lyin," Trell said as Josh smiled. "I'ma ask her."

I was too busy being hypnotized by the money I held in my hands to be worried about what Josh and Trell were talking about. "I'm savin my money," I said.

"Savin?" asked Trell.

"For what?" followed Josh

"I don't know yet I just know I can't go to high school broke."

We all smiled.

"Freshman year of high school. I can't wait," said Josh gazing up to the sky.

"Me either," said Trell licking his lips. "Norview High ain't never seen a nigga like me before. I swear this gon be some of the best times of our lives, watch."

"Hell yeah," said Josh as we continued our journey to the crib.

If it's one thing I'm sure of it's that if me Josh and Trell get together, there's gonna be some type of argument. Trell's pretty ass always thought he was better than everybody at everything, Josh's white ass thought he knew everything and my ass just always seemed to get caught up in the middle of their bullshit. But what can I say, they're my homies. I couldn't imagine life without them. From the moment I met them in Mrs. Ebert's six grade class, they made me feel right at home. A feeling I hadn't felt in a long time.

After my Pops died my Mom couldn't really afford the rent in Wellington Oaks anymore and with my Daddy being a former foster kid, he didn't have any family we could lean on, so we moved to Tidewater Park Projects in downtown Norfolk with my Grandma and my Mom's youngest Brother Damon.

Grandma's rent was dirt cheap so she didn't charge us anything which was cool cause my Mom was able to get a little part time gig to take care of us and still go to school full time.

Living with my Grandma wasn't anything new, I had lived with her the first four years of my life before my Mom and Dad had got their place. But this time it was different. Everything was different, the entire world. Not a single night went past where I didn't have some sort of nightmare about my Pops dying. I never told my Mom or anyone what I had seen. Fuck that, I just kept it inside.

Besides, my Mom had so much on her plate, I didn't want to bother her with my problems. I was only five when we moved back in, but I knew my Mom well enough to know that she wasn't the same person anymore. She still laughed and joked, read bedtime's stories and all that good stuff but there was something missing. When I looked into her eyes I saw pain and worry. This damn sure wasn't the same Mom who had the power to brighten anyone's day by saying something as simple as 'hello'. So I did my best to stay out of trouble.

Luckily that wasn't so hard considering the fact that my Grandma was crazy. She had earned her license in ass whippings and wasn't afraid to use it. I can still picture her sticking her head out the front door everyday at 6 and screaming, "Pete get your lil butt in this house, you know your Mama don't allow you out all times of the night."

Talk about embarrassing, all the other kids my age could stay out as late as they wanted. They were all like 21 year olds trapped in six year old bodies. Words can't even explain how much I wanted to be like them. Who wouldn't? Especially living in Tidewater Park, it was like a world of its own. There was no need to leave the Park for shit.

Candy ladies in every court. The food truck stopped by every night. Every weekend there was at least 3 or 4 Selling Parties going on.

Of course I never did drugs but I know for a fact you could get anything you needed. I can't count the times I overheard my Uncle telling someone to meet him around

11

the corner before he'd make his way to his shoe box under his bed. The same one I just so happen to bump into every time he left the house.

And let's not get to talking about clothes. Tee-Tee and her sisters boosted and they had anything you needed; Roca-Wear, LRG, Coach, Gucci, Jordan's, Air force 1's you name it Tee-Tee had it.

Car fucked up? No problem, Johnny Mac could handle anything from a full body paint job to an oil leak. He was an ol black ass nigga. Word on the street was that he used to be light skinned but he loved car's so much he started sweating engine oil and it transformed his ass or some shit. I don't know how true it is but I know he got my Mom's hoop ride back on the road more than a couple times.

The entertainment in the projects was endless. Bootleg movies and cd's were floating around everywhere. My Mom didn't believe in buying bootleg shit, she thought that it was stealing. But Grandma and my Uncle didn't give a damn. We had every movie before they hit the theatres and every CD before it hit the shelf. 3 for 10? Mom's was tripping.

But the scheme that really took the cake was my Grandma's best friend, Charlottes Grandson Kevin's. He had scored a job working at the Navy Exchange. It was some big ass military mall where they sold everything, even all the latest clothes and electronics, resulting in Kevin coming up with the scheme of a life time. I guess security didn't really expect those military nigga's to steal so they were loose as hell. And that was the biggest mistake they could ever make.

Once Kevin found that out, he got his homies to come up there and rack up. You're supposed to have a military I.D. to buy shit but Kev was at the register so that wasn't an issue. All his homeboy's would come up there, put hella shit in their basket while Kev pretended to ring everything up, but in reality all he'd really ring up was probably a 50 cent piece of candy just so a receipt would come out.

After that, his homies would walk on out casually, receipt in hand straight to their whip. Then they'd retreat back to the park and make a killing. I swear they did that shit for about a year before Kev got locked up. And the crazy thing is, he got locked up for robbing a pizza man, the Navy Exchange never even caught on to what he was doing. To this day that nigga's a hood legend.

Of course since I was in the house at 6 every night I didn't really get to witness any of that shit I just mentioned. I just know it because at school and the little time that I did spend outside the kids used to talk about it all day.

Oh yeah, did I mention there were kids every where? That's another great thing about Tidewater Park; a parent never had to find play dates for their kids. No bullshit, there was probably at least 5 kids in every crib. And if there did just so happen to be a crib that only had one kid who actually lived there, I guarantee their Mom's best friends kids, cousins or boyfriend sister baby mama kids were there. I guarantee it.

From having my own room to going back to sleeping in the same bed as my Mom and baby bro was hard. But again, I could deal with it. I had a perfect view of the whole hood and this shit was 20 times better than Wellington Oaks.

Looking out that window was better than being in the movies. I saw women jumping men, men jumping women, prostitutes getting slapped, kids getting whipping, drive-by's, block parties, kids having tumbling competitions on old dirty mattresses, feigns smoking crack, nigga's rolling weed, nigga's getting drunk, niggas falling out after getting too drunk, niggas getting shot, girls getting shot, kids getting shot, police running in cribs, niggas running from the police, local rappers shooting videos, famous rappers shooting videos, niggas sneaking in their girlfriends windows, girls fighting their mom's, whole families fighting other whole families.

I saw it all and my Mom hated it. So when she finally graduated from nursing school she searched endlessly for a job before finding one about twenty minutes from Richmond, Va. in a small town called Norview, only a population of a bout ten or fifteen thousand people. It was about a two hour drive from Norfolk but who cares? Despite everything the Park had to offer I couldn't wait to move. It had been six years and I was still having nightmares about my Dad, my Mom was still not back to her regular self and Korb, well Korb was the same but you get the point.

From the second we moved to Norview I realized I was far, far away from Tidewater Park. There were big beautiful trees, big ass lakes, Mom and Pop stores everywhere, nice cribs, they had a few ghetto spots too but even they had nothing on Tidewater Park.

The people here were so friendly and for the first time in years I saw white people. Lots of them. The only white people I was used to seeing before was the police or white boy Louie and his family but they weren't really white. I mean their skin was white but they dressed, talked, and acted like straight up niggas. These new white people in Norview were really white. I'm talking about walking their dogs in shorts and flip flops in the winter time white.

And even though you catch a lot of them with confederate flag bumper stickers or tee-shirts they were still some nice ass crackers. The blacks still hung with the blacks and whites hung with the whites but everyone was living peacefully. It was like some shit Dr. King would be proud of.

Don't let me forget to mention our crib. Mom's got a sweet ass 3 bedroom with an upstairs and 2 bathrooms. She had been saving so she bought all type of dope furniture from IKEA. We was living large if I do say so myself.

Still the best thing of all, I had my own room. And it wasn't just some little closet sized room like I had in Wellington Oaks. Nope, this time I had some ol player shit. I had a TV with cable, a queen size bed, play station 3, walk in closet, big ass dressers. It was the shit. I threw up posters of all my favorite entertainers like Lil Wayne, and Michael Vick, I always wanted to do that shit. I even through a picture of my Dad on my Dresser. For years I couldn't even look at his face. But things were different now. I wasn't even having nightmares anymore.

I was happy, Korb was happy and I could tell my Mom was too. She even met two cool Nurses who worked with her, Aunt Fonda and Aunt Tina. Things were really starting to look up. And with Trell and Josh around, things couldn't get any better. Life was good.

15

"Yo ain't that Sho down there?" asked Trell pointing down the street to Sho, who was walking towards us smoking a cigarette.

He looked like a million dollars. I remember seeing some comedy show where Jamie Foxx said that when he first saw Prince in person he had some sorta glow around him; well that's exactly what Sho had. He was seven-teen and probably the coolest nigga in Norview history. He had been in and out of detention and group homes since he was 12. Whenever there was trouble in Norview, nine times out of ten. Naw scratch that, ten times out of ten Sho was involved. There wasn't a kid in town who didn't respect him. The nigga had the key to the city, he was special. And since I was his first cousin, I was special too.

Sho was my Mom's oldest brother's kid. When we first moved here we didn't even know each other. My uncle had babies every damn where but as soon as we were introduced he treated me more like a little bro than a little cousin. I couldn't have asked for a better role model.

"What's poppin?" said Sho as he greeted us all with dap.

We all said "What's up."

"Man don't tell me yall been up all mornin cuttin some fuckin grass," Sho said as he looked down at our gardening tools.

"Yeah," said Josh. "What's wrong with that?"

"Yeah, we gotta get paid," said Trell, flashing his 50 dollar bill.

"Yeah I guess you right," said Sho. "But I know otha ways to get paid." Sho was a professional thief, if you had it and he wanted it consider it gone. "Yo did yall hea bout that party tonight?" asked Sho as he did a little dance.

"Hell yeah I'm definitely trying to be in there," Josh replied.

"Who the hell told you bout it, white boy?" barked Sho.

Hangin out with Josh you were bound to hear at least 10 references to the color of his skin a day. Like I said all the whites stuck with the whites and vice versa but to me and Trell, Josh was just a lighter version of us. And it wasn't even like he was trying to be black or anything. He was just a cool ass kid. Me and Trell even gave Josh permission to say nigga. We got tired of him saying 'The N-word' when telling a story. He never actually said it but if he did it wouldn't have mattered he was my nigga either way.

Josh looked over to Trell with a devilish grin and answered Sho, "Tinka."

I couldn't help but laugh as I peeped the look on Trell's face. He and Josh had both been trying to smash Tinka for the longest time. Like most everybody our age they were on a race to lose their virginity. I to, wanted to lose mine but to tell the truth I ain't know what to say to girls. I had been practicing in my mirror a lot but I hadn't quite gotten it down pat yet.

"True, I'ma hit yall lil niggas up lata to see if yall hittin it up or not," Sho said looking at the time on his g-shock. "Nicole's Mom don't get off till 7 and we gotta lil

17

business to handle," he said, smiling showing off all 12 of his gold teeth.

He dapped us all and continued walking down the street as we all said, "Alright Sho" in unison.

"Yo we gotta be at that party," said Trell as we continued walking down the street.

"Hell yeah," I said smiling from ear to ear. "I know it's gon be jumpin stupid hard."

"Damn right, I can't wait," said Josh rubbing his hands together. "But in the mean time, yall feel like getting your asses bust in a couple games of Madden?"

"Man I'm the King of Madden and yall know that," I said.

"Hell naw I'm the King," followed Trell.

"Well how about yall put your money where your mouth is," Josh said with sly grin.

After leaving Josh's crib I could hardly walk a straight line. The thought of going to my first High School Party had me trippin. I couldn't help but picture all those old school Uncle Luke videos and House Party Movies I'd seen. My brain was filled with images of booty's bouncing everywhere. To a 14 year old virgin this was going to be the closest thing to sex. Not to mention I was going with Sho. This was a dream come true.

As I approached my porch I saw Korb and his best friend Rell chilling, sippin on some kool-aid. I had so much nervous energy and excitement built inside of me that I was forced to smack the cups out of their hands and began terrorizing.

"Mama," screamed Korbin as I held both he and Rell in headlocks.

"Let me go," screamed Rell.

All I could do was laugh. Beating up on Korbin was one of my favorite past times. Plus Sho told me that if I ain't want him to be a bitch, thats the kind of shit I had to do.

I was just about to double sumo slam them when my Mom came rushing to the door panicking. "Oh my God, Korbin. I thought someone was really trying to kidnap you," she said with her hand placed over her heart.

I let go of Rell and held Korbs face up to my Mom. "Kidnap? Have you seen this boy lately? I'm surprised he's allowed to even come out in public."

In actuality Korb was really a cute kid but it just did something to me to call him name's any chance I could get.

"Whatever Pete," said Mom as she made her way over to Korb. "My baby's gorgeous." She kissed Korb on the cheek.

Korb looked over to Rell, embarrassed and wiped the kiss off. "I'm not a baby. Eww."

We all laughed as Mom and I made our way into the house. Aunt Fonda and Aunt Tina were sitting down on the couch. They both smiled when they caught a glimpse of me. Man, I love them. Neither one of them had kids of their own so I was sorta like their son too. It's cool most of the time, unless I'm with all three of them and men can't keep their eyes off of them. That shit pisses me off. But hey even Stevie Wonder could see how beautiful they all were. Still, I wish men could just keep their eyes to themselves. They were my girls.

"Hey my Peta Wida," said Aunt Tina as I walked over to give them both a hug.

"Hey Aunt Fond, hey Aunt Tina," I said hugging them both.

"Hey Pete," said Aunt Fonda as she pushed me away with her hand over her nose. "Boy, you smell just like outside."

I proudly stepped back before pulling out the cash I had earned today. "That's how it is when you a workin man."

"Wow, what are you going to buy me with all that money?" asked Aunt Fonda as her and Aunt Tina both sat back down.

"I don't know. What do you prefer the Benz or the Lex?"

"I think I'd prefer the Lex."

"Alright, alright. I got you next week. I need this money right here for the party tonight."

"Party?" asked my Mom. She was now sitting on the couch next to Aunt Fonda and Tina. I knew she would have something to say. But I knew this was the best time to spring it on her. She's always in a good mood when her friends were over.

"Yep. Me and the homies are going."

I was trying a new method. I usually gave her a little childish whine whenever I wanted something. But since I'm trying to go to a teen party I thought it would be best if I took control and showed her I was growing up.

"Are you asking or telling me?"

I could tell by the sound of her voice she wasn't digging the whole *'taking control'* thing so I went back to old faithful. "Mommy please. You gotta let me go. It's the first party of the summer everybody's gonna be there."

"Where's the party?"

"At Chantal's down the street."

"And are her parents going to be home?"

"Of course they are." I really didn't know if they were going to be home or not. To tell the truth I prayed they would be nowhere in sight. You can't really grind comfortably on some ass with somebody's old ass Daddy staring dead at you.

"Well ok just be home by 11."

11? What the hell is wrong with her? I'm 14 years old. What if some chick wants me to sneak into her crib for a little late night rendezvous. This is crazy. "Ma its 2008, parties don't even get live till 12."

"Well pretend like its 1968 and have your butt in this house by 11."

"But Ma." She gave me the look that let me know that if I didn't shut up things could get worse. Still I had to say one last thing. I looked over to Aunt Fonda and Tina. "Yall see what I gotta deal with?"

21

"Pete, you're only 14 years old you have plenty of time to stay out all night," said Aunt Fonda as Aunt Tina and my Mom nodded their heads, agreeing.

I shook my head and walked up to the staircase. I took one last look at Aunt Fonda before saying, "I see you're working with the enemy. You can forget about that Lex." We all laughed.

When I got to my room I turned on some Gucci Mane and hopped in the box. I scrubbed my body as hard as I could. I knew it might get hot and steamy in the party and I wasn't trying to be the nigga with the musty balls.

After about thirty minutes I hopped out the box and jetted to my room, popped open the closet door and pulled out my new LRG fit my Mom had copped me for my B-Day a couple weeks ago. I had only worn it once and that was when I went to see my Grandma out Tidewater Park, so no one in Norview had even seen me rock it yet. I had been waiting for the perfect time to whip it out and what better time than now.

With my favorite Gucci Mane song *'I'm the Shit'* still blasting and my new fit on, I felt like a superstar. I stood in front of my body sized mirror that hung from my closet door and used my cell phone to take some pictures of me. This shit was definitely going on MySpace and Facebook.

Even after I was done snapping pictures I still couldn't pull myself away from the mirror. I was looking good. Boy, was I feeling myself.

When Sho finally called and told me he was on his way to my crib I could've fainted. The time was finally here. I strutted downstairs slowly; I decided to hold in my

22

excitement, it was time to be mature. When I made it to the bottom of the staircase my Mom and Aunts were all staring at me as if I was about to go to Prom or something. They always did shit like this. If I didn't hurry up I'd be taking pictures and hearing stories about their first times going to a house party. I definitely didn't feel like hearing all that so I headed straight for the door. "Bye yall," I said without making eye contact with any of them.

"Bye Pete," they all yelled as I closed the door.

When I stepped outside Sho was already sitting on the porch. I thought I looked good but this nigga was 10 times fresher than me. He had the latest J's and a True Religion fit, not to mention his fitted cap matched everything to the T. This nigga looked like he was supposed to be posing for the Source magazine or something.

"What's up," I said. We gave each other dap.

"What's good lil nigga? You ready to get right?" he asked as he whipped out a bag of weed and smiled.

"Come on man, put that down my Mom's in there," I said, quickly looking back at the door. I couldn't believe this nigga was actually flashing drugs on my porch. Does he not know who my Mama is? "What's that for?" I whispered.

"Nigga, what you think it's for," he answered, tucking the weed back into his pockets. "Call your homies and tell' em to meet us at the pier. I'm about to show yall boys how to live."

Man, this wasn't in the plans, I had never really even thought about doing drugs. Yeah, I saw Sho high all

23

the time but he always looked sleepy and shit. Why in the hell would I want to be sleepy in a party? I was tryna be hype in that bitch. But how could I tell him no? Plus it can't hurt just to try it. Can it?

Sho and I walked down to the pier. It was this small dock behind a bunch of tree's and shit. No one really ever went over there so it was the perfect spot to smoke. I was nervous as hell the whole walk over, I was trying to come up with ways to tell Sho why I couldn't smoke. So far I hadn't come up with one single reason that Sho wouldn't have a comeback for. But Josh and Trell were on their way up here. They didn't know what we were about to do but hopefully they could come up with some type of an excuse.

After about 15 minutes of throwing rocks into the lake, Trell and Josh arrived and the first thing both of their eyes saw was Sho sitting on the dock fiddling with the weed.

"Yall bouta smoke?" blurted out Trell.

"Naw we bouta smoke," replied Sho as he looked at Josh and Trell dead in their eyes. It was obvious this was a demand.

"Whoa man. I can't smoke. I've got asthma," said Josh.

Damn why didn't I think of that. So simple, yet so perfect.

"Well I hope you bought your inhala," said Sho.

I knew if that didn't work, nothing would.

"But what if someone smells it on us in the party?" asked Trell.

"So? Yall niggas needa chill with all this bitchen. Yall wanna party with the big dog's, yall gonna learn to live like the big dog's." We all sat silent. There was nothing else to say. "So I'm guessin don't none of yall niggas know how to roll a blunt.

We all shook our heads.

"Man yall niggas pitiful. 14 years old and can't even roll a damn blunt. What is the world comin to?" he said as he pulled out a cigar from his pocket. "I'ma teach yall one time and one time only. Watch and learn."

We all got a closer view of Sho and studied as he unwrapped the wrapper and split the cigar down the middle. He then released the guts into the lake before sprinkling the weed into the cigar and rolling it up until it looked like some brown overgrown cigarette. He was done in less than 2 minutes and had made it look so easy. It was obvious that he was a pro.

"Voila," said Sho holding the blunt up to the sky.

"That's it?" asked Trell.

"Yep. Simple as a mo'fucker. One of yall niggas got a lighta?"

Trell and Josh shook their heads as I searched through my pockets.

"Bro, you know your ass ain't got no lighta," Trell said looking over at me.

"Nigga you don't know what I got," I said.

I knew I didn't have a lighter. Guess I was just trying to be cool. They all continued to stare at me as I pulled nothing but lint from my pockets.

Everyone laughed. "Amateurs," said Sho pulling a lighter from his pockets.

We all silently watched as Sho sparked the blunt and began hitting it. He looked as if he was gliding through the gates of heaven each time he inhaled. Maybe this wouldn't be so bad after all.

I was the closest person to Sho, so naturally he handed the blunt over to me. I slowly grabbed it.

Damn. I was scared but I knew the longer I thought about it the harder it would be. So I closed my eyes, put the blunt to my mouth and inhaled. I immediately blew the smoke out. Yes, I did it! That wasn't so hard. I opened my eyes with a feeling up triumph. All eyes were on me.

"Nigga what the hell you doin?" asked Sho.

What the fuck did he mean what was I doing? I swear I just did the exact same thing he had done.

"I'm smokin. What it look like I'm doin," I said with the blunt still in my hand.

"Nigga it look like you don't know what the hell you doin. You gotta get the smoke inside your chest," he replied as he pounded on his chest while inhaling then exhaling. "Then you release that shit. Try it again."

I took a deep breath and looked around. They were all still watching me. The pressure was on. So I tried once more. This time holding the smoke in my chest. Instantly smoke surrounded my lungs and took over as I coughed.

"You almost got it. Just do it smootha. Don't let the weed beat you up."

I regained my breath and once again everything was silent. I felt like I was taking the game winning free throw, so I put the blunt back up to my mouth and hit it one more time. Inhaled the smoke until I felt it reach the middle of my chest and released it with no problems. I did it! I know I did it!

"Yeah. Just like that. Now pass my blunt. 2 and P, puff puff pass baby," said Sho snatching the blunt from me and passing it over to Josh. I couldn't wait to see him fail. I saw them snickering the entire time I was trying.

Josh took a drag and just like I thought, FAIL. He eventually got it and Trell did the same. We kicked it for a while laughing and joking, feeling accomplished. We all had finally gotten the hang of this smoking thing.

When the blunt was gone and I was officially high, it didn't take any time at all to determine how I felt about it.

I felt great! I know I'm a virgin and all but I felt like King Dingaling. I felt like I could fuck for 10 hours straight. I felt like I could build a spaceship. Like I could climb Mount Everest. Or I'd just hit the jack pot for a billion dollars. I felt like Buster Douglas when he knocked Mike Tyson's ass out. I felt like smacking asses. I felt like smacking niggas. I felt like the Motherfucking Man!

And from the looks of things I wasn't the only one feeling that way. We were still chilling on the pier off into

27

our own zone when Josh said, "I can't wait to get in that party."

"Hell yeah," said Trell. "It's gonna be bitties everywhere."

"Man, yall needa stop worryin bout these bitches," said Sho as he pulled out a big ass stack of money filled with 20 and 10 dollar bills. "And start thinkin about this right hea. This shit'll get you anything you want in the world."

"What are you talking about?" asked Josh. "We made 50 dollars each this morning."

"50 dollars? 50 dollars?" screamed Sho. "Man that's fuckin chump change. I'll shit 50 dollars."

"Well I don't think I can do any crimes to get cash. I'm too pretty to go to jail," said Trell as he caressed his acne free face.

"What?" Sho screamed once again. "Nigga every black man go to jail at least once in his life. These cracka's hate us and they'll do anything to get our black asses off these streets."

I looked over to Josh. I wanted to see how he felt about Sho saying cracker like that. But he didn't seem bothered. He knew how Sho was.

"I don't know Sho. My uncle's a cop and he's a pretty cool guy," said Josh.

"Yeah he's cool to you," Sho said before pointing to himself, Trell and I. "But he hates our black asses. You don't see all these damn confederate flags swingin round hea. You lyin to yourself if you think shits all good. For a white boy to go to jail he gotta do some ol crazy shit. While we get locked for J walkin."

"Fuck that, I still ain't goin," I said dapping Trell and Josh up.

"Hell yeah I'm with Pete. I'ma just stay my black ass outta their way," said Trell.

"Nigga you can't," said Sho. This nigga was angry. I could see veins popping out of his neck. "Your life ain't shit but a game to them dog. You just gotta play smart."

"What you mean play smart?" I asked. I always had to make sure I understood everything Sho said. He was famous for quizzing us on his lessons.

"They gon catch you sometimes, you just gotta know how to get lose," Sho said as he stood to his feet. I knew he was feeling it. He was a hood professor.

"Get lose?" asked Trell. Trell was obviously thinking about those pop quizzes too.

"Yeah you gotta be smarta than them cracka's. If they ain't catch you in the act of doin whateva the hell they said you did. Then they ass don't know shit," said Sho.

"So how they arrest you if they don't know nothing?" I asked.

"Cause its dumb niggas like yall who tell them everything they need to know."

"What?" asked Trell.

We were really into this. I still kept looking over to Josh. He looked as if he was listening too.

"Nigga who would take you in a room and ask you a million questions if they already knew the answers?"

"So they just trying to see if you crack?" I asked.

"Exactly." Sho shouted. "That's why I act like Helen Keller when they got me in that bitch."

"Helen Keller?" asked Trell.

Trell was a dumbass. He was OD'ing with the questions now.

"Damn I ain't been to school in three years and I know more than your ass."

"That's the girl who couldn't hear or see," said Josh.

"Yep, that's why only four words come outta my mouth," said Sho as he counted on his fingers. "I …Need … A … Lawyer."

"But what if they tell you if you talk they'll let you go?" I asked.

"Don't believe a damn thing they tell you. Just sit there and be quiet," said Sho as he rolled up his shirt sleeve exposing a tattoo on his upper arm that read 'Neva Snitch' in bold letters. "The numba one rule a man should live by 'Neva Snitch'. It's all about loyalty. I am my brotha's keepa," he said before his mood suddenly changed from serious to happy. "Alright that was the Sho lesson of the day. Yall tryna hit this party or what?"

We all sprung up, excited. "Hell yeah," we shouted.

"Let's go," I said. My high was even better now that I was standing up. With all the talking Sho did I had forgotten that I had even smoked.

We all stumbled our way towards the dirt path. If someone didn't know any better they would've thought me, Trell and Josh had just inhaled some laughing gas.

"Yo. I think I'm high," said Trell.

"Me too," followed Josh.

"Of course yall high. Yall smoked a woola," said Sho.

"A wooler?" Josh asked.

"Yeah nigga, weed with crack sprinkled in it," Sho said calmly.

Our eyes all popped out of our heads and our smiles quickly vanished. "What?" we all shouted.

"Calm down crack ain't neva hurt nobody," said Sho. "Stop actin like some ol pussy ass niggas.   "

I immediately stuck my finger down my throat trying my hardest to gag. Trell picked up some old half full Aquafina bottle off the ground and splashed it onto his face as Josh dropped to the ground hypervinalating, screaming, "I think I'm dying. I think I'm dying."

Sho fell to the ground laughing uncontrollably. "Stop, stop, stop. Yall killin me. I ain't put no damn crack in it. Chill out."

31

We all looked at Sho and burst out laughing. For a minute I thought I was a certified crack head. I saw my entire life flashing by. Thank God that was a joke.

Walking into that party felt like a dream. Actually it was better than a dream. I don't think there's a word in the English language to describe the feeling. The room was dark and everyone seemed to be moving in slow motion. Girls were everywhere and I don't know if it was because I was high but they all looked amazing. Short skirts, daisy dukes', halter tops, this had to be how heaven looked.

All eyes were on us. Well they were actually on Sho but we were next to him so it was just like they were looking at us. Plus Sho didn't even seem to notice all the obvious attention bestowed upon him. He was so smooth. He walked straight through the crowd of teen's screaming his name "Sho", "What's up Sho," "Hey Sho," only to give a couple head nods. This nigga was a neighborhood superstar. Me, Josh, and Trell made sure we stayed as close as possible.

Especially Trell, he made sure that there was no way anyone could miss him. "TRELL ... IS ... IN ... THE ... BUILDING," he screamed over the loud music. A couple people looked over to him but Sho's spotlight was too strong.

He led us to an empty corner of the party where we kicked back against the wall. Even in the corner I could still feel countless eyes beaming in our direction. This was officially the V.I.P. section.

We weren't standing there for 2 minutes before some chick seductively walked over to Sho and started grinding all up on him. And I'm talking really grinding. I definitely wanted a piece of that action.

It seems as if Josh and Trell wanted some too. "Yo I gotta get one of these shorties," said Trell as he looked out into the crowd.

"Me too," said Josh before locking his eyes into a particular section of the party. I looked over and there was Tinka, dancing by herself on the opposite side of the room. "And Tinka's right there," said Josh as he rushed towards her.

"Oh hell naw that's my girl," said Trell as he speeded over to catch up with Josh.

I was now alone. Josh and Trell were over there trying to win Tinka's heart(pussy) and Sho was now dancing with a completely different girl and this one was even freakier than the last. Suddenly I felt out of place. Everyone was dancing around, having a good ol time and I was stuck on the wall, dolo. I prayed to myself that some chick would rush over to me like they did for Sho. But after about an hour the only thing I had done was watch Sho switch chicks every song and Josh and Trell continue to fight over Tinka. A couple girls had looked my direction and some had even walked over but of course they were only making their way over to Sho.

There were even a couple songs when the nigga had two girls at one time. Shit was ridiculous. Every time I'd look over to him he'd point to one of his girls as if I wanted him to pass her to me. But fuck that I wasn't gonna settle for his hand-me-downs. Even though most of the girls looked damn good I still was determined to find my own.

33

After a while I was starting to get frustrated and my high was coming down. It was already 9:30, only had an hour and a half left to work magic. So I scrolled my eyes through the party. There were plenty of guys dancing with girls but I didn't want to go out there by myself. If stupid ass Josh and Trell would get off of Tinka's nuts maybe I'd have some confidence but those niggas was over there making a Tinka sandwich by now. All three of them looked like they were having the time of their life. Faggots.

I continued scrolling my eyes through the party until I spotted some girl staring dead at me. At first I figured she was looking at Sho but as I took a better look it was clear to see that it was me she was watching. And this wasn't just any girl, this was a pretty girl and she wasn't just staring, she was giving me the *'I want you'* eyes. Well at least that's what it looked like to me. But considering the fact I'd never had a girl before I wasn't really too sure. I needed some confirmation. But how would I know?

I looked over to Sho and to my surprise he was already looking at me. He pointed with his head and mouthed the words, "Who's that?"

"I don't know," I mouthed back.

"Well nigga you betta find out," he mouthed sternly.

I looked back over to the girl and she was still staring. Only now she was smiling. Boy did she have a beautiful smile. The party was dark but I could still see her ocean deep dimples. I began panicking.

'What do I do, what do I do' I thought. I looked back over to Sho. He was still staring at me. I quickly turned back to my admirer. She too was still staring. It was now or never. I was on my way to High School. It was time

34

to be a man. So I closed my eyes, took a deep breath and mustered up enough courage to walk over to her.

The walk over seemed eternal as I repeated under my breath "Don't say anything stupid," over and over.

By the time I had finally gotten over to her I realized that I had forgotten one major fact-- I had no idea what to say. She was now only a foot away from me and her face was even more beautiful. Her hair was done up all pretty in some type of braids that I'd been seeing all the popular girls wear. And not only did she have dimples but she had the cutest little mole on her right cheek. Even the scar on the corner of her forehead was sexy. She wasn't even dressed like any of the other girls. I don't know what the hell you call the outfit she had on but the pants came to her knees and she had a little button up with lots of little beaded jewelry. She wasn't showing hardly any skin; still she stuck out like a sore thumb.

Realizing I had been standing there for about a minute without saying one word I said the first thing that came to my mind. "Yo."

I couldn't believe I had just said that. Yo? Yo? That's not the type of shit you say to a girl. She wasn't my homeboy. I had to be the dumbest nigga in this bitch.

"Yo," she said back, still smiling, staring, waiting for me to continue talking.

I thought long and hard for my next line. Still all I came up with was, "What's your name?"

Unfortunately at the same time I popped my question, Juveniles *'Back That Ass Up'* came blasting through the stereo resulting in her not hearing a word that I'd said .

"Huh?" she asked.

"What's your--," I said before realizing that there was no way possible she'd hear anything that came out of my mouth. So I thought fast. "Can we talk outside?" I screamed pointing to the door.

There really is a God; she smiled, nodding her head. Boy she was sexy. She then turned to her friends. I recognized them all. They went to school with me. A couple of them were even in my class. How hadn't I seen this girl before?

I quickly took my attention off of her friends and noticed that this unnamed bombshell had a phat ass. It was perfect. I could tell by her face and the girls she was chilling with that she was my age but boy, that booty was grown. Damn.

She turned back around and I noticed that one of her friends had given her a bottle of pepper spray. That was kind of weird but fuck it at least she was coming outside.

We made our way to the front door. I was strategizing what I could say to her but nothing was coming to mind. I was a nervous wreck, I exhaled.

When we finally got outside we sat down on Chantal's porch next to one another. The porch light brought out even more of her beauty. Her skin shined bright like a diamond. I was sitting next to an Angel. Maybe that's the reason I somehow felt completely comfortable. She had some sorta calming spirit.

"So what's your name?" I asked as I fell victim to her big brown eyes.

"Sharee. Pete," she said with an attitude.

It's funny. I know I should've been wondering how the hell she already knew my name but instead I was thinking about how wonderful my name sounded falling from her tongue. She said it in a way that no one had ever said it before. She sorta sung it. There was no way she could be from Norview. We're southern but she had a little extra country twang on her. I wanted to ask for her to say it one more time, instead I decided to play it cool and ask her the obvious.

"Whoa. How'd you know my name?"

"I just know things."

Neither one of us had took our eyes off of one another yet. This was getting good.

"You just know things, huh? So what other things you know?"

"Well I know you and your little friends like to wake people up with lawn mowers at 8 in the freakin mornin."

Lawn mowers? She must live around my neighborhood. But where? How could I have ever missed a girl like her? Still I had to play it cool. "Ay, a man's gotta make his money."

"Well a man needs to learn to wait till I wake up to be making all that noise. It's the summer time fool."

She still spoke with so much attitude. Sexy attitude.

"Maybe if I had your numba I could know when you're up."

I couldn't believe I had just said that. Where did that come from? Since when did I know how to spit game? I was liking this. I was liking this a lot. And if I didn't know any better I'd say she did too.

"I don't know. You might be some sorta thug like your cousin Sho. And I don't do the whole thug thing."

I gotta admit I was kind of flattered that she put me and Sho's name in the same sentence. But if she didn't like thugs then a thug is the last thing I want to be. Still how did she know so much about me?

"Whoa. You been stalking me or something?"

"Stalkin?"She said it like I had offended her. Like she was too good to ever stalk anyone. She was. "No fool. I just moved to Norview from Memphis and my cousin Ciara gave me the scoop on everything and everybody around here."

Ciara, she was one of the girls Sharee had been in the party with. She was in my Social Studies class last year. Her ass got on my damn nerves. She was one of those females who was always mad about something. If she had told Sharee about me then I know it wasn't good.

"Oh, well I'm far from a thug," I said as I gave her one of those looks I had seen Larenz Tate give Nia Long in 'Love Jones'. "But Memphis huh? What brings you to my neck of the woods?"

"Well--" Sharee was rudely interrupted by her cousin Ciara. The loud music completely ruined the mood.

38

"Girl you betta bring your tail in hea. Your song on," said Ciara, sticking her little peanut head out of the door.

"Oh snap," Sharee said. She hopped up quickly as if she wasn't just engaging in the best 3 minute convo of my life. I gave Ciara an Ice Cube gangsta mug before focusing back on Sharee.

"What about your numba?" I asked as I smiled, showing Sharee she wasn't the only one with dimples.

"I'll take yours," she answered, returning the smile as she reached for her phone. "What is it?"

"834-4343."

"Ok. Maybe I'll give you a call."

What did she mean by maybe? Did she not feel what I felt? But fuck it who am I kidding I'd take a maybe from her any day. Still I was playing it cool. "That's what's up."

Sharee and Ciara darted back into the crib.

I was thrilled. I didn't know what to do with myself but before I could even fully comprehend what had just occurred I was bumped by some girl storming her way into the party.

When I looked up to see who it was, my heart dropped. It was Nicole. Sho's Nicole, everybody knew Nicole was crazy. Shit, almost as crazy as Sho. Someone must've told her about all these girls surrounding him. I had already seen Sho and Nicole

39

fight each other tons of times so I knew this wasn't good. I had to warn my nigga.

I rushed into the party praying that I could somehow run into Sho before Nicole caught him all hugged up. I pushed my way through the party but it was too wild. They were playing *'Knuck if you Buck'* and the entire party was going nuts. This is one of those songs that make everyone jump around, pushing people. I knew this would be the perfect soundtrack for Nicole. I couldn't let it go down.

Too late. By the time I could get to a view of Sho, Nicole was 2ft away from him. Sho's back was facing the party. It looked as though he was tonguing some chick down. I could only watch from afar as the mayhem began.

"Who the fuck is this bitch?" screamed Nicole as she grabbed Sho by the collar, turning him towards her.

"Oh Shit," yelled Sho. I could tell he instantly knew who was behind him. Usually Sho was so cool but Nicole seemed to be the only one who had the power to make him tense up.

"Bitch?" said the girl Sho was just kissing. I couldn't help but to gawk at her. Nicole was cute and all but that girl was bad. Super Bad with big ol titties and a booty to match. "Who you calling a bitch?" she said as she attempted to step up to Nicole. Obviously she was new around here.

As Sho stepped in closer between the two, Nicole stood quiet, staring her down. "Chill out," hollered Sho as the music came to a screeching halt and everyone looked over to what was about to erupt.

40

Suddenly Nicole haymakered the shit outta Sho's other girl. The party went into a frenzy. Everyone rushed over to get a closer look at the battle. Blinds were being broken. Pictures knocked off the wall. It was going down. By now I was unable to even see the fight anymore. I didn't even know where Trell or Josh was, nor could I see Sharee. All I could hear were people screaming, *'Oh shit'*, *'Hit her ass'* and *'Oooh'*.

Chantal, the girl who was throwing the party was also heard. She kept saying shit about her Mom killing her. I think she jinxed herself because seconds later we heard, "What the hell is goin on up in hea?"

Chantal's Mom burst into the house, face full of rage. Chantal may have been right, she was going to kill her. Everyone's eyes now shifted over to her except Sho, Nicole and his other girl, who continued scuffling.

No one seemed interested in the fight anymore as everyone in the party scattered towards the door. It was like a chain reaction and I had to follow the action. I did another quick surveillance for Trell and Josh but still no luck. I was out.

As soon as I stepped foot out the door I heard someone yell "The Jakes". There was an instant riot. Whenever anyone mentioned the police we all were trained to jet and that's exactly what we did. Everyone was moving in all different types of directions. No one was trying to take that ride home in the police car. For some, that could result in a severe punishment, cancelling out all future parties. I definitely wasn't trying to lose my party privileges so I thought quickly. Instead of running towards the front yard like everyone else I dipped into the backyard.

41

It had to be some sorta gate I could hop. My night life was in jeopardy.

When I got to the backyard, there was a small shed unattached to the house. If it was open I could hide out until the coast was clear. First I had to make sure the door was open.

Jackpot, it was. I eased open the door and crept in. It was pitch black.

I took a breath of relief when out of nowhere a small bright light flashed. "Oh shit," I screamed, practically jumping out of my body. I damn near had an early heart attack until I noticed it was Sharee. She was holding her cell phone light up.

"Now who's stalkin who?"

I struggled to catch my breath. "Yo you scared the shit outta me. What you doin in hea?"

"You're not the only one who knows how to run from the police. My Mama would kill me if I came home in a cop car. She didn't even want me out tonight."

"Yeah my Mom be trippin too. She wants me in the house by twelve."

I had to lie to her. Eleven o'clock was embarrassing. If I gotta stay out to twelve so be it. Besides, my Mom's probably asleep already anyway. She usually can't even stay up past nine-thirty.

"Twelve? You're lucky. My Mom told me eleven." I'm still glad I lied. It's ok for a girl to have an earlier curfew than a boy. Sharee looked down at her phone before rolling her eyes and stating, "Nine-fifty-seven. I'm still supposed to be partyin right now.

"Why you lookin at me like that? I ain't the one who was fightin."

"Yeah but your people's was. I told you yall was some thugs." I couldn't really tell if she was serious or not. "Don't forget I still got this," she said after reaching inside of her purse pulling out the pepper spray.

"What? What kind of nigga do you take me for?" I asked as I motioned for her to put the pepper spray away. "You can put the peppa spray down. I'm safe. Trust me."

Sharee smiled and shook her head. "Yeah, yeah that's what they all say."

She never put the pepper spray away but I knew she was just playing. I could sense that she actually liked me. I think this is just what they call playing hard to get. Sho told me a lot of girls did that.

"You're crazy," I replied as I smiled. "At least you don't have to be all nervous about callin me tonight, I'm right hea," I said as I continued smiling, hoping to be charming.

"Who said I was callin you?" she asked as she looked around sarcastically. All I could do was laugh. What can I say, the girl was funny. "What you laughin for I ain't jokin," she said as her smile grew as we gawked at one another.

I wasn't positive I was getting anywhere with Sharee earlier but seeing her blush gave me all the confirmation I needed. I had her right where I wanted. I just needed to keep her there.

"Oh yeah. You said you were from Memphis, right," I asked as she nodded. "What brought you hea?"

Sharee's facial expression suddenly changed. It was a look of pain. A look of hurt. I immediately felt concerned. What could it be that would make her entire mood change the way it did? I had never really spoken too much about my Father's death but something inside me told me that I could tell Sharee my story. Something told me she would understand. I could feel the pain from her face and it felt familiar. I knew she'd understand.

In no time I found myself telling my my life story to her. She was the first person I'd ever told that I'd seen my Father murdered. I didn't even realize what I was doing. Everything was just spilling out. The entire time I spoke she didn't say a single word but looking into her eyes I could tell I was right. I knew I could trust her. I was prepared to let loose all my inner most thoughts if she'd let me.

Too bad we were interrupted by Chantal's Mom holding some bazzoka like gun. Sharee and I both screamed, through our hands up and backed up.

"Get the fuck outta hea." We didn't waste a second following her orders. In the blink of an ey we both ran as fast as we could. "Hell yall doin in my damn shed? I'll kill yall lil mo'fucka's. Fuck wrong with yall?" she shouted to us as we ran for more than a block hand in hand.

We would've probably never stopped if we would've never been abruptly cut off by a black Acura with

44

tinted windows. Still holding on to one another, we both all most ran into the car.

Again, Sharee screamed. I had already done enough of that for the night though. I knew I had to be a man this time.

Thank God it was Sho. "What's up? What yall runnin for Yall needa ride?" he said after slinging the drivers side door open, stepping out.

Relieved, I released Sharee's hand and said "Hell yeah."

I was psyched that it was Sho. Not just because he was there to witness me with Sharee but the wheels he was whipping were the shit. Twenty inch rims and I could see T.V.'s through the windows.

I looked inside, Sho's homeboy Boogie was in the passenger seat smoking a cigarette. We both nodded over to one another.

Like Sho, Boogie was a crazy motherfucker too. Only he stayed locked up too much for him to be as popular. Shit, Boogie's I.D. probably had a detention home address. He damn sure spent more time there then out here.

"I'll walk", said Sharee, noticeably uneasy.

Call me crazy but before Sharee said that, I had never thought to think that Sho might not supposed to be driving that car. I looked over to her before walking a little closer to Sho.

"Yo where'd you get this?" I whispered.

"Tell home girl we'll drop her off and then me you and Boog can burn up," said Sho, blatanly ignoring my question as he pointed to a rolled up blunt sitting in the ash tray "Oh yeah. I saw them niggas Trell and Josh. They was lookin for you. Them pussy niggas went in the crib already now."

I looked down at my phone. No wonder Trell and Josh hadn't called, it was completely dead. At least they were safe. I wonder if Sho gave them a ride. And how did he steal a car this quick? Wasn't the police out here?

I had to snap back to reality. I looked over to Sharee; she was staring right in my face. I usually loved when she did that but right now isn't the time. Riding around with Sho sounded great but I had to be in the house in a couple minutes anyway.

Plus I can't chance ruining anything with her. I could tell from the look in her eyes there was no way she was stepping foot in that car. I looked over to Sho. "Naw man her house is just down the street," I said as I yawned. "Plus I'm tired I'm just gonna call it a night."

I could tell Sho thought I was bitching out. I think he spared me a lecture because Sharee was there.

"Alright I'ma hit you up tomorrow. We can hit up the mall or something," he said.

"Alright," I followed before dapping him up and moving along.

On the way home Sharee didn't say a word. I prayed she wasn't mad at me. I had no idea what to say to her though. I was confused and didn't even really know what I had done wrong.

By the time we arrived at her front door I was still trying to figure out a way to get a kiss. Besides Truth or Dare I had never made out with a girl before. But tonight seemed like the perfect time.

We stood face to face as she finally spoke again. "Thanks for walkin me home. I had a nice time talkin to you," she said, finally smiling.

"No problem. I did too. Does this mean I'll be gettin a phone call soon?"

"I told you already. Maybe," she said softly before turning around, floating to her doorstep.

When I got home, surprisingly Mom, along with Aunt Tina and Aunt Fonda were still up sitting in the exact spots I'd left them in. I'm not 100 percent sure but I'd be willing to bet a million dollars that they were up all night participating in their favorite past time, gossiping.

"Hey Pete. We were just talking about you," said Mom.

"Hey," I said attempting to make my way up stairs. I didn't feel like small talking with them. Plus I wasn't positive that the weed odor had disappeared from my clothes yet.

"Hey Peta Wida. Did you have fun?" asked Aunt Tina.

"Yeah it was cool."

"Well I'm glad you had a good time and thanks for coming in on time, it's nice to know I can trust you," said Mom as Aunt Fonda and Aunt Tina looked over smiling.

47

"No problem. Goodnight. Love yall," I said as I continued walking up the stairs.

"Love you too," they all replied.

I trotted up stairs still thinking about how great my night had turned out.

I woke up the next day to a phone call from Josh. We didn't have any lawns to cut but he wanted to head down to the rec and shoots some hoops.

Trell had spent the night at his crib and they wanted to know what happened last night. He said they were on their way to my house before I could even said it was ok.

So I got up to wash my face and shit. My Mom was at work and Korb was at some little summer daytime camp. I couldn't help but think how perfect it would be if I could ever somehow get Sharee to drop on by. Sho said sex in the daytime was the best because you could see all the crazy faces girls make.

After I put on all my clothes I heard the sound of the doorbell. I knew it was Josh because he was ringing it like his mind was bad. He always did that when he knew my Mom wasn't home. I ran down the stairs and went outside, the air was breezy, a huge contrast from yesterday. This was the type of day where nothing could go wrong.

Trell and Josh wasted no time with their interrogation as they stared at me from My Mom's two porch chairs.

"Yo, where the hell were you last night? We looked all over for you," asked Trell.

"Hell yeah, we thought the Police had got you," said Josh as they both stared, anxiously awaiting a reply.

I thought I was a nosy ass nigga but these two may be the new world leaders. I tried to keep a straight face but I couldn't help but to smile. "Nope."

They knew something was up.

"Then what the hell happened?" asked Josh.

"You was with the dimple faced girl I saw you with, won't you?" asked Trell. Damn, I didn't even know they had seen me with Sharee. In a way I was happy. They had never seen me with a girl. I'm glad the first one they saw me with was bangin. I smiled. "Did you hit?" asked Trell.

"No," I replied quickly.

Even if I did I wouldn't tell these niggas. Sharee's a special girl you don't just go around telling her business.

Naw fuck that what am I thinking if I ever hit her I'd have to tell them. They my niggas, besides I don't think any man in the world could keep a secret like that. I mean damn I'm only human.

"Damn nigga why you say no like that?" asked Trell.

"Cause it ain't none of yall business what we did."

"Hold on, let me get this straight. Are you defending chicks you don't even know?" asked Josh as he and Trell burst into laughter.

49

Them niggas was getting me hot. I don't care how long I knew them. Aint nobody just gonna be speaking on Sharee like that. Angry, I stormed off the porch. I ain't even feel like looking at their asses no more. Them niggas sharing dirty ass Tinka and want to talk about me. Fuck them.

Togehether they ran behind me mocking, "Ah shit Pete's in love," said Josh. "Never thought I'd see the day."

"Hell yeah," followed Trell. "But at least we know he ain't gay now."

They burst out laughing even harder this time.

I looked back furiously. Me, Trell, and Josh had gotten into plenty of fights versus one another and this was about to be another one. I couldn't' take it anymore.

Lucky for them the most amazing thing happened to me. I saw Sharee. She was walking up behind them, holding on to a dog leash that had some little hairy puppy attached to it, looking even better than she had in the party. My heart pounded as I forgot all about Josh and Trell's bitch asses.

After peeping me staring back like a deer caught in the headlights they turned around. "Oh shit, Josh there's his wife right there."

I don't think Sharee heard what they said but she definitely knew we were talking about her. She was looking right at us.

"Look at him making googly eyes," said Josh.

They were having the time of their life. I still didn't care. I pushed pass them and made my way over.

Again I didn't know what I was going to say but my legs were walking without my permission. Luckily I didn't have to say anything. She did.

"Hey Pete I was just about to call you." I couldn't believe the words that had just came out of her mouth. Call me? I was speechless. "I was gonna ask if you wanted to walk my Aunt's dog over to the dog park with me. It's so nice out here.

My brain was functioning again. "Hell yeah I'll go," I said, forgetting all about being cool.

"You sure? I see you're with your friends," Sharee said as she nodded over to Trell and Josh who were staring down at us.

Fuck them, they was getting on my nerves anyway.

"It's Ok. I kick it with them every day. Plus I've never been to the dog park," I followed as I looked back at them smiling.

"Well Ok," she said, blushing once again.

Together we began walking. Trell and Josh were still standing in the same spot as we walked past.

"I'll see yall lata," I said smiling as they stood their shocked as I kept it moving. Now who they punk asses gon joke?

"Have fun," they both screamed to us.

Me and Sharee small talked our way down to the park. It's funny; she didn't even know that I hated animals. But fuck it, who cares? I'd do anything to be in her presence. Boy, she smelled good.

When we hit the corner, Police were everywhere. I looked down to the ground and low and behold, they had Boogie and Sho face down side by side in cuffs. The stolen car from last night was parked a little further down the street surrounded by police. Both doors were still open. It appeared as if they'd attempted to run with no avail. The block was poppin. Norview residents don't really get this type of action too much.

I noticed Sharee tensing up. She began walking faster as I struggled to keep up. When we finally reached the spot where Sho was, I looked over to him. He was looking right at me and this nigga had the nerve to be smiling.

I'm not sure if he was happy to be getting locked up or happy that I was with Sharee. Confusion consumed me as I debated on what my facial expression should be. Should I smile back or nod my head? I knew I couldn't just walk past like I didn't see him. In a way I kinda wanted to burst into tears. I hated when he got locked up. Life was so much better with him around. And with the summer just starting, this was the worst thing that could happen. I was planning on making plenty more appearances with him. Damn.

Still I decided to be strong and to just nod my head. He continued smiling and nodded back.

Sharee was walking even faster now. Again I was struggling to keep up. When we finally made it to the next street, she gave me the best surprise I could ever ask for. She grabbed me by the middle of my shirt and planted a big wet juicy kiss right on my lips. I thought I was confused earlier but now I was just plain ol lost. Still, I loved it. Even with Sho facing time and my summer taking a drastic turn I suddenly felt like this could very well be the best summer of my life.

Chapter 3

The first day of High school and I was already late for my first class. Not to mention I had no idea where I was going. I had walked Sharee to her class and now I was alone in this huge building. My class was the first freshman class to enter. The school was brand spankin new. I had never been in the old one but I heard it was a dump. This one was the shit. At least that's what everyone had been telling me. Honestly, to me it was just a school. Who gets excited about a damn school?

As I walked down the still freshly painted hallway I saw kids in class already working hard, sharpening pencils, and raising hands. It had finally dawned on me that summer time was over and I'd be forced to do some work. With all the fun I had this summer I had completely forgotten how much I'd hated school. Maybe the fact that I was going to high school had blinded me but the thought of learning pointless things that I was sure I would never care about or need in life was making me sick to my stomach. Sho always said that anything school could teach him he could learn on Google and I have to say I couldn't agree more.

I wandered aimlessly through the empty hall for about 10 minutes before some old ass security guard asked to see my schedule and escorted me to class. He acted like he had an attitude or something, like helping students out wasn't his job. I could already tell we were going to get into it one day.

When I finally walked into my class I had everyone's attention, which I didn't mind because I had picked out the perfect outfit for back to school, fresh white air force ones and a dope ass LRG shirt with the shorts to match.

The teacher, Mrs. Harley was standing in front of the class holding a roll sheet. I could tell I wasn't gonna like her either. She was short and fat with big ass bi focal glasses. She looked like the type who probably had some fat ass husband and fat ass kids. From the frown marks on her face I could tell she hated her life and would try her best to make me hate mine too.

"And your name is sir?" asked Mrs. Harley.

I was hesitant to speak because I couldn't help but notice that she had the most crooked teeth I had ever seen. She didn't even look human. I know teachers get insurance. Why the hell is her grill like that? Doesn't she have a mirror and if not I'm sure somebody told her about her damn teeth before. Shit, she pisses me off good enough I might tell her.

"Pete Turna," I said trying desperately not to stare at her teeth.

She looked over the roll sheet. "I don't have a Pete Turner," she said before staring back at me. "I have a Samuel Turner but no Pete Turner."

She talked with one of those cocky attitudes, like she thought she was better than me or something.

"Yeah that's me but I go by Pete."

"Well, when the roll says Pete I will call you that. Until then, Samuel, find a seat and take out a sheet of paper."

Man, every teacher I've ever had agreed to call me Pete. It wasn't like I had some crazy ass nickname like Pookie or something. Bitch.

I scanned the class and spotted Trell looking equally as fresh as me sitting in the back of the room staring at me along with the rest of the class. Noticing an empty seat next to him, I walked over.

Trell and I had been in the same classes all through middle school so I knew this would be cool.

"Whatsup Samuel," Trell whispered as I sat down. I flicked him off and pulled out a sheet of paper from my binder. "How in the hell you late on the first day? I thought you said you was walking with me and Josh this morning."

"Sharee wanted me to walk with her and when I got to her crib she was having a bad hair day so--" I whispered back.

"What?" Trell asked cutting me off. "You ditched us for her again?" Looking at me in disgust, he shook his head before, saying "Sucka."

Trell didn't have a girl. He was too immature to understand the sacrifices you make in relationships. The entire summer I was forced to hear him and Josh tell me just how much of a sucker I was.

"Whateva man," I said, forgetting to whisper.

"I'm not going to have to separate the two of you am I?" asked Mrs. Harley as the entire class turned around.

In unison we both shook our heads before awaiting her to begin talking again. Since I had sat down I hadn't heard a word she had said. "I want everyone to write down five things about yourselves. I'm going to give you two minutes."

"I'm high as gas," Trell whispered.

He must've dropped some visine in his eyes because they were still pearly white. Ever since Sho had introduced us to the wonderful world of weed, we had been hooked. It had gotten to a point where we smoked at least four times a week.

"Yall smoked without me?"

"Nobody forced you to walk your wife to school."

"Whatever."

"Ay is Sho still gettin out the Detention Home Friday?"

This was a clear sign that Trell really was high. He always talked his ass off whenever we were blowed. I had just told him yesterday that Sho got out Friday.

Still the thought of Sho getting out put a smile to my face. "Yeah."

Sho had been locked up for the entire summer. Luckily he wasn't driving the car when they got pulled. Boogie was, so they just charged him with a simple Joyriding. I couldn't wait till he came home. He wrote me a couple weeks ago and told me that his probation officer was making him go back to school until he turned eighteen in February. I really didn't understand why they were doing that. Sho hadn't accumulated a single credit in the three years he'd been in high school. It seemed pretty stupid to make him go to school now.

Still, I was thrilled that me and Sho would actually be in the same school. I might not have been able to hit all the parties up with him this summer but being seen with him in school would most definitely boost my popularity.

"Yo this school year is about to be poppin," said Trell. He must've had some of the same thoughts that I had about Sho coming to school with us because he was now the one who had forgotten to whisper.

Instantly I felt a pair of eyes burning a hole in me.

"Mr. Turner, I want you to go first," said Mrs. Harley.

I had completely forgotten what the hell she had even told us to do. The only thing I could come up with was, "I didn't get a chance to finish. I can't find my pencil."

"Well I have plenty on my desk," she said pointing over to it as I stood to my feet. "And bring your belongings along with you since you and Mr. Gordon can't seem to concentrate next to one another."

Again the entire class was staring back at us. I sucked my teeth, packed up all of my shit and made my way to the front of the class.

I grabbed a pencil off of her desk and noticed that she had a cup of coffee sitting. Everything in me wanted to spit in it but I decided not to when I realized everyone including Mrs. Harley was still watching me. So I made my way to my new desk in the front of the class and took a seat making as much noise as I possibly could.

Mrs. Harley then called on some tall kid with braces. "Mr. Lopez would you like to go next?"

I zoned out. I didn't care about what the hell 'Mr. Lopez' was talking about. I was too busy wondering what Sharee was doing. During the summer we spent almost every day together. But now I gotta worry about 17 year old seniors with cars trying to steal my Angel away from me. How could I compete with a guy with a mustache and muscles? The thought of Sharee with another nigga was making my blood boil. I felt sweat dripping down my forehead. I'd kill somebody over her. Ok, maybe not kill, but I'd definitely feel like it. She's my baby.

I was rudely broken out of my zone by my Mrs. Harley. "Samuel, Samuel, Samuel," she said.

I was trying my best to ignore her. The bitch was annoying as hell. Kept calling me Samuel. I told her big ass that won't my name. She had plucked my last nerve.

"That ain't my name." The entire class gasped. I guess they were surprised that a student would act like that on the first day and I gotta admit I was pretty surprised my damn self. I had never talked back to any teachers. I don't know what's gotten into me.

As steam rose from her scalp she stared me down berore looking over to the door. That's when she peeped the same bitch ass security guard from earlier walking by. Intantly she motioned for him to come inside.
"Well maybe you can tell Mr. Perry who Samuel is."

He stood at the entrance of the class with his hand on his hip. "Do we have a problem?"

His punk ass just knew he was important. I bet he wouldn't act so tough if we were all grown. I made sure I stared him in the eyes. I wanted him to know that he didn't put any fear in my heart. Sho had always said that staring contest were sometimes the best way to challenge a man.

"Yes, would you be kind enough to escort this young man to the office. It seems as if he has forgotten how to conduct himself in a classroom over the summer."

"Yes Ma'am," he answered as we continued our stare off. "Come with me," he ordered.

Once again, I packed up all of my shit but before leaving I felt the need to take a second off of my staring match with Mr. Perry to give Mrs. Harley a quick unfriendly mean mug. Her deformed looking ass tried to act like she didn't see me but I know she did.

Afterwards I continued my dual with Mr. Perry before g-strolling my way out of class. Fuck it; I ain't feel like doing no work anyway.

When the bell rung for dismissal I felt like I had just been released from prison. This was by far the worse day I had, had in months. And judging from the other hundreds of students who were stampeding towards the door I wasn't the only one who had felt that way.

As I headed to the exit I noticed Josh walking up to me. The grin on his face let me know that he had already heard about what had happened in Mrs. Harley's class. There were only two lunches here and neither Sharee, Trell, nor Josh was in mine so I figured they had already talked about it.

"What's up Man?" said Josh before dapping me up. "I heard about what happened."

"First day of school and they already called my Mama."

"They called your Mom?" asked Josh appearing to feel my pain. We both knew my Mom ain't play that getting in trouble in school shit.

"Yep and I got detention next Monday."

We made our way outside. The sun illuminated the sky as students laughed and joked around as music blasted from the speakers of the upper classman cars. This shit looked like an episode of Saved by the Bell or something. Everybody looked all happy and here I was looking sap, probably the only dumb ass who had fucked up on the first day. I shoulda kept my big mouth shut. Damn.

"My nigga Samuel," Trell joked as he walked up from behind.

"Everybody got jokes huh," I said attempting to keep a straight face. It was too hard though. Trell and Josh's goofy asses had me weak with laughter I couldn't help but to crack a smile.

"My name is Pete," Trell said mocking me. He and Josh laughed even harder now. I couldn't help but to join in.

Unfortuately our moment was quickly halted as I felt a light tap on my shoulder followed by a voice that was all too familiar. It was Sharee. "What's this I hear about you going to the Dean's office today?"

I hated when Sharee did shit like this. It gave Trell and Josh an even bigger reason to say she had me on lock. So I did what any smart man in my situation would have done. I tried to kiss her. "Hey baby," I said leaning forward for the kiss.

Sharee quickly backed away, "And why haven't I seen you all day?

I looked over to Trell and Josh embarrassingly. They got the hint. "We'll catch up with yall lovebirds later," said Josh.

I knew Josh and Trell like the back of my hand and it was clear as day that they were thinking I was a sucker. Shit, maybe I was. "Alright yall," I said as I dapped the two of them up.

"Alright Pete," they both said before looking over to Sharee. "Bye Sharee."

"Bye," Sharee said as they walked away.

I saw them giggling about something. I'm sure it was about me. But I couldn't worry about them.

"So how was school?" I asked Sharee as I smiled hoping this would ease the tension. Her face immediately told me that she wasn't going for it.

"Don't try to change the subject. Ciara told me she saw you get taken into the dean's office by a security guard," Sharee said as she stood there staring at me with her hand on her hip. I didn't know what to say. All I could think of was how I couldn't stand Ciara. Her nosey ass needs a damn man. Always up in somebody's business. I wish she won't so damn ugly. I'd hook her up with Trell or Josh. "I'm listenin," she said.

"Mrs. Harley kept callin me Samuel," I said without making eye contact.

"And."

"My name is Pete."

Visibly annoyed, Sharee began power walking away from me back into the building leaving me with no choice but to chase behind. I hated when she acted like this. It's like she think she's my Mom or something. Still, there was a part of me that kind of liked it. She actually cared about me. Plus she looks dumb good when she was mad.

"Don't you have cheerleadin practice?" I asked.

"Yeah," she said, still power walking.

Judging from the number of students still lingering around I realized that I may have been wrong about everyone hating school as much as I did. I guess they were all going to some practice or something. But I'll be damned if I play some dumb ass sport. Sho always said it was a waste of time if you weren't some superstar athlete who

63

was going to the NBA or something. Why waste energy when you could be somewhere chillin?

"Where the gym at?" I asked as I continued to follow her. It seemed as if we had been walking forever.

Sharee looked at me with one of her annoyed looks again. "I told you, you should've come to freshman orientation."

"Sho told me only suckas went to orientations."

As soon as those words came out of my mouth I knew I had made a mistake.

"Dang Pete, if Sho told you to jump off a bridge would you do it?"

She smacked me upside my head. This was definitely something I hated. I looked around to see if anyone had seen it. Last thing I want to be known as is the kid who gets beat up by his girlfriend. Luckily the coast was clear. "Man--"

Sharee cut me off. "Man nothing," she said as she stopped and grabbed me by the arm. "Where is Sho right now?"

I knew she'd hit me with that. She always did. She never said it in so many words but I knew she didn't like Sho very much. "What that got to do with anything?"

"You keep followin his every word and you gonna end up right in there with him."

"Ok Mama," I said as she shook her head and began her power walk once more. Of course I followed.

64

"Whateva Pete. Just know I refuse to be spending my precious nights writing jail letters."

We stopped in front of the sign that read 'Girls locker room.' "You're over exaggerating."

"No I'm not but I gotta go I'll call you later," she said as she began walking away.

"So I don't get a kiss?" I asked, gently pulling her back towards me.

"Nope you're on a punishment."

Sharee loved to be a tough guy but I know she can't resist me.

"Stop playin baby. Gimme a kiss," I said, pulling her even closer to me.

"Move Pete."

She was smiling so I knew this was only a game of hard to get.

"No. Gimme a kiss." By now we were practically nose to nose. Oh my God she looked so good. She puckered up and gave me one of those gay ass cheek kisses. "Do I look like your Grandma? Gimme a real kiss."

Without hesitation we embarked on a long passionate kiss before some woman stepped inches away from us, clearing her throat, making it obvious that she wanted our attention.

We both ceased lip locking and looked over to the woman. She was tall as hell and had some lopsided wig on her head. Looking up at her, she appeared as though should've been in the WNBA or something. I didn't know who the hell this lady was but as I looked at Sharee I could tell she did. She had that same look on her face when her mom caught me tonguing her down on her back porch one night when she was supposed to be asleep.

"Hey Mrs. Williams," said Sharee. The 'Mom' voice that she had just displayed to me was gone and she was now talking like some four year old toddler. Ironically she even sounded good doing that.

"How are you doing Mrs. Gardner?" said the lady as she stared at Sharee as if she could see right through her. I knew Sharee had to be feeling uncomfortable. I sure was. "You didn't inform me this summer that you had such a handsome husband," she continued, splitting her focus between the both of us. I assumed this was Sharee's cheer coach. She was always talking about her but she never mentioned she was so damn manly.

"Husband?" Sharee asked, as if she didn't know the reason Mrs. Williams was saying it. I was feeling real awkward so I just looked at the ground and counted the tile on the floor.

"He must be because young ladies don't just kiss any ol body like I saw the two of you just doing." I was still looking at the ground but I could see from my peripheral that Sharee was doing the same thing. "So are you going to introduce me to your friend?"

We both lifted our head. Mrs. Williams had found a way to stare at both of us at the same time. "Mrs. Williams, this is Pete, my boyfriend." They both turned their attention over to me. "Pete, this is Mrs. Williams, my cheer coach."

I put on the most mannerable voice I could muster up and said, "Nice to meet you Mrs. Williams."

We extended our hands for a handshake.

"Nice meeting you too Pete. And what grade are you in mite I ask?"

"9th, it's my first year."

"Great. And are you on your way to any practices?"

Damn she was nosey. "No ma'am." I could tell that wasn't the answer she was looking for.

"And why not? The idol mind is the Devils workshop. I can't have my precious Sharee involved with a hoodlum."

Hoodlum? Who even says the word hoodlum anymore?

"I just like to have as much time as possible to study. I would love to be the class valedictorian some day."

I looked over to Sharee. She was shaking her head mouthing the words *'Valedictorian'*.

"That's wonderful." She smiled. I think I won her over. "Now come on Sharee. You're late for practice. "It was a pleasure meeting you Mr. Future Valedictorian."

"Nice meeting you to Mrs. Williams." I gave her one of my phoniest smiles before focusing my attention back to Sharee. "Bye Sharee."

"Bye Pete." We attempted to give a quick peck but we both realized Mrs. Williams was staring directly at us

67

and decided to opt out. "I'll call you lata. Unless you're gonna be too busy workin on your valedictorian speech." She smiled.

I loved her. "I'll take a break for you baby," I said as I smiled right back at her

"Aw," said Mrs. Williams. Her nosey ass just wouldn't leave.. "Now get your butt in the locker room," she said as she pushed Sharee along.

I already knew my Mom would flip out about me getting in trouble on the first day. I was just hoping she'd spare me a punishment since it was my first time getting in trouble this year. Plus I came in by curfew the whole summer. Of course I snuck out a few times but she never caught me so that doesn't count. I deserved to be cut a little slack.

Still, I sat in my room doing homework. It always makes the punishment a little leaner when she sees me doing something good.

After drifting in and out of pointless homework and day dreaming my Mom burst in my room the second she got off work.

"Hey Ma," I said smiling, hoping my giddiness would be contagious.

"Don't hey Ma me."How dare you disrespect a teacher?"

She was looking angrier than I had seen her in a while. I guess my giddiness wasn't contagious at all.

"Ma, I told her my name was Pete."

"Told her?" she asked as she walked closer to me? "Told her? She's an adult you don't tell her anything. You're gonna write her an apology letter."

"Apology letta?"

I acted as though I was shocked even though she'd been making me write them for as long as I can remember.

"Did I stutter? And I better not find out you're talking back to any other teachers," she said before turning around and leaving the room, slamming the door shut.

Even though she fussed and I had to write a damn apology letter I still couldn't help but to be glad she didn't put me on punishment. I could still go to the game with Sho Friday when he got out.

Suddenly my door burst back open. It was Mom. "And don't go outside for a week." She slammed the door once more.

Shit!

Chapter 4

The next couple of days at school were same ol same ol. I'd managed to get by without getting into any trouble and now it was Thursday, one more day until the big game but more importantly one more day until Sho would be home and sadly my black ass was still on punishment.

Sharee had practice again so I got to walk home with the fellas. This was by far the highlight of my day.

"Bro, it's only a week, my Mom grounded me for three weeks before," said Josh.

I had been venting to the homies.

"Yeah but me and Sho was posed to hit up the game tomorrow," I said.

"So. You act like you his girl or somethin," said Trell and like always both of their punk asses burst out laughing.

"Yall think yall so funny," I said. "You gotta admit that was pretty funny," said Josh. He was right. Even though I was really upset that I couldn't go to the game, I still couldn't help but laugh at their crazy asses. I had been spending so much time with Sharee that I had kind of forgot how funny these niggas was. As we laughed and joked all the way home I realized I'd have to find a way to kick it with them more often.

When my Mom got home from work I had already found a way to get through all the meaningless homework

70

I'd been assigned and was now kickin it on the couch watching some old re runs of The Steve Harvey Show. "Hey Pete," she said all jolly and shit.

"Hey Ma," I replied not even turning to look at her. I always did this when she had me on punishment. I guess I hoped she'd somehow not be able to take me not talking to her, breakdown and take me off of punishment. It's never worked but I'm not the type to give up.

"Where's your brother?"

"Upstairs."

"OK. How was school?"

"Cool," I said as I heard her fumbling through today's mail.

My phone rang. I knew it was Sharee before I had even looked at the caller I.D. I had Jagged Edge's *'Promise'* as her ring tone. I knew the homies would joke the hell out of me if they'd ever heard that shit so I always made sure I put it on vibrate whenever they were around.

We talked; excuse me, she talked for about five minutes before I heard Mrs. Williams crazy ass in the background shouting *'Breaks over'*.

As soon as I hung up the phone the doorbell rung. My Mom had left the room so I answered.

I opened the door and immediately wiped my eyes; I couldn't believe what I was witnessing. Out of all people in the world Sho was the last person I was expecting to be standing on the outside of that door. Any other time I'd be elated to see him but he didn't get out until tomorrow. I

71

stepped outside closing the door quickly. "Yo what the hell you doin hea?" I whispered.

"Damn nigga. What kind of greetin is that?"

Sho was smiling showcasing his still polished gold grills. He even had on a brand new outfit with the latest Ken Griffey Nike's. He didn't look anything like a man who had just got out the bean. Like always, I was confused.

"I thought you got out Friday" I said still whispering.

"Man, I had the days mixed up." Sho was always a top notch liar so I didn't know what to believe. He had already done every crime under the sun; escaping from jail certainly wouldn't be a stretch. "Nigga I ain't break out. Damn I'm crazy but not that crazy," he said as I stood speechless. "Let's walk to the store. I'm starvin."

Never in a million years would I imagine I'd say this but for the first time ever I was happy to be on punishment. Call me crazy but I really wasn't in the mood to be having police and helicopters surround me.

"Can't, Mom's got me on a punishment," I answered.

This time Sho was the one looking confused. "Punishment? Parents actually do that shit in real life?"

At that moment my Mom came barging out the front door. "Pete--."

She was cut off by Sho. "Hey Aunt Mary."

I had made sure that my Mom hadn't heard about Sho getting arrested this summer. She always knew he got in a little trouble from time to time, but she had no idea of the full extent to exactly who Sho really was. And I was determined to keep it that way. It wasn't any of her business.

"Hey Shomar, I know you didn't just come to my house and not ask to speak to me."

"Never. I was just asking Pete about you. I missed you."

"Aww." My Mom was always so gullible. "Give me a hug. You are so handsome. Looking just like your Daddy," she said as they hugged. "Have you seen him lately?"

"Nope, he's still M.I.A."

My Uncle Cliff was different. A lot of guys were dead beat Dad's but he took the cake. He was a dead beat son, dead beat brother, dead beat uncle, dead beat friend, dead beat boyfriend. It's pretty safe to say that he just won't shit.

"That's a shame. We haven't seen him either."

"Yeah you know how he is."

"Unfortunately I do but it's so nice to see you Shomar. I don't think you stopped by here the entire summer. I hope you've been staying out of trouble."

I giggled to myself. Only if she knew.

"Of course," Sho said.

"You better be," she said before turning her attention over to me. "Don't be out here long."

I looked away as I spoke. "OK."

She walked back into the house closing the door behind her.

"Man I'ma holla at you later. I'm hungry as hell," said Sho.

"Alright man."

We dapped each other up and I walked back into my cell.

Korb had come downstairs and he and my Mom decided to take over my spot on the couch, so I headed upstairs to my room.

"Hold on Pete," said my Mom. Before I even turned to look at her I already knew that she was gonna tell me something pointless like always.

To my surprise she was holding my I.D. card in her hand. I don't know how I keep losing that shit. Maybe it was time for a wallet. But then again if I had a wallet I might lose everything all at once.

I walked over to retrieve the I.D. I knew she'd have something to say. "Didn't I tell you to keep up with this? You need to have it on you at all times, it's important."

She had told me this at least ten times already. She acted like I was losing it on purpose. I just couldn't help it.

"Ok Ma," I said as she handed over the I.D. "Thank You."

I turned back around to head upstairs.

"You're welcome. Did you do your homework?"

"Yes Ma." I replied, continuing my path.

"You don't wanna watch TV with me and your brother?"

"Naw I'm tired. I think I'm gonna take a nap."

I was lying about taking a nap initially but right about now it didn't seem like to bad of an idea.

I looked back towards Mom and overheard her say "I guess we're not cool enough for him," as she kissed Korb on the cheek.

"Eww," he said. I couldn't help but laugh.

"Hey boo. You sleep?"

I was awoken from my slumber by a phone call from Sharee. I always put the phone on speaker when I was in my room. Holding a phone to my ear always felt awkward for some reason.

I looked over to my alarm clock. It was 8:30. I had been knocked out for almost three hours. "Yeah I was," I said yawning.

"Well I'm glad you got some rest cause we're about to be on the phone all night."

She put infancies on the *'all'* and I knew she wasn't lying. Sharee can talk. Most of the time I don't even have to listen, all I have to say is, 'Foreal', 'You lying', or 'You right about that', from time to time.

"Says who?" I asked jokingly.

"Says me. You got a problem with that?"

"Nope."

I looked down at my phone, Sho was beeping in. I told Sharee to hang on for a sec and clicked over. "Hello."

"Ay nigga, bring your ass outside. I'm in front of your crib."

Was this nigga crazy or what? I know I told him earlier that I was on punishment. Plus it was a school night I had to be in by 9 anyway. He knows that. Ain't too much changed since he's been gone.
"What? Man you know my Mama ain't lettin me come outside."

"Nigga Aunt Mary go to sleep at 8. I know she sleep. Bring your ass."

Damn he was right.

"Man." I thought for another excuse but couldn't find one. "Hold on." I crept over to my Mom's room and opened the door. She was sound asleep. I thought about lying to Sho and saying that she was awake but I hated lying to him. He always seemed to know. So I closed the door and walked back into my room. "Alright man. Gimme five minutes."

76

"Alright."

I clicked back over as I put my clothes on. "Hey baby. Do you mind if I call you back?"

"Call me back? You always have somethin betta to do then to talk to me."

"Shar--."

She hung up before I could even finish my sentence. I started to call her back but that seemed kind of stupid. I'm actually kind of glad she hung up. Now I don't have to make up a lie about where I'm going.

I threw back on the clothes I'd worn earlier, grabbed my I.D. from off the dresser and tip toed my way to the back door.

I crept to the front yard ninja style and just when I thought I'd almost made it to my destination safely my heart dropped. Sho was parked directly in front of my crib in some shiny black car flashing his head lights at me. He can't be serious. Who the hell steals a car the day they get out? This nigga was insane. I desperately wanted to dart back into the house but I already told him I was coming, I couldn't just renig like that. So I dragged my feet, which now felt like they weighed 100 pounds apiece over to the whip, took one last look up to my Mom's window, sucked in some air and plopped down in some stranger's car.

"Yo where'd you get this whip?" I asked, reclining my seat back as far as I could, the same way Sho always did. I looked around at the spotless interior wondering why the hell I even asked that dumb ass question. Guess I was hoping he had some sorta reasonable explanation.

77

"I borrowed it," said Sho nonchalantly as he pressed down on the gas and sped off.

"Again man?" I already knew what that borrowed shit meant. I wasn't stupid. Or maybe I was for even getting in this hot shit.

"Calm down, somebody left the keys in the ignition. They must've wanted me to have it." I sat stiff in my seat looking straight ahead as Sho looked over to me. "Chill out. The Police don't start looking for a car till its missing 24 hours. I only need it for a lil while."

"So what you need me for?"

"I just wanted to kick it with you for a while. Damn."

I felt him still looking over to me. I was still sitting stiff looking out the window. I was beginning to panic, every car that came near us started resembling the police.

"Man I can't believe I'm in a stolen car when I'm posed to be in the house on punishment."

"Dog, we not gettin caught. It won't my fault I got tore off last time. Plus I'ma have you home in no time. Stop actin like a female."

"Alright. But if we get caught I'm sayin you kidnapped me," I said trying my hardest to loosen up.

We both laughed. "Alright that's a bet." He and I both knew I was lying. "So what's up with you and the lil bitch I heard you be fuckin with? You hit that ass yet?"

If anyone else would've called Sharee a little bitch I would've snapped but that's just how Sho is. He can't help it. He was born that way. "I'm workin on it."

"Workin on it? How much time you need nigga?"

I really didn't want to talk to Sho about Sharee. He's just like everyone else; he doesn't understand how special she was. I'd wait forever for her. Even if I was beginning to run out of lotion.

"Dog she's a virgin."

"A virgin? Nigga how you know?"

"How else? She told me."

"If she told you she could fly would you believe her?" He stared at me like I was supposed to answer or something. I turned away and began peering out the window again. "A bitch'll tell you anything. They some slick mo'fuckers."

"Man she's only 14. Why would she lie?"

"14? Man I know 12 year olds who out here takin dick. And why wouldn't she lie. She a bitch that's what bitches do." Sho was doing a little too much. I was ready to go home. I won't trying to hear all this bullshit. Just cause all his girls are hoes and sluts doesn't mean Sharee is. "Man I'm teachin you a valuable life lesson." He stared over to me. "Look at me dog," he said as I looked over unenthusiastically. "Trust no female in this world, they all the same. Even your Mama."

"What?" I blurted. Sho must've smoked a wooler or something today, he was trippin.

"She might be the best Mama in the world, but at the end of the day she still a female," he preached as we pulled up to Sho's crib. He lived in the poor section of Norview, 'The Cut'. The apartments kind of reminded me of Tidewater Park but it was a lot smaller and the people didn't seem as ghetto. I mean you had your lowlifes but it was tolerable. I guess the other Norview residents rubbed off on them or something. "Rememba. You can love any girl in this world. Just don't trust em," he continued before opening up the car door. "I'll be right back. I gotta run in the crib for a second, I forgot somethin."

Sho hadn't pissed me off many times in my life but that shit he was talking just made tonight one of them. And on top of that I was in the hottest hood in Norview sitting inside a stolen car. I was becoming more and more aggravated with the silence so I decided to turn on the radio. Showtime the local DJ was on. *"Yo, Yo, Yo, it's ya boy Showtime and it's time for 'Real Talk Radio'. And the question of the night is 'Can you trust the opposite sex?' Hit me up baby- Alright, we got a caller."*

"Yo am I on the radio?" said the caller.

"Yeah man you're on right now."

"Oh Ok. Well hell naw you can't trust'em! I just caught my girl--"

I instantly turned off the radio. That was the last thing I was trying to hear. Sharee's a Queen and that's all it was to it.

Sho was only gone for like five minutes but it seemed like hours. Rain had even started to pour, making things seem a hundred times worse. When he finally returned we pulled off briskly. I continued staring out the window hoping he'd sense my attitude and take me home.

"Damn I hate rain," he said as he turned on the wind shield wipers. Now not only was I scared that the police would pull us over but I was scared that Sho didn't know how to drive in the rain. It wasn't like he was some sorta experienced driver or something.

"Ay did I tell you I'm bouta be a Pops?" Sho asked as he grined from ear to ear, allowing me to see my reflection in his gold teeth.

"Foreal? Who'd you knock up?"

With all the girls Sho was messing with before he got locked up it could be anyone.

"Nicole nigga. You know she had to be my first BM."

"Damn cuz. Why you ain't strap up?"

Sho's smile quickly changed to a look as if I had just talked about his Mama or something. "Strap up? Nigga that's for suckas. I need all the feelin."

"So you happy?"

"Hell yeah. I just hope it's a little boy to carry on my legacy."

81

Sho having a baby completely took my mind off the fact that I was in a stolen car with no idea of where our next destination would be. I couldn't wait to have a new little cousin. This was going to be cool, another member added to the fam. Sho's news was so good that I mistakenly ignored the fact that he had just ran the hell out of a stop sign.

But the red and blue lights that flashed behind me sure hadn't. "Oh shit," said Sho. He was visibly nervous. We both looked over to one another. I began to panic. Sweat sprouted from my pours as I struggled to fight back a gang of tears.

"We good. Just sit back I got this."

Sho pulled over to the side of a dark empty street. My stomach dropped to my knees as I hoped and prayed that this was just a dream. This couldn't be real.

Some tall cock strong cop walked over to the window. "How yall boys doing? Yall aware that yall ran a stop sign?"

Despite the little steroid abuser look he had going on his blue eyes had a friendly sparkle to them, he actually looked kind of nice. He was even smiling. And not one of those *'I got you now smiles'*. He was genuinely smiling, which was pretty weird considering the fact that he was getting soaking wet from the rain.

Everything inside of me wanted to blurt out *'The car is stolen but I have nothing to do with it.'* Instead I sat there saying nothing. Hoping Sho had some sorta plan to get us out of this.

"Yeah I know officer. I'm sorry," Sho replied. actually sounding sincere.

"It's OK just let me see your license and registration."

License and registration? We don't have either. Ah fuck I'm going to juvie. Damn, damn, damn. First talking back to teachers now this. My Mom's gonna disown me.

"No problem officer," Sho said before reaching over to the glove compartment. My heart eased up a little, guess he did have a plan.

The tension in my body was slowly easing away when out of nowhere Sho pulled a gun from the compartment and in the blink of an eye he shot the Officer slam in the head.

Blood splattered everywhere as my thunderous screams echoed through the car. Sho abruptly pulled off failing to even watch his body hit the ground. I was hysterical. "Oh shit, oh shit. What the fuck? What the fuck Sho?"

He turned to me, eyes bloodshot red, shouting, "Yo shut the fuck up."

Tears shot down my face. "Yo you just killed a cop," I stuttered.

"Nigga fuck that. I gotta seed on the way I ain't going back to jail."

I continued crying as Sho sped over to some dark dead end street and hopped out. He wiped his finger prints off the car with a bandana and tossed it to me before tucking the gun onto his hip. "Wipe your side off." My teeth chattered and body trembled as I struggled to wipe down the inside of the car. "Come on," said Sho as he motioned for me to follow him as I stumbled out to wipe down the outside.

He led me to a gate a few yards away from the whip. I attempted to hop but as I tried to move forward I realized that I couldn't move. My pants pockets had gotten stuck. Sho continued running as I veimately attempted to get loose. It seemed like I was eternally trapped, Sho was getting further and further away as the rain struck down on me, piercing my face like hundreds of little needles. I was losing my mind.

Finally I sprung loose after ripping my pants pockets. They were my favorite jeans but that was damn sure the least of my worries. I hurdled mud puddles and dodged branches trying frantically to catch up to Sho who was now running through some gigantic field. It seemed like it would take forever to get to the wooded area Sho was running towards, still I ran as if a stampede of starving wild animals were charging after me. I had to, my life depended on it.

When we finally stopped, we stood ankle deep in a sticky mud puddle surrounded by mosquitoes. "We gotta find a ride. The cops bouta be all over this shit," said Sho trying pirfusively to catch his breath.

"Call your Mom," I said unable to look Sho in the eyes as I spoke.

"Call my Mom? Nigga you crazy? My Mama ain't even got no fuckin car," he replied as I remained silent analyzing the ground. My brain was no longer functioning,

84

it had been on overload. "I'm bouta call Nicole. I ain't want to get her involved but I got to. She the only one who can come scoop us."

I've never felt this way, the insides of my body felt as though someone had chewed my heart into a million pieces and it was sitting at the pit of my stomach. Vomit suddenly exploded from my mouth uncontrollably as I fell to my knees. By the time I was finished Sho had gotten off the phone. "She on her way."

I made it home safe, walked into my room eyes cocked resembling a soaking wet zombie. I fainted onto my bed face first staring blankly into the room. Over and over I tried my best to fall asleep but the image of Sho killing that Officer replayed in my mind as my Dad's murder scene simultaneously bounced around in my head. I hadn't thought about it in years but suddenly I couldn't get it off my mind. I knew how it felt not to have a Dad around and now I was probably involved in taking someone else's fathers life. I hated myself. I layed there all night praying that I would wake up from this nightmare. I never did.

I walked to school in a lonely daze. No Sharee, no Josh, no Trell. No one. My phone was turned off. Human contact was the last thing I needed. I studied the cracks in the cement as I walked. The faces of the drivers who drove past gave me the chills. Something inside me told me that they knew everything that had happened last night. My world was spinning.

When I finally arrived at school no one was in the hallway. I'm not sure if I was walking slow or if I had left the crib late, my mind was too cluttered to really know but either way I was happy I didn't run into Sharee or something. Too much shit was going on to have to hear her bitch about me not calling her back or walking her to school today. Fuck that. It was already bad enough Trell was in my 1st period class. He knew me too well not to notice something was wrong. Luckily Mrs. Harley had made my seat in the front permanent. This way I could avoid him.

As I approached the class I heard loud chatter, rapping and the sound of kids having fun. I 360 scanned around to make sure I was in the right spot. This couldn't be Mrs. Stanfield's class; she'd never go for anything like this. I looked at the room number, '245', yep I was at the right class. What in the hell was going on?

When I walked in everything immediately made sense. We had a substitute, some young black man who couldn't be more than 23 was sitting behind the desk playing with his cell phone as almost every kid in the class went buck wild. He didn't even ask me for my name, he just nodded his head like I was his homeboy or something.

"Yo Pete come hea big dog," said Trell.

He was sitting in the back of the class and my old seat next to him was vacant. There was no logical reason why I couldn't sit beside him. Slowly I proceeded to walk over, trying my hardest not to look how I was feeling. But with my head still dragging the ground I'm not too sure if I was accomplishing my goal too well.

"Yo you heard about what happened to Josh?" asked Trell before my ass could even hit the seat. From the look in his eyes I could tell it wasn't' anything good. Still I didn't want to risk him finding out that something was wrong so I just shook my head, he might be able to sense something from my voice. I was going to stay quiet as much as possible.

"You know his cool ass Uncle he used to talk about? That nigga dead."

"Huh?" I asked. I had heard perfectly clear what he had said but I knew I had to have heard it wrong. This couldn't be real.

"Yeah, the Policeman, dude got popped last night. They say they found him slump in a pool of blood in the rain. Shit's crazy. It was all over the news. I tried to call you this mornin but your phone was dead. Yo we gotta go see Josh after school. I know you on punishment and all but I know your Mom gonna understand. I talked to Josh this mornin and he all was fucked up. Shit's sad."

My eyes were pointed towards Trell but it was obvious I was no longer present in the room. Before he had said any of that I was sure that I had reached an all time low but I was wrong. Dead wrong. This feeling that I was having was something like no other. This was the kind of feeling that nothing could make better. Not even Sharee. Usually her smile could take away any pain but not today. I didn't even want to see her. If I would have just stayed on the phone with her none of this shit would've happen. I didn't need a reminder of that shit.

So without muttering a word I jetted out of class, burst through the school's front doors and ran all the way home. Fuck school, fuck everything. I didn't care anymore.

I ran nonstop to the crib, darting in and out of traffic, jumping fences, dodging dogs, until I finally made it to my room. My body was weak and my head seemed to be housing a massive heart, once again I fell face first onto the bed. I tried my hardest not to think of everything that was going on but I couldn't, I laid there soaking my sheets with tears for at least an hour before gathering everything I had in me to finally sit up.

I remember last week I had a cold and my Mom had bought a bottle of Nyquil so I could get some sleep. It had worked like a charm. It was time for me to hit it again; I couldn't bare this pain any longer.

I rushed down the steps, opened the kitchen cabinet and there it was. My problems were solved. Well at least for half the day. Last time I took some I was asleep for about four hours but the amount I was prepared to drink should have me past out all day. I popped open the top and guzzled, fuck a tea spoon.

When I made it back upstairs I flopped back onto the bed and before I knew it I was out for the count. The next thing I remember was my Mom's blurry face hovering over top of me.

"Pete," she said as she glared at me smiling as if I was some innocent child. I was still drowsy as hell from the Nyquil when I fixed my eyes and squinted over to my alarm. It was 5:30 I had been sleep since about nine and I still felt exhausted. It was taking everything I had in me not to ignore her and go right back to sleep. That was the most peace I'd had in the last 24 hours.

I wished she'd quit smiling at me, I hadn't done anything good. She must not have heard that I had completely ditched school today. And she damn sure had no idea of what I had been involved in last night. This was the first time I'd seen her sense it happened. She was already at work when I woke up this morning. I dropped my head; I couldn't bear to look at her anymore. I was ashamed.

She plopped down next to me on the bed as I sat up, rubbing my eyes trying to wake up. "What's up Ma?"

"Pete I've been doing some serious thinking and I want you to know that disrespecting a teacher is completely inappropriate behavior. But I don't think you're a bad person. I just think you're going through some little stage. You're just trying to find yourself. And with your Dad gone I know it has to be pretty difficult. Still that's not an excuse. You still have to work hard, trust in the Lord and make better decisions." I nodded my head. "And I have confidence that you're going to do just that." She smiled again. "So I've decided to allow you to go to the game. It's your first high school game and I really don't want you to miss it. These are going to be some of the best years of your life." She smiled at me as if she was doing me a favor or something. She had no idea that I had suddenly come down with a life threatening cold and I wasn't leaving this house for a long, long time. "So put on your clothes on Trell's down stairs. Thank him and Sharee for helping me change my mind. Trell told me what happened to Josh's Uncle and he said you were really disturbed. They both felt you needed to get out and get your mind off of things. They told me you'd cut your phone off and everything. They begged me to let you go."

She was smiling even harder now. I didn't know what to do. Trell was downstairs. I couldn't just leave him hanging. Especially considering the fact that I was part of the reason he had no one to go to the game with.

"Thanks Ma."

I tried my hardest to look happy. I had to go. There was no way around it. Hopefully Trell has some weed. I needed it more than ever.

"You're welcome," she said as she reached over for a hug. "I love you."

"I love you too Ma."

She walked out the room as I flopped back onto the bed. I couldn't wait for this to be over. That sleep was priceless. No worries. No guilt. If I could I swear I'd sleep my entire life away.

I stepped into the game sober as a cobra. Trell had talked a hole in my ear about everything from Josh to all the new girls he'd met. Of course the only thing I was interested in was how Josh was doing. He said he hadn't really spoken to him much but he still sounded pretty bad. It took everything I had inside of me not to burst into tears. Just the thought of Josh being hurt because of me had me tripping.

The game was filled to capacity as usual. Norview residents don't really have too many activities to indulge in so for some these football games were their lives. Even though Norview hadn't had a winning record for as long as I can remember, mo'fuckers acted like the players were professionals or something. They knew all the players' names, stats, GPA, everything.

This was the first game in the new stadium and I could feel the excitement in the air. Still, this did nothing for my mood. Like earlier, I felt like all eyes were on me. Only this time everything seemed unclear. My eyes had become so watery that I could hardly even see the faces of the hundreds of people in attendance. I carefully followed Trell to a seat with some niggas he'd met in school this week. I'm not even sure if I spoke. Probably not. I was back in zombie mode.

That was until my eyes were rewarded with a shot of Sharee. She flew out onto the field looking like treasure. She had her cute little cheerleading outfit on, fitting her perfectly. I eyeballed the crowd trying to see if anyone else was watching her. I couldn't really tell but I knew they were, she was bad.

She appeared as though she was scanning through the crowd looking for me. When our eyes finally connected she released the hands down most stunning smile I'd ever witnessed. Thanks to her I was no longer seeing a blur. Everything was crystal clear. I guess I was wrong, her smile still had the power to make me forget all of my problems.

Just like that, everything was cool. I even found myself conversing and laughing with Trell and his friends. Nothing much but I was having an alright time. Apparently Sharee had forgiven me for ducking her in school and never calling her back the other night because she couldn't keep her eyes off of me. I love her.

What a change of events. Everything was going great. The game was good and Sharee was doing a hell of a job. She was the only freshman on the squad and on top of that she had the entire crowd turned up. Maybe the other cheerers were doing good too but I wasn't paying them any mind. It was Sharee's world, they were just living in it.

But like everything that had been happening to me lately my smile was snatched away when I took my eyes off of Sharee for a split second, there was Sho, standing at the bottom of the bleachers looking directly at me. It was spooky. Not just because he was wearing all black but there was something different about him. Maybe he had a murderer look to him now or something, I don't know. I was just trying to figure out what the hell he was doing here? He had just killed a cop last night. Is he crazy? He slowly began making his way up to me. My good time suddenly came to an end and my brain was suddenly malfunctioning. I wasn't ready to talk to him.

And it seemed as if I would never have a chance anyway. About eight giant deputies were marching towards him. My heart pounded. Damn. Sho was about to go down and he didn't even see them coming. I searched for a way to warn him but my body wouldn't allow me to move. When they finally reached him I felt a tear hit my cheek. I knew Sho would be gone forever.

With the grace of God they kept walking right on past him and made their way further up the bleachers. Only now they were looking directly at me. I was probably wrong earlier about everyone watching me but now I'm one hundred percent sure their attention was directed my way. In fact the entire crowd had been drawn over to me by now. Petrified, my eyes scrambled for an escape, unfortunately there was nowhere to go. I panicked as one of the officers pointed square at me. I knew I wasn't tripping now. They strutted over to me, each appearing to have machete sharp horns bursting from their heads. Even with everything seeming to move in slow motion I was still unable to think straight. So as they got within arms distance, I went with my instincts. I swung as if I was fighting my way out of Hell. I felt myself connect right before I blacked out.

The next thing I knew I was face down on the stone cold steel bleachers, still holding the entire crowds attention. Everything seemed silent. I looked over to Trell. He looked baffled. I looked down to Sharee; tears were flowing down her eyes as Mrs. Williams held her back. I looked down at Sho. He had his right index finger over his lips. I closed my eyes.

So there I was sitting in some small ass room, no windows, dim light, just me, a table and a couple of the most uncomfortable chairs fathomable. My clothes were all ripped up and I hadn't seen my face yet but I was sure it was swollen. After the police dragged me out the game they had bought me here. They read me my rights, at least I think they did. Everything was still fuzzy; I really can't fully recall what the hell they did. I just remember them talking some shit about me being a cop killer on the way over.

Then they threw me in this room. I don't even have any idea of how long I'd even been in this bitch. Nothing was registering in my brain, I couldn't muster up one complete thought. Except for one; ramming my head into the wall. At this point death was the only logical remedy. Anything would be better than going to jail.

I know Sho said every black man goes to jail one day but I'm not even a fucking man. I'm 14 years old. The thought of being raped was eating me alive. Before I felt frozen. My emotions were vanished. But that shit was over. The urge to weep was building fast but I refused. And the fact that I ain't even do shit made it even worse.

Let me rephrase that, I ain't do shit that was worth going to jail. I mean what was I supposed to do, go tell the Police as soon as it happened or something? Who would do that? Besides they didn't even give me a chance to do it. Of course I'd never snitch on Sho but this was supposed to be him in here keeping his mouth shut, not me. I can't believe this. I wonder what he's thinking. Shit, I wonder what everybody's thinking.

My Mom, after everything she had just told me. Look at me, I'm in jail for murder. The brick wall was looking better and better. My eyes were fixed on it as I contemplated my next move when suddenly some big black Detective walked in. He looked at me devilishly as his eyes seemed to be ripping on my soul. His hideous face was blank but I'm sure inside he was bubbling with joy. I stared back.

"How ya doing Samuel, I'm Detective Fraley?" he said.

If I would've never seen his face I would have sworn he was a white man. He sat down slowly inching his chair closer to me. I looked away.

Sho's voice suddenly popped in my head *"Nigga who would take you in a room and ask you a million questions if they already knew the answers? That's why I act like Helen Keller when they got me in that bitch."*

Hearing Sho's voice gave me a sense of peace. No longer was I scared. Ok, I'm lying, maybe I was still scared but I knew there was nothing this hoe could do to me. I was in control. He couldn't make me talk. Talking wouldn't bring Josh's Uncle back. I had no reason to say anything.

94

"So you like to go around killing cops huh?" I looked at him for a second before turning away. This crazy motherfucker was smiling. This whole situation was creepy as hell but I refused to crack that easy. No matter what thoughts were running through my head. Sho had already schooled me. He's probably used to talking to dumb ass niggas with no sense. He got the wrong one. "Oh you a tough nigga huh?" he followed.

I continued to look away although I was dying to look him in the eyes and say, *"Nope I'm a smart nigga."* But I really wasn't in the mood to get my ass whipped again. The swelling on my face seemed to suddenly have a pulse.

For about five minutes he stared silently as my eyes strolled the room. His ass was still smiling. I really couldn't figure out his angle so I balled up my fist and clinched my teeth preparing for a punch when all of a sudden he slammed his hand on the table causing me to jump back. He then slowly picked It up, revealing an I.D. My eyes locked down on it and I realized it was mine.

"I hope you're ready for a big black dick in your ass."

My eyes never left the I.D. but I know his big bald headed ass was still smiling. I couldn't believe it was mine. I discretely checked the outside of my pants to feel for it. I was so fucked up this morning I didn't even notice that I didn't have it. But where did he get this from? Did I leave it in the car? I must have. But how? I never even took it out.

"You got anything you need to get off your chest?" he asked as he poked my chest with his pointer finger as he spoke.

"I need a lawyer," I finally said with my voice crackling. This was too much. I covered my face with my hands as Detective Fraley stormed out.

A tear fell from my face as two white pigs opened the door and trotted over to me. "Get up," said one as the other slapped more cuffs on me. I did as they said; I was too weak to fight. My life was falling from beneath me.

The cops escorted me out of the interrogation room down a long white hallway. There were rooms on both sides. I think they were interrogation rooms too but I didn't bother to look inside. I kept my head down. When I finally looked up I saw my worst nightmare. My Mom, standing next to some more officers at the far end of the hallway. Without wasting a second she rushed towards me the moment her eyes caught a glimpse but the officers restrained her.

She screamed a scream that could wake the dead and mumbled words but they weren't the least bit understandable as she stretched her arms out trying desperately to somehow grab a hold of me. As I got closer her words became clearer.

"My baby," she repeated over and over as the Officers continued to hold her back. I couldn't bear to look her in the eyes and not be able to touch her so I pretended as if she wasn't there. I closed my eyes as I got closer. "No. No. Not my baby," she screamed as I turned the corner and walked past.

As I placed my back up against the wall to take my mug shot picture, all hope that this was just a nightmare disappeared. Every event that had occurred within the last twenty four hours was real. It was officially official.

I was charged with the Capital Murder of Officer John McNair, use of a fire arm, operating a stolen vehicle, and resisting arrest, all felonies. They were placing me in an adult jail and charging me as an adult. I was on my way to the lion's den.

I sat in the back of the squad car, motionless, I was approaching hell.

As we drove through a revolving barbed wire gate I peered out at the 10 story brick building that would now serve as my home and as the gate slammed I saw everything I cherished violently snatched away from me. I was trapped. Images of killers and rapist from all the movies I'd seen flashed before my eyes. There was no way I could survive here for long. Home was so close, yet so far away. Still I had faith that Sho knew what he was talking about. He wouldn't lie, well at least not to me.

In the meantime I was gonna have to make the best out of this situation. But as I entered the cold and dry jail it seemed impossible. There was a feeling of emptiness that seemed to plague. The air was stale. Actually stale wasn't even the word. The air was dead. Like the spirit of so many men whose lives were washed down the drain were still lingering around. Or maybe it was the fact that every deputy looked at me as if they wanted me dead. I don't know but as the officers dragged me around I decided that nice ol Pete was out the window. I was transforming into Sho. Everything he stood for, everything he'd ever taught

97

me would be utilized. No one was going to hurt me. No one.

"Get his ass over here," said one of the Deputies' as I walked into some big white empty room that was filled with about 12 C.O.'s. They surrounded me with their mouths watering. I had no clue what was going on. But I made sure my face stayed emotionless. I even made sure I wasn't thinking of any punk ass shit. They looked like they could sense fear.

I don't know, I guess they all just wanted to get a good look at me or something because after a minute of them all just staring at me, one of the officers dragged me over to a smaller room connected to the larger room that I'd just been in. There were black and white jumpers all over the floor. I had seen those jumpers on the news all the time when they were interviewing prisoners. I used to think they looked kind of cool. I was a fool.

"Strip," screamed one of the pigs. There was now only three of them in here with me. A fat one, tall skinny one and a regular sized one. The fat one was the speaker.

They all stood in front of me with their arms crossed with identical smirks. You could fill the hatred from a galaxy away.

I couldn't help but to lose my emotionless face. What the fuck did he mean strip? There were three fucking men in here. I had already told myself that I would die before I got raped. There was no way I was stripping in front of three crackers who wanted me dead.

"Strip?" I asked, attempting to sound as hard as I could.

"Yeah nigger. Strip before we strip you," fat ass bellowed. I was stunned. I had never been called that before. Never. I guess this was a sign of things to come. But I wasn't going out like a sucker.

"For what?"

All three officers died laughing. "So I can stick my dick in your little black butt," said fat ass.

"We're gonna kill that lil ass hole of yours," said the tall one finally breaking his silence.

Again my eyes were starting to water. But fuck it. I said I'd die before I got raped and that's exactly what I was prepared to do.

"Take your damn clothes off nigger," shouted fatty as I stood there with my teeth and fist clinched, I was ready to go to war. "We wouldn't dare touch you. The niggas upstairs will handle that for us. Now Strip."

I was confused. I stood there for a second before I began undressing. Still, my fist remained balled as I looked around carefully. I took everything but my underwear off and stood tall. My body trembled as my feet seemed to be sticking to the ice cold floor.

"Take all that shit off boy. We gotta make sure your black ass ain't got shit on you. We know how yall are," said fat ass as his two flunkies continued staring at me never losing their smirk. I couldn't believe these motherfuckers wanted me to get butt ass naked. And what the fuck did he mean make sure I ain't got shit on me? What could I have in my underwear? But with all the foul shit happening I gave in. This was no worse than everything else. I dropped my underwear. "Now lift your nut sack, squat and cough."

The only thing I was left to do in this situation was to huff and puff. These gay ass motherfuckers seemed to be enjoying this shit more and more by the minute. I slowly followed their commands. Still, I was still prepared to die. I don't see how niggas could come in and out of jail all the time. I hadn't even made it to a cell and I already knew once I got out this bitch I was never coming back again.

"Put that shit on," said the taller one as he tossed me an oversized jumper before stepping on my underwear just as I was about ot retrieve them.

"Do you see that sign right there?" he asked, pointing to the wall. The sign read 'No Colored Underwear'. Mine were blue and red polka dotted. I looked around to see if there were any piles of underwear lying around. "You ever heard of free balling boy? You better tell Mommy to put some money on your books fast. You don't wanna make it that easy for Big Ray Ray to have a good time."

They all burst out laughing like they weren't talking to a 14 year old.

Approaching the cell my heart pumped like it was going out of style. My legs were shaking so much I don't have any idea how I was moving. I heard the loud voices of what sounded like hundreds of men screaming and yelling as I walked past countless cells filled with dark faces. There was a distinct echo. If I didn't know any better I would think that they were having fun. Still I wouldn't allow myself to look too hard. I didn't want to draw any extra attention to myself.

We finally stopped at a giant steel door. This didn't look anything like the other cell I'd just walked past. I could hear people inside but I couldn't see anything. The blue steel door was completely shut. The only light that came out was from what looked like a tiny mail slot in the middle of the door.

The guard typed in some sorta password into a small keypad on the side of the door before pressing his index finger on it. I think it checked his fingerprints or something. Looks like it would be pretty hard to break out of this bitch.

The cell door slowly opened, I braced myself and went into full gangster mode. I put on the meanest face I could muster up.

The light from the cell nearly blinded me. It was a huge contrast from the dim windowless hallway I had previously occupied. The block was hella big. There were niggas everywhere. Some shooting dice, some playing cards, some watching a little ass TV propped up inches away from the ceiling in the corner; there were even about five men who looked like they were having some sort of church service or something at these little cookout style tables they had lined up against the left side of the wall. The rest of the block was full of about 20 or so steal bunk beds precisely placed about four feet from each other in rows around the block.

The entire room went silent as the C.O. pushed me into the cell, immediately closing the door. "Have fun," he said as I took a huge gulp.

I stood at the entrance holding a blue duffel bag. All eyes turned to me. A group of inmates shooting dice close

101

to the entrance began speaking. "Damn we babysitting now?" said one of them as I stood in place trying to figure out my next move.

"That ain't no baby, nigga that's the mo'fuckin cop killer. You don't rememba seeing his lil ass on the news last night?" said another.

The inmate took a closer look at me before saying "Oh shit, I like the lil nigga already. What's up lil cuz?"

Even though it seemed as if they were cool, I still didn't trust it. I simply nodded my head and began steadily walking down the block. I heard one of them say "Oh shit he think he hard," as the others laughed. Still I didn't turn around.

Inmates silently watched as I made my way down the block, face tight, fist balled. Through my pereipheral I noticed one inmate in particalr staring pretty hard. He was sitting on the bottom of his bunk. His mouth was pretty much shut but I still could see the gleam from his gold teeth. His unkempt beard and huge scar in the middle of his forehead led me to believe that he was a stone cold killer. There was no way my mean mug would be any match for his.

"You don't have a clue what to do, do you?" he asked as I stepped closer to him. I was shocked. I was planning on walking right past him. But I couldn't just ignore him.

So I nervously replied "No." I wanted to lie and act tough like I'd been here plenty of times before but I'm pretty sure I looked my age so I didn't go with that one.

"It's a free bunk on top of mine. Put your shit up there," he said.

I had no choice but to oblige. I didn't want to look like a bitch and be taking orders as soon as I got in here but it was either do what he said or continue searching the block like a dummy.

"Thanks man. What's this bag for?" I asked, holding up the blue duffel bag I'd been toting around, the guards had given it to me earlier.

"You put your tissue, socks, drawers and food and shit in there. Guard that shit with your life cause niggas don't play fair round hea," he answered. I nodded my head and threw my shit to the top bunk. The bed was hard as a rock. "How old is you anyway?"

"14."

"14?" he asked as he shook his head in disbelief. "Damn. This ain't the place to be lil nigga. But you might as well get used to it while you here. I'm Dada."

"I'm Pete," I said attempting to give him some dap.

Instead DaDa balled up his fist initiating us to tap knuckles. "Niggas play with they dick too much to be touching hands round hea."

For the rest of the night I sat on my bunk observing and thinking. It was four in the morning and most everybody in the block was still awake doing the same shit they'd been doing when I got in here. I still hadn't said anything to anyone but DaDa.

I couldn't stop shaking my head in disappointment,

I couldn't believe where I was but after hearing that inmate say he saw me on the news, I knew for a fact the whole town knew by now. I wondered if they thought that I had really done it.

Did my Mom think I'd done it? I was too embarrassed to even call her. I didn't' even want to think about her.

I wondered what Sharee was thinking. She hated thugs and I was being charged with the murder of a cop. She's gotta hate me now. How could I explain this to her?

And Josh. Damn. I know for sure he hates me. But he knows me better than anybody. He should know I didn't do it. Shit, he probably knows Sho had something to do with it. Maybe Sho would turn himself in. Hell naw, what am I thinking I know better than that.

I wondered how long I'd have to stay in here before they realized I didn't do it. How the hell did they get the I.D. in the first place?

I was going crazy with all these thoughts so I tried to think of something positive. It was damn near impossible as I looked around at all of Norviews hardest criminals surrounding me. As s matter of fact, this ain't even just Norview's hardest criminals. Richmond was so crazy that they didn't have enough room to store all of their gangsters so they had to throw some in our jail. Damn, why they gotta be here? If it was just Norview criminals I'd feel a little better but I always heard Richmond niggas was missing a couple marbles. Shit!

I looked down at DaDa, he was one of the few niggas who was actually sleep. Just looking at him I could already tell he was from Richmond. Still, I'm so glad that I met him. He seemed cool. I wondered if he'd teach me how to make a shank. I just hope he won't the nigga I had to be shanking. I hope not because I don't know what kinda shank would cause any harm to his body, probably just make him angry. Actually he looked like he might like a good stabbing, judging from all the scars and tattoos all over his body he might be the type who enjoyed pain. The nigga even had a tattoo on his eye lids that's only visible when he closed his eyes. It read 'Fear God'. I ain't never seen no shit like that before. Of course I seen rappers do crazy shit like that but never just a regular ass nigga. I couldn't take my eyes off of him.

"Is it somethin you want down hea lil nigga?" asked DaDa opening his eyes, startling the shit out of me.

I quickly laid back. "No."

"You gotta be able to feel a nigga lookin at you in this bitch. You get caught slippin one time and it could be your last. I'm just tryna teach you how to survive. You in a Man's world now lil nigga. Whetha you killed that cop or not."

I closed my eyes and went to sleep. I had some long day's ahead of me.

Chapter 5

"One more minute" screamed C.O. Barnes, a tall older black man standing in the corner of the visitation room. This was the first time in the seven months I'd been here that I was fortunate enough to be the sole inmate occupying the room. Usually it was at least five of us in here clutching a oversized phone receiver, talking to our people's who sat separated from us by some bulletproof glass window that split the room in half.

Today my Mom was visiting me. Actually she and my lawyer were the only ones who ever visited. It wasn't so much that no one wanted to, it's just that my Mom wouldn't allow them to. She wanted me all to herself. I guess I'm cool with that.

"Ok Pete, tomorrows the big day. I want you to speak clearly and look the judge in the eyes. Don't look away," said Mary as tears formed in the corners of her eyes.

"Ma, I know. You told me a million times."

"I know, Pete I love you. We're gonna get through this," she said as tears slowly eased down her stressed riddled face. "Put your hand on the glass." I hated when she got all emotional. I couldn't help but to shed a tear as we both lined our hands up congruently on the glass. "Close your eyes." We both closed our eyes tightly as my Mom called out to the Lord. "Lord please grant my son with the will and energy to make it through these trying times. Let him see that with you he can make it through anything."

"Times up," shouted the C.O. in the corner.

"Continue to keep us strong through the night," continued Mom. "Lord, guide us. Please Lord let us acquire all the knowledge that you have set forth for us to learn in this situation Lord. We refuse to let this ordeal be in vein. We trust you Lord. We need you Lord. In Jesus name we Pray. Amen."

"Amen" I repeated as we both opened our eyes.

"I love you Pete."

"I love you too Ma."

"Call me tonight. Ok?"

"Ok."

I strolled down the eerie jail hallway on my way back to my Maximum security block side by side with C.O. Barnes.

"Whadup Pete," screamed inmates as they lined up against the bars of their standard low level cells.

"Whadup, Whadup," I shouted back.

"Tomorrows the big day, ain't it?" screamed another.

"Yeah man," I replied.

"We prayin for you baby boy."

"That's whatsup. I appreciate it."

Life's funny. As long as I can remember, my Mom always told me that God answers prayers. And like always I really didn't pay her any mind. Of course I prayed when something bad was going down. Or when there was something that I really wanted. Who doesn't? But as far as getting on my knees every single night and asking some guy I couldn't see for random things, I never really saw the need. What for, when the person who really seemed to control everything was right across the hall. My Mom. Don't get me wrong I believed in God and everything, I just always felt that asking my Mom for shit was just way more logical.

That was until last summer. It was then I realized that Mom couldn't control the things I wanted anymore. So I began hitting my knees every night. And I must admit, Mom Dukes was right, I prayed to get some money in my pocket. The next week, me, Josh and Trell came up with a plan for cutting grass. I prayed to meet a girl, WOILA; Sharee. I prayed to have a great summer, Bam.

Everything seemed to fall right into place. So when I asked God for popularity there was no doubt in my mind that I would be *'That Nigga'* walking down Norview High's Hallways. I wanted everyone to know me. Watching Sho walk through crowds and having everyone scream his name enticed me. I wanted in. And soon, I got exactly what I asked for. Not only was I the most recognizable face in jail but I was the most recognizable face in the entire Norview. I guess I gotta be more specific with my prayers.

In the last seven months my case had spun the entire town upside down. You know I haven't been there to witness it, but according to all the letters Sharee and Trell had been writing me, shit was getting real. The whites hated the blacks and the blacks hated them just as much. It turns out Josh wasn't the only one who loved Officer McNair. Hell no, every white person in town did. And the fact that my Mom was so active in the community and just an all around happy ass person, every black person was on her side.

See, there are two major churches in Norview; Norview Holiness, which was the black church and Norview Baptist which was for the whites. There were no signs that read 'Whites Only or Blacks Only' or anything but it was just understood.

So of course Officer McNair's entire family were members of Norview Baptist. Each week they started holding special offerings for his family and shit. He had three kids under ten and a pregnant wife so you already know everybody felt sorry for them. Plus they say his wife made some heartfelt speech at the funeral thanking the Police for their hard work and for catching me and shit.

While on the other side of town my Mom had gave a speech about how them crackers had taken her baby away from her. She supposedly had the whole church in tears.

And just like that the town was divided. Soon arguments, threats, and even occasional fist fights between the blacks and whites was normal. Someone even spray painted the words 'Cop Killer' on my Mom's white picket fence.

Shit's crazy. Still, with everything that was going wrong in my life, my relationship with Josh still stuck out like a sore thumb. My nigga was gone. My first true friend. A friend who bought me endless memories would probably hate my guts for the rest of our lives. Man, I must admit the thought of snitching just so Josh knew it wasn't me had definitely crossed my mind more than a few times. The pain of losing someone as special as Josh is one I'd never wish on anyone. Well, no one but those pussies who'd spray painted my Mom's gate.

"Ay Jesse, Tell Byrd to send me over some oatmeal pies," screamed an inmate. Inmates always borrowed shit from their homies in other blocks. Usually I would be down for helping another inmate out. But not right now. I was in my feelings. Ever since I got in this bitch I had these wild ass mood swings. Just a minute ago I was happy, speaking to all the other inmates but in a split second I had switched over to fuck you mode. So fuck him and his damn oatmeal pies. I walked down the hallway ignoring him as he yelled my name. "Jesse, Jesse."

Oh yeah that's what they call me around here. They say before I had gotten here it was some dude named Jesse who looked just like me. At first I wasn't feeling it. There were so many cool nicknames they could've given me. Why the hell did I have to get stuck with some bullshit? This Jesse nigga could be some ol Biz Markie looking mo'fucker. But after repeatedly attempting to resist I realized there was no use and just went with the flow. Fuck it I was Lil Jesse.

"You not gonna get them oatmeal pies?" asked C.O. Barnes.

"Naw," I replied without looking up to him. I didn't want to be to mean to Barnes. He was the coolest C.O. we had. But when I'm in 'Fuck you Mode' his ass could get it to.

"You sure?"

"Yeah," I replied sternly, this time looking him in the eyes.

Barnes was pushing it. I don't give a fuck if he did just let me have ten extra minutes in visitation. He had one more time to say something to me.

With every second I spent in this place I seemed to be growing more and more aggravated. The dry air had yet to set in with me. Sometimes I felt myself losing breath. The air was still dead and I refused to get used to it.

Dudes in here are crazy. They be sweepin and mopping the floor. Making niggas take off they shoes when they step into their area. Fuck all that. These niggas acting like this they home or something. This ain't no damn home . This is hell and I'll be damned if I showed any kinda respect for this hell hole. Home is where the heart is and my heart for damn sure ain't here. My heart is out there. Out there with my family.

"Alright dog," said C.O. Barnes as he opened up the electric door for me to get back in the block.

"Alright man," I said as I slowly walked in.

Mostly everyone was asleep. It was 3:00 pm. Time schedules in here are a little different than they are out there on the land. While everyone's asleep in the real world. We're up.

Our schedule was simple. Breakfast Trays were served at 5:30 sharp. But in here breakfast was different considering the fact that generally no one had been to sleep yet. After breakfast, it was our time to sleep. Everyone sleeps until about 11:00, that's when lunch is served. After lunch we're back to sleep again till diner at 4:30. After diner everyone was usually up for the remainder of the night doing everything from gambling, arguing, gossiping or any other thing that would pass the time. You know, normal jail nigga shit. Of course you had some niggas who had their own schedule. Like the niggas who were all gathered around at the T.V. right now, but for the most part everyone really followed the protocol. And I was one of them.

"Whadup Jesse," said the group of inmates watching T.V..

I nodded and headed to my rack. After visitation niggas don't usually have too much to say. They understood that. No one said anything else. Niggas in here showed respect. I came in here thinking shit was going to be all crazy but that's a far stretch from how it really is. Yeah, you had people who came in being disrespectful but they were usually the ones who got their ass beat all the damn time. You showed respect and you was good.

Unless you were white. They were outnumbered by probably a thousand to one ratio in here. I heard ever since they built this jail they'd been getting their asses kicked. Probably because they resembled all the officers and judges who'd been responsible for holding our asses in here. And of course the recent black versus white beef didn't make shit any better. In fact shit had gotten so bad that just last week they had to create a whole new separate cell for whiteys. They might run the world but once you step foot in one of these cell blocks it was the land of the black man. In a weird way I guess I kind of grew to feel proud about that.

I stripped down to my underwear and wrapped my head in a broken up sheet that served as my do-rag. Back at home my Mom always had to force me to brush my hair but in here I was a wave fiend. Everyone was. Even if you have the nappiest head in the world. (Like myself).

112

There was this thing we all did. We'd cover our hair with soap and wrap an old cut up sheet around our head. We'd keep it on for about a week straight. After that week, woila; you'd magically have a head full of waves spinning. I don't know what kinda secret wave forming solution was in the state soap but it was the truth. Whoever created it needs to win some type of award or something.

I hopped up on my bed and closed my eyes. Tomorrows the big day. My life was in a stranger's hand. I couldn't even think about it without my entire body falling weak. I was either going to the crib or going to my new crib, a maximum state prison for the rest of my life. Just the thought of never going home again had me nearly having a panic attack. So like always I thought of the one person who always seemed to bring me up during times like this.

Sharee. Even though I felt so lonely without her, reading her letters made me feel just a tad bit closer to her. Don't judge me but at times I even smelled the paper that she wrote on. The scent of her was something that I could spot a mile away, it soothed me.

She was my Goddess, she almost wrote me as much as my own Mother. And considering the fact that my Mom wrote me every day that was huge. In each letter Sharee always filled me in on whatever was going on. School gossip, Sho's latest girl Drama. She was even the one who had told me that Sho had finally had his kid. He had a boy. A little Sho, this world better watch out. I loved when she told me about Sho. Probably because he never wrote. I don't really know how to feel about that. And that was exactly the problem, I didn't know what to think and worse, I didn't even have Sharee to talk about it too. I wanted to tell her everything that went on so bad and I couldn't. It was killing me

113

As I studied her letters I started to feel a tear making its way to my face and the walls seemed to be caving in on me. Man, I gotta learn how to control my emotions better. I could feel a breakdown brewing so I jumped off the rack, forcing myself to be strong.

I through my jumper back on and walked over to the homies watching T.V. I really didn't feel like talking but I'm cool with all of them and I know they ass would have me feeling a little better in no time. Niggas like them sometimes made time speed by. God really did a number when he created these fools. They were all unique in their own crazy way.

I swear to God Byrd was the funniest nigga I'd ever seen. He was on his way to doing a 28 year bid for some botched robbery him and some of his homeboys did but you'd never guess it. He joked all day, every day. The nigga woke up joking, went to sleep joking, joked while he took a shit, I swear the nigga need to be on somebody's T.V. show. He was one of those niggas that everybody loved. Well, almost everybody.

When Byrd wasn't easing the tension of being in jail with his humor, he was busy gunning one of the female nurses or C.O.'s down. Now of course getting a gun into a maximum security block was virtually impossible, so obviously I'm not talking about an actual gun. Gunning a bitch down in here was indecent exposure. Whenever a female deputy or nurse would walk into the block niggas would usually hop in their bunk stare the female down and get to gunnin! The sane thing to do was to make sure you kept your little man inside your jumper while you gunned. Which wasn't so hard being that our jumpers were huge. But Byrd was different, he'd actually whip it on out. He didn't give a fuck. Consequently he got caught A LOT. The

114

C.O.'s would always rush in to take him down to the hole for a few days. And it never failed, as soon as they bought him back he'd be right back to the Byrd we all knew and loved. Joking all day and gunning hoes down. Dude definitely had a few screws loose. But who cares the block wouldn't be the same without him.

Then you got my nigga Skinny. He was in here for 10 counts of Armed Robbery but if you looked at him you'd never believe it. He was short, skinny as a twig, wore big ass bifocals and talked like Carlton from Fresh Prince of Bel-Air. He'd just graduated from Hampton University before he landed in here and he made sure he let you know any chance he could get. Skinny was the type of nigga who thought he knew everything. That shit got on everybody's nerves but he was one of those niggas nobody took serious, so niggas just ignored his ass or said the blocks famous line towards him *'Shut the fuck up Skinny!'* Still five minutes later he'd be back to correcting niggas again.

That was until he corrected the wrong nigga, A.J. A.J. was from Brooklyn. Word on the block was that he'd killed a 7-eleven clerk for giving him the wrong change. And from the looks of him I didn't doubt it for a second. He was the type of nigga who I tried to stay far, far away from, everybody did. That's why I don't have any idea what Skinny could've possibly said to piss A.J. off. All I know was that when A.J. said those famous fighting words *'Strap Up'* the entire block went silent.

In jail everyone knew what *'Strap Up'* meant. It meant it was time to take your jailhouse slippers off and strap up your tennis shoes. It was about to go down!

No one said it but I could sense everyone felt for Skinny as he went to his rack to lace up his shoes. I had never even thought about Skinny squaring up with anyone let alone squaring up with the biggest nigga in here. Something inside me wanted to hop in for him. But then something else told me to sit my little ass down and get a front row seat in the *'Cage'* along with everyone else on the block.

The cage wasn't actually a cage it was just in the back corner of the block where we held our fights. Don't ask me why they named it the cage. It was like that when I got here. I just go with the flow.

Let me get back to the story. I still remember it like it was yesterday, A.J. paced around the Cage as Skinny walked in looking right through everyone who was looking at him. He was focused. Still, no one believed he had a chance in hell. As he walked into the cage I closed my eyes and said a prayer. I knew he needed it. He was a brave soul.

To everyone's surprise Skinny wasted no time. He swung first connecting with A.J.'s jaw. The entire block gasped as excitement erupted throughout the room. Even if Skinny didn't get another lick he would've gained our respect forever.

Luckily we never would have to worry about that. A.J. never landed a hit. Skinny whipped his ass up and down the cage. Turns out this nigga knew more than we gave him credit for because he hit A.J. with some moves that only some tae quon doe expert would know. I had always thought Skinny was wrongfully accused of all the shit they say he did but after seeing his face beaming down over A.J.'s beaten body I saw something I'd never seen. He now had the face of a hardnosed gangster. It's safe to say nobody in the block looked at him like we used to anymore. He was the truth.

But Lying ass Larry damn sure wasn't. And you'd think someone who had a nick name like that would get the hint that niggas knew he was a liar. But nope. He lied like his mind was bad.

Larry was supposedly locked up for killing a guy who raped his sister. But since he was Lying ass Larry who knows.

Hearing lies in jail wasn't anything new. Niggas lied all the time. Every day I heard stories of how they were 'this' or they had 'that' when they were on the streets. I was pretty used to it. But lying ass Larry was on a whole nother lever. He'd lie about any and everything. Anytime anyone told a story his ass just had to have been there too. He was a basketball player, football player, gangster, poet, singer, songwriter, loving Father, great husband, pimp, counselor, mechanic, plumber, sky diver, chemist, drug dealer, weed coinsurer. He could do anything under the sun. It got to a point where I just would go talk to him for a good laugh. His wild stories got me thorough some rough days.

But the nigga who really got me through some rough times was Dre Skii. Hands down he was the best rapper I'd ever heard in my life. Better than Pac, Biggie, Jay-Z, Lil Wayne, anybody. Never in life had I heard anyone spit with so much passion, so much charisma. With him in the block, it didn't even matter that we didn't have a radio because he was always coming up with some dope ass raps. Whether it be just some random freestyle about what had went down that day or a full length song about the trials and tribulations of his life, the songs were always fire. Anytime a new guy would come to the block claiming that he spit, we'd tell Dre to kick something. And it never failed, as soon as Dre was done, they would all suddenly lose all passion for rapping. Dre was unreal. I can't count

117

the number of times Dre's rhymes had the entire block shedding tears. He'd beat on the walls and make you feel every word that slid out of his mouth deep down in the pit of your soul. Each line he spit felt more important than the last. Too bad he was sentenced to 55 years. Supposedly Dre and some friends had jumped a guy and the guy died and so did Dre's dreams of being a rapper. Every night before I went to bed I made sure I prayed for him. It didn't seem right for God to create someone so talented and for the world to never hear them. That shit made me think about how there was probably niggas who balled better than Jordan or smarter than Martin Luther King Jr. who were stuck in some penitentiary for the rest of their lives. It's crazy right?

Just like Buck. Buck was an ex crack head/current alcoholic. He was an O.G. in the block, he had been getting locked up before most of us was even born and it ain't hard to figure out why. Buck was straight up crazy.

A few months back he had been telling us about how if he beat his charge he was going straight. A life of crime was in his rearview. He was embarking on a whole new life. And what do you know, he beat his case and was released. We were all so happy for him. Seeing someone from the block actually get to carry their ass to the crib was something we celebrated. We talked about Bucks crazy ass all day until later that night we were watching the eleven o'clock news and guess who we see. Yep, Buck. His old ass was on the damn news for robbing some white lady at gun point. Next thing we know his ass was getting thrown back in the block talking about, "They framed me." He fed everybody some lie about how it wasn't him even though someone had caught it on tape and it was all over the

118

internet. Still it was funny hearing his story. In a way I guess it's kinda better that he was in here.

So as you can see going over to watch T.V. with these guys would definitely be something interesting.

When I arrived at the T.V., the first thing I saw was my face plastered on the channel four news. I guess they were talking about my case. I for damn sure ain't feel like hearing that shit.

"Yo. Could yall please turn that shit?" I asked convincingly as they all looked over to me.

"Say no more," said Dre Skii who held the remote. He flicked through the channels.

"Ay turn to VH1. For the love of Ray-J on," said Lying Ass Larry. We only had four channels. The news, PBS, VH1 and some channel for country music, shit that we'd never watch any other time. Still it wouldn't be hard for us to discover our favorite channel, VH1. With reality T.V. taking over the world they hands down had to have the best. Where else could you watch a show with 20 something gorgeous women walking around half naked fighting over a C list celebrity? The prison Gods really looked out for us when they created shit like that. For niggas locked up it ain't get no better. It goes without saying, there was a lot of gunning going down when this shit was on the screen.

"Oh shit, that look just like Roofus," said Buck as we watched some Pedigree commercial.

"Roofus? Who the hell is Roofus? And why the hell he look like a damn German Sheppard?" asked Byrd as we

119

all laughed. It was something about the way he said everything that was always funny as shit.

"Man Roofus was my pet Rock wilder," said Buck staring at the T.V., reminiscing.

"You do know that was a German Sheppard, right?" asked Dre Skii.

"Naw I think that was a Rock wilder," said Lying ass Larry.

"Larry shut yo lyin ass up," said Byrd.

"Yeah I know that was a German Sheppard but that's how Roofus started lookin after we started smokin crack. He was my best friend," said Buck as he dropped his head, truly saddened.

We all looked around at each other confused, not believing what we'd just heard.

"You and your dog smoked crack together?" I asked?

"Hell yeah. That was my nigga. I won't gonna just walk around high and leave him out. Ain't no fun if the homie can't have none."

We all just shook our heads as *'For the Love of Ray-J'* came back on. Believe it or not this wasn't nearly the craziest thing said around here. We were all used to it. It's some interesting shit that goes on in this world and being in here you were guaranteed to find some of that shit out. Guaranteed.

"Yo. You think that nigga Ray-J really be fuckin these hoes?" I asked staring at all these half naked women surrounding Ray-J, wishing I could be him for just one day.

"Hell naw that nigga gay as hell," replied Dre Skii.

"You crazy. You must ain't see his sex tape with that bitch Kim Kardashian," said Skinny.

"Man, I saw that bullshit. But if you ask me, Dre's right, that nigga gayer than a Mo'fucka. Kim had that big phat ol booty and his ass all in the camera winkin and shit, makin love to the bitch. A nigga like me would've caught an assault charge on that pussy. I woulda beat it up," bolted Byrd.

"Shit, but hey at least he fucked that bitch. Niggas with money can fuck anybody. Look at them hoes up there. If that nigga name wont Ray-J them hoes would walk right past his lil gay ass," replied Dre Skii.

I could look in his eyes and tell that he knew that was supposed to be him up there hogging up the limelight.

"Man, these thirsty bitches'll fuck a roach if they think he got some money," said Byrd

"Bitches ain't shit," added Buck

"Hell yeah fuck them hoes," followed Lyin ass Larry.

"Why the hell did God even create them for/" asked Skinny.

"Shit, I know why he created 'em," said Dre Skii smiling.

"Hell yeah," followed Buck.

I couldn't help but to smile.

"What the hell you smilin for lil nigga? You know you don't know shit about why these hoes hea for," joked Byrd.

"Shit, you crazy," I said trying to be as convincing as I could be.

"Nigga, you ain't neva had no damn pussy," said Buck.

"Shit, nigga you must don't know who the fuck I am."

They all burst out laughing and began dapping me up.

"That's what I'm talkin about lil nigga," said Dre Skii.

"Shit, I was fuckin at your age too," added Lyin ass Larry.

"Hell yeah those was the best times," said Skinny.

"Who you tellin? All the bitches had them tight little pussies," said Buck.

They all got super excited as they remininsed.

"Man, now all my bitches got them big ass car tunnel pussies," said Byrd.

"Hell yeah, dog," said Dre Skii.

"So if you go home tomorrow-" said Buck.

"Naw Lil Jesse definitely goin home tommorow. No doubt. You gotta be positive my nigga," said Dre Skii.

"Alright my bad. 'When' you get out tomorrow and them little bitches throw you that pussy. And they definitely will throw you that pussy. Cuz you gonna have that glow," said Buck.

"Glow?" I asked.

I had no idea what they were talking about but judging from their reactions it was something really, really good.

"Hell yeah. The glow. Everybody gets the glow for about a month after you get out," said Dre Skii.

"For some reason bitches just can't resist you. It's like you're the chosen one or somethin. It kinda makes going to jail worth it a little bit. That shit don't last forever though so while you out there gettin all that pussy, appreciate it," said Byrd.

"Yeah you gotta cherish that shit," followed Lying ass Larry.

"Yeah and don't just cherish it. Eat it," followed Buck. "Eat it like it's your last meal young nigga!"

"Man the lil nigga know he supposed to eat it," said Dre Skii.

"I don't know dog. These lil niggas out hea ain't livin right. You eat pussy Lil Jesse?" asked Byrd.

"Hell naw," I blurted. Sho had always told me that, that was a no no.

123

"What?" they all screamed.

"What the hell wrong with you boy?" asked Buck as if I had commited a deadly sin or something.

"I thought you was a man," said Skinny, shaking his head.

"I am. That shit just nasty," I said hoping they'd understand.

"No. the hell it ain't," screamed Byrd.

"Well it can be if it's the wrong bitch," said Dre Skii.

"Yeah you can't just go round stickin yo face in everybody," added Lyin ass Larry.

"But for the ones that's worth it. Eat it right and they'll love you forever," said Buck. "And when you get real advanced you gotta start lickin that asshole," he said looking me dead in the eyes.

For some reason this made all of them extra excited. But they got even happier when C.O. Barnes screamed "Trays,'

Immediately everyone woke up and jetted over to the door to C.O. Barnes, who handed us the trays. He was with his usual worker, some old gray hairded guy. I don't know his name. He never talked he just filled our cup up with the jail house tea from the cooler. Which happens to be some of the worst tea you'll ever locate on earth.

Today we're having baked chicken, string beans, and rice and Gravy. That's usually reserved for a Sunday diner but I guess they were feeling generous for a chance.

124

Most likely they just had some extra chicken for some reason. I seriously doubt they just wanted to do something kind for us.

Usually I'd hurry over but I hadn't had much of an appetite today. Too many butterfly's were flying around in my stomach. So I decided to trade my tray for some honey buns and donuts. I'd probably get hungry later on. I had enough canteen food stashed away to make myself a little meal if I had too.

After diner it was mail time. A lot of niggas names seldom got called. Some niggas was all alone in this world. Thank the Lord I wasn't one of those niggas. Not a day went by when I wasn't granted at least one letter. There was one week that they was giving all my mail to some other guy named Samuel Turner but after three days with no mail I knew something was up and I got that shit situated.

Today when I opened the mail I got the usual inspirational poem from my Mom and a cute little card from Sharee with some little flower on the front. The inside simply read 'Just Thinking About You'. As usual Sharee wrote a little something in there for me "Always remember you are special. And if no one on this earth has your back. I do."

Instantly I felt better. I hopped on top of my rack and began looking for my pad and pencil. I felt like writing Sharee.

As soon as I put the pen to the pad DaDa walked up. "I hope you ain't bouta write no letta."

"Yeah what's wrong with that?"

125

"Neva write a letter the day before you're set to go to court. It's like saying you plannin on being hea to get it"

"Ok," I said.

I had no choice but to listen to DaDa. He was always schooling me on some real shit. He's the first person to tell me that *'If you do the crime you gotta be prepared to do the time'* and *'Never step into a man's world if you're not prepared for men consequences'* Sometimes I'd listen to him and I'd swear I was talking to Sho. They were just alike. DaDa was just an older, more mature version.

Just like Sho, everybody respected DaDa. He was the coolest nigga in this bitch and not once did he ever act tough. But trust, niggas knew, they knew not to fuck with DaDa. He just had this look to him that let you know he didn't play no games. Not once had he talked about who he was on the street, he let everyone else do the talking.

Of course since he never said anything I don't know how true everything is but niggas say he was like some Drug God. They said he had about 10 butta whips, a big ass crib and bitches like a rap star. I always wanted to ask DaDa about it but if he never said anything I guess I wasn't supposed to either. Plus just by looking at him I knew it was the truth. Before I get out this bitch I'ma make sure we have a little talk. I wanna be just like him when I hit the streets.

"Wake up Lil nigga," screamed Byrd as he stood next to me. I opened my eyes. I didn't even realize it but I guess I'd taken a little nap. "Your ass been down today so we got a lil somethin for you. Since this might be, I mean since this is gonna be your last day," he said as he pointed over to the Bench where almost the entire block was gathered around. There was all kinds of jail house food. Swole is what we called it. It looked like a cell block cookout. "We want to make sure your last day in this bitch is excitin."

The whole block was staring at me. I felt special.

"Radio do yo thang," said Buck to Radio. Radio was the guy on the block who could recite and beat box just about every popping song known to man. Every time he did his thing he had the entire block crunk. Immediately he started hitting the blocks number one jam, 'Shoulder Lean' by Young Dro. Everyone loved to do the dance. It was funny as hell to see a bunch of cock diesel grown ass men laughing and dancing around. Times like this would be a horrible time for kids to take a 'Scared Straight' field trip, after seeing shit like this they ass might think jail was one big party.

After about an hour everything was going great. The food was on point, Radio was keeping the hits coming and Dre even gave us a preview of a new song he had been working on. As usual Larry was Lying and Byrd was keeping our stomachs in a knot.

The night was going so good I almost didn't wanna leave. Well I won't take it that far but tonight was the best night I'd had since I'd been here. It seemed like every one was living through the fact that I might be going home and having a life. I just hoped I'd get a chance to go.

With all the excitement. I had forgotten the first thing that Dada had taught me. *'Guard all your shit with your life at all times.'* And it must've been fate or something because as soon as I thought about it, I looked over to my bunk and spotted A.J. creeping by. I turned my head and acted as though I wasn't paying him any attention, still peeking from my peripheral. And just when he thought he had the perfect time, a time when everyone was in there own little world, he swiped me. He quietly snatched my entire bag from my bunk.

This nigga was trippin. I snapped, "Ay nigga what the hell you doin?"

All the commotion instantly went to a screeching halt as A.J. looked over to me, he was caught red handed.

"What? Nigga you don't need this shit. You goin home tomorrow," said A.J.

I could tell that he was embarrassed because he couldn't even look me in the eyes as he spoke.

"What? Nigga put my shit down!" Something inside me became nervous. This was definitely a time where I was supposed to scrap. But how could I? A.J. was huge. But DaDa told me to never show fear. "Nigga strap up," I yelled.

Everything was in slow motion now. I couldn't believe what was happening. I didn't even see any of the other inmates. It was just me and A.J.. As I walked, miraculously all fear I had disappeared. I had been in this bitch mad at the world for the last seven months and I needed someone to take out my anger on. Fuck it, even if I don't land a punch, simply swinging would be enough to let off some much needed energy and steam.

I was halfway over to my rack to get my sneakers when I heard a, Pow! I looked over and DaDa had creamed A.J. and the entire block was following his lead. It was crazy. Everyone was beating ass, I rushed over to get in a few licks. This was wonderful. I was able to get my stress off and not even have to take a hit. Seeing my feet connecting with his helpless body was just what I needed. This felt great. I was in the zone, forgetting where I was. I think I may have even been smiling.

Shit was perfect until I felt a sudden pain in my side. I instantly screamed before dropping down to the ground. I felt like I had been shot. I looked up and realized I had been. I had been in such a daze that I didn't even notice that the goon squad had burst into the block with their guns drawn. I had never experienced this. I had heard about them but I had never seen them in person. It was about 10 of them dressed in all black, suited and booted like some super heroes. They had these little pellet guns in their hands and they were ordering everyone to the wall, nose to the back of the head. I ignored my pain and rushed over to the wall as they destructively searched through all of our shit. All I could think of was Sharee's letters. I prayed they didn't ruin them. I needed those things. It's crazy just when I thought jail wasn't that bad I was reminded of how this place was hell.

The courtroom was packed. My Mom, Grandma, Aunt Tina and Fonda were all there. My Mom had left Korb at home. He knew what was going on but she didn't want him to see me like that. I couldn't blame her. I didn't

129

even want to see myself like this. There were camera men and women everywhere. My life was a movie.

Officer Mcnairs entire family was there too, including Josh. When the Sheriffs bought me in he was actually the first person that I noticed. My first thought was to smile. I hadn't seen him in so long, I thought of all the fun we had together. Unfortunately the feeling obviously wasn't mutual. He threw me a look of disgust that I'll never forget. Josh was always so upbeat. To see him look at me with rage, killed me. But what can I say, I guess that's how I'd look to if I had to look at the supposed killer of my Dad.

I wish it was some way I could let Josh know exactly what I was feeling. Maybe than he'd understand. Naw scratch that, ain't no way he'd understand. It was time I just counted my losses. Josh was gone outta my life and he was never coming back. I decided not to look over to him anymore, I was feeling low enough. But when you're involved in a murder, is there a such thing as low enough? It was bad enough I couldn't even look at my own family.

I looked over to them but I couldn't look anyone in the eyes. Again, something inside me wanted to let the judge know everything that happened and tell the court I was sorry. But I knew that was out of the question so I just took my seat and looked straight ahead.

For the next hour I sat, shaking as sweat drenched my jailhouse jumper, feet shackled listening to the prosecutor, some white bitch and my lawyer go back and forth.

Honestly the prosecutor didn't have shit on me. That was the main reason the blacks in town had been fighting for me. They had all ganged up and held donations for my lawyer fees and everything. They all believed that I really didn't do it. Or maybe they did think I did it. They just knew my Mom and wanted to help her out. Guess that's basically the same reason all the white people were against me.

The only evidence the prosecutors kept talking about was that damn I.D. I had been thinking about it every day since Detective Fraley had slammed it on the table. They said they found it a few yards away from the vehicle by a gate. And it was then I remembered how I had gotten stuck on the gate. The I.D. must've fell out of my pocket. Damn, it's funny how the one thing my Mom always told me to keep on me is what landed me in here. I knew it was a reason I never listened to her ass.

Still that wasn't really enough to say that I actually had anything to do with the murder, so after 2 hours it was time for the judge to release my fate. My entire life flashed before my eyes.

Everything I had ever been through, my Dad, all my fun times with the homies, my Mom and Korbin , all those late night talks and walks with Sharee, all the times Sho gave me some game. But what really stood out was the moment Officer McNair got shot. I couldn't help but wonder if I deserved to go to prison. My crime held a minimum life sentence. I quickly decided that I didn't deserve it.

Besides, the guys who killed my Dad didn't even get anytime. They never even got caught. Fuck that I needed to go home. God knows I'm sorry. There's no use in sending me to prison. What would that solve?

I looked at the judge square in his little squinty blue eyes with the most innocent face I could deliver. Sweat continued to drench my body as my heart beat through my chest at 100 miles an hour.

"In the case of the State vs. Samuel Turner. I find the defendant not guilty on Capital Murder," said the Judge.

I heard my family let out a huge sigh. "Thank you Jesus," my Mom shouted.

On the opposite side I heard gasps of disbelief "Bullshit," shouted one man. I couldn't help but to smile.

"Order. Order," said the judge banging his gavel. "Silence. Anyone else who interrupts will be held in contempt of the court." The courtroom was silent. "On the charge of occupying a stolen vehicle. I find the defendant not guilty. On the charge of occupying a fire arm. I find the defendant not guilty." I was going home. "And on the assault on a law official I find the defendant guilty and I sentence him to a mandatory 2 years in Beaumont Youth Correction Center." Damn. I had gotten so caught up in the murder that I had completely forgotten the fact that I had fought the police on the night of my arrest. "He will remain incarcerated until we can ship him off. Court adjourned."

Some goofy looking officer walked over to cuff me as I finally looked my family in the eyes. Everyone's faces were filled with joy. "I love you Pete," my Mom shouted.

"I love you more Mom," I said looking back as tears streamed from everyone's eyes.

The officers quickly grabbed me up and reminded me of where I was. I was also reminded that the judge said

I had two more long years to do. He snatched me up and drug me away from my family. Two fucking years, damn.

When I walked outside to get into the jail van I took a whiff of the fresh air. Court dates were the only time I was able to get a taste. It was also the only time I got a little sunlight. Since coming to jail I had gone from a smooth chocolate complexion to more of a dry caramel color. I appreciated every second spent soaking up the sun, it felt amazing.

There were News Reporters and Camera's everywhere. There was even a large metal gate that blocked about 200 people from me. It was crazy, the whites held sign like *'Cop Killer'* and *'Murderer'* and shouted things like *'You're going to hell'*.

While the blacks held signs like *'Keep your head up'* and *'Innocent'*. They were yelling things like *'We knew it' 'Thank God'*. It was surreal.

The local Newscaster Bob Sanders walked up to me out of nowhere and thrusted a microphone to my mouth. "How does it feel to have charges dropped after spending seven months in jail?"

I looked around still in awe of everything that was going on and said "It feels good, real good." I knew I had to say more. "But I would also like to send my condolences to the McNair family. I'm deeply sorry for your lost."

The Sheriffs then yoked me up and escorted me to the van. "He deserves to die," screamed a white man. I looked up into the crowd and saw an object flying directly at me. It missed me by an inch. When I looked down to see what it was I recognized that it was an old slave looking doll with a tiny Neuse around its neck. I couldn't believe that shit. I looked out into the crowd and it really hit me. I was the reason for all this hatred. I thought I'd feel good if I beat the case but I still felt awful. I lowered my head and made my way onto the bus.

As soon as my ass hit the seat, I heard a bunch of commotion from outside. I looked up and there was a huge riot ensuing between the whites and the blacks. For the first time I saw firsthand what was going on and it was all my fault.

By the time I got back to the block word had already spread about the trial. I could've sworn I had just graduated from high school instead of beating a court case. But there were so many people who were never going home that they were just happy to see me make it. Even though I had to still do two more years that was peanuts to a guy doing life. Most everyone in the block has already done at least two years anyway. They called anything less than five years easy time.

"You official now lil bro." "That's how you beat the Mo'fuckin system." "It's a shame this lil nigga only 14 and kept his mouth shut betta than some of yall snitching asses."

Niggas was showing love. I felt like a jail legend. Everybody said I was gonna be good in Prisons all over Virginia. That was cool and all but I never wanted to see another jail cell for the rest of my life. See, most of the niggas in the block still talked about hittin licks and selling drugs when they got out. All jail seemed to do was tell them what not to do next time.

"The white man ain't tryna hire no felon," they all said. Maybe they were right, hell how would I know. I ain't

never had a job a day in my life. Hopefully they weren't right but if they were, when I finished these two years, I had gained enough knowledge in here to make it through anything. I hated that I had to go through this shit. But I came out like a champ. I had survived what most people never could imagine and I wasn't even 15 yet. I was feeling invincible.

Before long I'd managed to speak to everyone who mattered on the block, everybody except DaDa. He had stayed in his rack reading the entire time. I knew it wasn't anything personal. He just wasn't the type of guy to be all mixed up with a crowd of people so I made my way over.

DaDa looked up and smiled.

"You dodged a big ass bullet big dog," he said as I nodded my head. 'I seen a lot of niggas not make it out of your predicament. Comin off with two years is sorta like comin off with nothing. You know why you beat that case, right?"

"Yeah," I said. "The prosecutor ain't have shit on me."

DaDa smiled and shook his head. "Nigga do you know how many niggas doin life and double life and the judge ain't have shit on them?" he asked as I sat silent. "Thousands. You beat that bitch cause of money. I heard about everybody donatin all that money for that good ass lawya. That's what beat that case right there."

I had to agree and he was nice as hell to my Mom, she really liked him. "Yeah he was a pretty good lawya," I said.

135

"Man fuck that lawya. He just got a good ass name."

I was confused. "Huh."

"I guarantee you a damn court appointed lawya could've got your ass the same results. It ain't the lawyer who gets you off. It's what he represents. Money," DaDa said before staring at me for about a minute as if to make sure what he was saying was sinking in. "Money is what beat the case. Money runs the world. Nothin's more important and nothin will eva be."

I sat silently listening. It was funny. He was saying almost the same exact shit Sho used to tell me.

DaDa talked to me for about an hour on the importance of money. He still never told me what he did for a living but I knew.

What stood out to me the most was the last thing he said. "I'ma be out this bitch in a lil while and I like the way you held thangs down. You can be somebody one day. In two years after you knock out your lil bid. Make sure you holla at me. Trust me I ain't gon be hard to find. Fuck with me and you'll be a millionaire."

I didn't know what to say so I just nodded my head. By then the homies on the block were ready to party. Everyone had pitched in and we had homemade pizza. It's amazing what you can do with Ramen Noodles, Doritos, bbq Fritos, crackers, Slim Jim and a little nacho cheese. Locked up, this was like a gourmet meal. It was a million times better than the slop they served us for meals. We also had Buck's world famous Jailhouse cheesecake. I have absolutely no idea how he makes it but on my Mama I ain't never tasted something so good in my life.

Dre Skii had even written a song about being free dedicated to me. Again he and Radio rapped all night as we chilled out. I was going out with a bang. Damn, I'm honestly gonna miss these crazy mo'fuckers. I hated jail, don't get me wrong. I hated being locked up. Each morning I woke up feeling dead. The whole world was moving and I was stuck standing still. But the love I was getting right now made things almost worth it. Almost.

Chapter 6

After two long months of waiting in jail to be shipped off, I was awaken at 7 this morning. My time in jail had come to an end and I was on my way to Beaumont Juvenile Corrections. It was about a four hour drive from Norview and it's supposedly the toughest Juvenile Center in all of Virginia. So I packed up all of my shit, said goodbye to all my homies and set sail for my new two year journey.

By 3:00pm I was dressed in a pair of dark blue jeans and a light blue denim button up shirt and thrown in shackles onto a bus along with 15 other juvies. I sat alone in my seat watching the world pass me by through the window.

Today was my 15th birthday. I was upset that this would be the way I would be spending it but I was more upset at the fact that I was guaranteed to spend my 16th birthday in here too. In jail I thought it was hard living day to day not knowing what my fate would be. But at least I had hope that I'd be getting out soon. Knowing for certain that I was gonna spend more than seven hundred more days in this bitch was killing me. And that wasn't even the beginning of my worries. In jail I was locked up with people three and four times my age. Everybody knew I wasn't one of them. In here, shit's different. I was actually these niggas age and as I carefully looked around at the kids surrounding me it became crystal clear that all these nigga's belonged here. They all looked like they should've been casted in 'Menace II Society' or something. As time dragged on I started to feel more and more like an impostor. Besides fighting the police that day I still hadn't even been in a fist fight ever in my life. And even if I woulda actually fought A.J that day, nobody would've cared if I would've loss because at the end of the day he was a full grown man fighting a kid.

Here, everyone was equal. The only good thing I could think of was the fact that I had grown 4 inches since going to jail. I came in 5'5 120 pounds and now I'm 5'9 145. I'm no giant but at least I'm not a midget.

After a 3 hour drive we finally arrived at the facility and were ordered off the bus. I hopped down and stared shook, at the sight of my new home. It was colossal, like a million square feet, one story with an equally long gate to keep us caged in.

We walked silently shackled by our hands in a single file line into the facility. I don't know why but as my body got closer to the building I started feeling the sudden urge to hug my Mother. I really needed her. So I decided to do what she always told me to do in times like this.

"Dear Lord, I know I probably deserve to be hea. I apologize for the entire situation. But I do have one small favor to ask and that is for you to keep me safe in hea. Also keep my family safe while I'm hea. Bless, Mom, Korb, Grandma, Trell, Sharee, Aunt Tina, Aunt Fonda, Dada, Sho, everybody back on the block. And oh yeah Josh. Keep us safe. In Jesus name we pray Amen." I opened my eyes and through on my mean mug. These niggas might look tough but I knew how to look just as tough.

I had been sitting alone shackled to a steel bench for about an hour waiting to see my counselor. They had me sitting next to his door at the end of some long dim hallway. I dont feel like being in here but I guess it's better than having to interact with everybody else. This may be my last shot at having some time to myself for the next two years.

So far everything from Officer Mcnairs murder to Sharee had popped in my mind but my thoughts were interrupted when two staff members who looked like they weren't a day over twenty one brought some other kid down here and shackled him to a matching bench directly across from me. The kid didn't look all that gangster. In fact he looked kinda soft. He was short and kinda pudgy. He looked a little older than me. Maybe about 17 or something. Looking at him made me feel a tad bit more comfortable. Still, I slouched down a little more and looked away from him. I didn't feel like glancing at him and mistakenly sparking any type of conversation.

The staff members walked down the hallway and stood about 20 feet away from us and now it was just me and him.

After about a minute of complete silence, silence that I was completely comfortable with, the nigga started talking.

"This your first time upstate ain't it?" he asked.

"Yeah," I tried to be short so that he'd get the point.

"I can tell. All the first timers always look the same. It's easy to tell that yall don't know what the hell to do."

I didn't say anything back, I continued to look away. I didn't need him schooling me on nothing. Especially when he looked like a fat Urkle. He's probably the kinda nigga who got beat up around here and I most definitely don't want any parts in hanging with a nigga like that. I ain't tryna be guilty by association.

"Man I been in this bitch two Goddamn years. I just got switched ova to this facility a few weeks ago. I was in Tanners House. I was gettin in too much shit over there so I got transferred ova hea to finish out my last couple months. But shit, I ain't seen no girls in two fuckin years I'm happy as hell I finally get to see some titties."

I had been so nervous about coming here that I had completely forgotten that Sho had told me this was a co-ed facility. At least I got one piece of good news today.

I nodded, still not in the mood to talk.

"Guess why the fuck I'm in this bitch."

I really didn't give a fuck, but I had a feeling that he was the type of nigga who was going to tell me anyway so I simply said, "What?"

"Showin my damn dick to this girl," he said as he stared at me as if he wanted me to comment or something. Instead, I just sat there as he continued, "Ok so I'm in Detention right. Just me and this BITCH named Whitney Porter. We called her Whitney Porter Potty cause she was just nasty. Ok, so yeah, we in class and shit. And like I said, she nasty. So we talkin freaky and shit. Her parents ain't neva home and I was tryna get it poppin when we got out. So the teacher walk out and shit. The bitch ask me to see my dick. So I'm like fuck it why not. She said if it's big enough she gon let me hit that shit. So I whipped out quick as hell. Soon as she see my shit she smilin hard as hell. She couldn't wait to go home and ride that shit. Then Bam," he shouted. "Ms. Washington walk back in the room and I'm standin there with my dick in my hand. So this bitch Whitney start screamin and shit like I had just whipped it out outta nowhere or somethin. Next thing you know I'm servin two years and I'm a sex offenda. Shit crazy huh?" he asked as I nodded my head, still not giving a fuck about what he was talking about.

Again that didn't stop him, he continued his animated story. "But shit I'm just glad this shit is almost over. Two months left in this bitch. They tryna make me go to some group home next week to serve out the remainder of my sentence but fuck that. I ain't tryna be half free and shit. All that's gonna do is make me even crazier. I'd fuck around and run away and end up right back in this shit. Fuck that, that's exactly what they want me to do but I'm too smart for that shit. Hell yeah I'ma just finish the rest of my time in hea and carry my ass back to good ol Virginia Beach, no probation, nothin, just free as a bird. Ya feel me?"

Again I just nodded my head. This time realizing that he was nowhere near finished talking.

He looked around aimlessly as if he really didn't have anything else to say but just couldn't hold back from talking. "Yo this place is cool and all with the girls but I gotta warn you, everything ain't as sweet as it might seem."

What the fuck was this nigga talking about I ain't never once thought this place was sweet. I don't give a fuck if this place got girls in it or not. It ain't like I can fuck

142

them or something. I'm in hell and I know it. What the fuck is he talking about?

"Dog you gotta watch out for this nigga named Duck. Big ass nigga, you can't miss em," he said spreading his arms wide as if to show me exactly how large he was. "He the only black nigga walkin round with red hair. They say he was a beast in football. On his way to a full ride to college until some white bitch said he raped her and shit. And just like that, Juvenile Life. He in this bitch till he 21 fucking years old. Heard the nigga been making life hell for anybody he felt like fuckin with. And don't think the staff is gonna help yo ass out. Oh hell naw. Them niggas don't give a fuck. Shit, I heard they be placin bets on fights and everything. Shits crazy. Duck ass even got him a lil whip ass crew and shit. Everybody in that bitch crazy. Usually niggas align they self with the city they from. But every since Duck been in this bitch it don't matter where you from, if you ain't down with him he was gon put yo ass down," he said pointing to the ground. "Mostly all them niggas do is steal niggas cantine and shit. So if you ever get yo shit taken just be smart and take the L. There's a chance he might beat your ass and take your shit but it's still a slight chance he'll just take your shit. So I'm tellin you the smart thing is just to shut up. And oh yeah," he said as he looked around cautiously before whispering .

"It's supposed to be some gangsta ass nigga comin hea this week. I don't really know too much about him but I overheard some of Duck's homeboys talking about him. They say he bouta be Duck's number one nigga. Shit, the nigga might've came on the bus ova with you. Everybody been talkin bout this nigga. I guess he some kinda super thug or somethin. I ain't tryna scare you or nothin my nigga I'm just tryna look out. Shit, I wish I had somebody to show me the ropes when I first got locked up. I had to learn everything the hard way."

"Mr. Turner," said some short white man, peeking his head out of the room next to me as he waved down for one of the staff members standing at the opposite side of the hallway to unshackle me.

"Rememba dog. Stay away from them niggas the best way you can." He said looking me in my eyes as the staff came in to unshackle me. "I'm serious dog. I'm only tryna help. You don't wanna end up anotha victim."

I looked him dead in his eyes as he spoke. This time paying close attention to all that he had to say.

When I got inside the room it looked like your regular school counselors office, inspirational quotes and shit everywhere. Everything was neatly aligned across his desk. But what really caught my attention was a picture of him at his wedding standing next to what looked like a really beautiful wife. Now this wouldn't be unusual except for one small fact. It was clear as day that this nigga was gay. And not gay as in wack or something. He was a real live gay man. I could tell. Of course he didn't say *'Hey Pete, I'm gay.'* But I could tell. Everything about him just screamed out *'I'm gay.'* His hair, face, voice, body movement, everything. He was gay, gay, gay, I never had any problem with gay people. Well at least I don't think I did. I never really encountered too many. There were some boys I always knew were going to be gay when they got older. You know the ones who like to double dutch with the girls at recess instead of balling with the homies. We all knew they'd be gay in the future but up until now I hadn't encountered too many gay men. Was he really the one who should be counseling me on how to be a REAL man?

I watched as he sat at his desk sorting through papers. "Mr. Turner," he said with a feminine smile.

"How you doin sir?" I asked, feeling uncomfortable.

"I'm great. I'm Mr. Siegel and I'm going to be your counselor," he said as we shook hands. "My goal is to utilize these next two years the best way we can to insure you leave here a better person then you came," he said as he passed me a little booklet. "That's the daily schedule and the rules and regulations. If you have any problems, me or one of the other counselors are always here. Now Samuel."

Immediately I wanted to correct him but fuck it. I knew what my name was.

"This is a hands on facility. Which unfortunately means if you don't listen you will be physically forced to do so. Our staff doesn't really like to go that route but it's all on you. You will be placed in a dorm with 30 other low level offenders. Now low level doesn't mean anything bad. We have five levels in Beaumount. The 1st level is where you are right now. With time and good behavior you can be bumped up levels which will lead you to different dormitories. But as of right now you and the rest of your dorm mates will be in a bed by 7:30 and up at 5:30 from 5:30 to 6 you'll be able to shower, make your bed and all that good stuff. After that you'll go to the cafeteria for a 30 minute breakfast where you'll be able to sit with the other inmates in your dorm. I'd advise you to make smart decisions in who you choose to associate with. You look like a good kid who just made a bad decision. Don't make that decision even worse by choosing to associate with people who aren't on a positive path. Ok?"

I nodded.

145

"Ok where was I? Oh yeah. After that you'll be in class where, from judging from your paper work you'll greatly benefit. You've missed a year of schooling but if you work with us we'll have you right back on track for senior year in two years. Ok, 12:00 you'll go to lunch for another 30 minutes where again you'll be able to sit with your dorm mates. Then back to class for another two hours. From 2:30 till 4:00 will be reading slash study time. 4:00 till 4:45 will be rec time. After that you'll have a quick 15 minutes to get ready for dinner at 5. After diner you'll be allowed to write letters and make phone calls until 6:30. By then you're required to get everything situated for school the next day and at 7:30 it's off to bed. On weekends your schedule will vary. We'll have scheduled events and speakers set up for you guys. So as you can see we're into keeping you busy. I don't know if you've heard but this facility used to be pretty bad. But we're really cleaning it up with our strict structure. There will also be a staff member in the Pod at all time. Oh yeah and one other thing. I know by now you've heard that we are now co-ed but if we catch you attempting or participating in any inappropriate behaviors you will be severely punished and sent to Larchburg. That's a top level juvenile home that I'm sure you don't want to go. Is there anything you'd like to say?"

I didn't know how I felt about this shit. I had just came from jail where we made our own rules. Now I'm here and my day would be controlled everyday in every way. I gotta admit I do like the fact that a staff member would be around all the time. Even though that Urkel looking nigga just told me they didn't give a fuck about fights it still felt just a tad bit safer than being all alone. I know they ain't just gonna sit there and watch me get punished. Shit, if they do they can bet my Mom's gonna be suing they ass. Guaranteed.

And I'm glad I'd be able to catch up on school. Until now I had kinda lost all hope of ever being a senior in high school. I was going to make sure I didn't mess up that. I was already missing three crucial years. Still, with all that I only had one answer for Mr. Siegel's question.

"I wanna go home," I said looking him square in the eyes, hoping for sympathy, I couldn't get that Duck nigga off my mind.

After leaving Mr. Siegel's office I was given all my hygiene products; shower shoes, a notebook, and escorted to my new block by some silent Staff Member. Usually I would have enjoyed his the peace and quiet. But the silence was causing me to feel uneasy. It was kinda spooky.

On the way I noticed that this place seemed fairly different from jail. In jail, there was seldom a dull moment, inmates were free to scream, shout and do as they pleased within the block. However in here, you could hear a pin drop from 50 ft. away. It also seemed pretty clean, there were no dust bunnies floating around, the tile on the floor had a little sparkle to it and the air didn't really give me the same dead feeling I'd always had in jail.

Still this place and jail did have their similarities, they had the same type of maximum security blocks that I had just been caged in. But unlike jail there were no steel bars holding low level offenders, every dorm was electrically controlled with each steel door shut.

Taking that walk was total nostalgia from a year ago. Only this time I knew what to expect. And I wasn't happy. Thoughts of getting my ass kicked wouldn't seem to

147

escape my brain. This time last year, walking in my jail cell I said I would transform into Sho. But like the old saying goes, you live and you learn and I've learned that if I walk in here grilling niggas and acting like some tough guy I'd be in for a rude awakening. So I figured this time I'd be DaDa. I was just going to shut up and do my time. Keep to myself and with God on my side hopefully I could just go unnoticed. Being nonexistent was the goal. Hopefully that could work. Still times like this I wish I woulda took boxing lessons, wrestled or something. I'm sure then I wouldn't even be feeling quite like this.

It was around 8:30 when the mute Staff member finally tossed me into my new block, luckily my cell mates were already asleep.

Ok maybe sleep is the wrong word because as I tip toed through the dark dorm in search of my new bunk I saw every eye in the building staring back at me. I didn't want to stare too hard but I didn't want to not and look like a bitch so I just glanced at everyone as nonchalantly as I could.

Looking around I noticed the block was identical to my old one in the jail except in here there were only single bunks. And where the picnic tables were located in the jail, they were instead a small desk that a staff member sat and watched us from. Sorta like a teacher would in a classroom.

The staff member at the desk right now never even looked up to me, his eyes were locked on his laptop that supplied the dorm with its only light. Still, the room was too dark to really get a good look at his face but from what I could see he was just as big as the desk. I'll be damn if I ever tried to start some shit with him.

"Put all your shit right there," he said pointing to an empty rack in the middle of the floor. "I know one of the counselors already told you that I have the right to fuck you up. Stay in your place. Go to sleep," he said calmly, never leaving his seat.

I nodded. Maybe a year ago I would've cared about how that nigga had just talked to me but I been called so much and treated like shit so many times that I really didn't give a fuck. I had too much on my mind to be worried about some worthless staff member.

I kicked off all my shit and laid down. I thought about the fact that it was my birthday. I imagined how life would have been if I'd been on the outside. If none of this shit would've ever happened. If I would've just did what my Mom said and stayed my black ass in the house.

Shit, I probably would've been somewhere kicking it with Trell and Josh. I know we would've scored some fire ass weed. Probably would've all stayed at my crib or something.

Ah man, who am I kidding, my ass would've probably been with Sharee. This might've been the night I would actually get to hit her. Who knows, I might've already hit her if I would've been home. I been gone for nearly a year, aint no telling what would have popped off already, knowing her she probally would have gave me some for Chrismas or something.

Damn, Christmas. I couldn't believe I'd be missing them for another two years. Holidays in Norview were the shit. Everyone always walked around all jolly and shit. Just high off life. Especially 4th of July. Everybody would go to this huge field called Waterside to see the fireworks.

149

Everyone was like one big happy family. And my dumbass ruined all that. There probably wasn't even going to be anyone there this year. And it was all my fault. On that note, I closed my eyes. Some birthday.

The big fat staff member woke us all up, screaming like some drill sergeant at 5:30a.m. Everyone was ordered to get up and get in a straight line. I was half asleep and didn't really know what to do so I wiped the coal from my eyes and followed what everyone else did. They all slipped on their slippers, grabbed their towels and hygiene kits and walked over to the line, I did the same, only much slower. My body felt sluggish as I walked, I'd tossed and turned and barely got any sleep last night. I guess I was too used to staying up all night in jail. All in all my ass probably only slept for an hour or two total the whole night.

When I finally made it over to the line, I lifted my droopy head and an instant shot of pure fear woke me up when I discovered who was standing directly in front of me. A towering figure with a head full of red hair. I became dizzy as I layed my eyes on this massive creature. My worse fear stood inches away from me.

As we were ordered to walk, my heart pounded as I carefully stepped behind him making sure there was no way that I'd slip up and step on the back of his foot or something. He hadn't turned around and looked at me yet and I wanted to keep it that way.

After what seemed like an eternal walk we safely made it to the bathroom area and I was hit with another unwanted surprise. We were being forced to take community showers. It was bad enough I had to squat butt naked and cough yesterday. Now they want me to get butt naked with a room full of niggas I ain't never seen a day in my life and worse, get wet in front of them. Ah man, I'm starting to think these jails and shit are designed to make niggas gay or something. I mean what if one of these niggas is already gay? What if they get turned on by the site of water glistening all over my body. I'm not gay and I don't want to be a part of any man's fantasies. I wondered what would happen if I refused. What if I wanted to stay dirty? But the thought of drawing unwanted attention to myself stopped me and like every other nigga I removed my clothes and entered; making sure I never looked below anyone's neck.

The shower was huge. There was two sides with shower heads on both, all spread out about 3ft away from one another. As I entered I made perfectly sure that I looked straight ahead at my shower head the entire time as I held on to my soap for dear life. Luckily I didn't have to suffer for too long, we only got two minute showers.

After that we walked in a straight line to the cafeteria. Only this time I was far away from Duck. I didn't get in front of him either. I wanted him in my eye sight at all times. When we finally got to the café it was huge. There were about a hundred or so long ass tables that each fit about 20 people all lined up in rows. There was about 30 staff members all posted up throughout the café waiting for something to go down. But considering we outnumbered the staff by the hundreds I don't really see the purpose in them.

There were boys and girls scattered around everywhere. Tall niggas, short niggas, fat girls , skinny girls. I never even knew Virginia had so many Juvenile delinquents. It seemed like everybody was in here.

Well everybody except white people. Looking around it was damn near impossible to find one. There was no doubt that Sho was right all along.

We weren't allowed to talk while we were in line but now that we were at breakfast we could engage in conversation with niggas in our block as long as we kept our voices down. Disobedience could result in the entire pod being silenced for a week. Shit, I kinda wished we'd get in trouble so no one would try to talk to me. I had a feeling some little motor mouth was going to try and be Mr. Friendly. Or even worse Duck would have something to say.

When I got my grub it appeared to be ten times better than the trifling stuff they serve in jail. I had sausage, eggs and pancakes with orange juice on the side. I couldn't believe what I was about to devour. My mouth watered as if I hadn't eaten in years as I followed the rest of my pod to our seats.

I sat down at the end of the table as far away from Duck as possible and gazed into my tray for about five more minutes before sticking my fork in. If I wasn't in DaDa mode I know I'd be smiling from cheek to cheek.

Instead I put my face to the trey, carefully looking from the corner of my eyes like DaDa did, making sure no one was going to try any funny shit. As I ate I couldn't help but get the feeling that everyone was staring at me. Maybe I'm bugging but each time I looked up for a quick second it seemed as if everyone put their head back down or tried to act like they were doing something else. Shit was crazy.

And on top of that it was weird as hell that no one had said a single word to me. No one. Not even the nigga's sitting beside me. Nothing. But shit, beggars can't' be choosers. This is what I asked for so I guess I should be happy. Fuck it. Shit's just stupid weird though.

After breakfast I was escorted to my new math class. Like Mr. Siegel's office the classroom looked like your regular school room, nothing special. I had managed to be one of the first kids in class so I got first dibs on a seat.

I'm sure I don't have to tell you I chose to sit in the back. While sitting I watched the other students get escorted in and again they were doing the same weird shit everyone was doing in breakfast.

"Hi I'm Ms. Jones. You all have been assigned here for the summer. Hopefully we can get you guys ready to be in your correct grade next school year. There are five tutors in here who will all help you get to where you need to be. As you can see all of them are inmates just like yourselves. They've all been in your shoes before and are ready to help," said the teacher, an older white lady.

I definitely liked jail more than this shit. This school shit was wack. I was in a class with a bunch of weird ass mo'fuckers that I'd never seen a day in my life. On a good note, Duck wasn't in here but I still wondered if any of his homey's were, so I scanned the room in search of any goonish looking niggas. But they all looked like goons so that was no help.

As time slowly ticked away I was growing more and angrier and as usual I ignored everything Ms. Jones was saying. Fuck her. I can't lie though, the old bitch was kinda sexy. Actually all the girls in here were kinda cute. At least I think they were. I had been around niggas so long that I'm not actually sure if my opinion counted.

It's five girls and about twelve niggas in here including the tutors. I prayed that one of the female tutors would be the one helping me. I'd love to hear a female's voice in my ear as her feminine fragrance takes over my nostrils.

I guess God was giving me a belated Birthday gift because not long after that thought shot through my head one of the females glided over to me. My hormones started popping like Crisco.

"Hey. You havin problems with algebra?" said the girl.

Now I'm not sure but I really think this girl looked good. She about 5'5 and her face was spotless. I had noticed that all of the girls had raggedy pony tails but hers seemed to be really doing her justice. Judging by the way she walked I could tell she was about 17 or 18. She had that grown woman swag to her.

"Yeah," I said as I halfway looked into her eyes. I was scared to stare at her too hard. You never know this could be Ducks girl or something.

"Are you Pete?" she asked as she sat down next to me.

"Yeah," I said.

What the fuck was going on? How the hell did she know my name. I assumed my nickname was in my paperwork and Ms. Jones had told her or something.

She smiled, a weird kinda smile. But a good weird. "Cool. I'm Britney. What you know about algebra so far?"

Before I could tell her that I didn't know a damn thing and that I never understood how a letter could ever result in being the answer of any problem involving numbers, I suddenly felt her hand against my thigh inching its way up to my crotch.

Had I died in went to heaven? Naw I must be still sleep from last night. But fuck it I'ma enjoy this dream.

We stared at one another seductively as she continued to ramble on about algebra as if I could pay attention to anything that she was saying. After awhile she started sounding like one of the parents off Charlie Brown.

The only thing on my mind was the fact that I was getting my dick massaged in the middle of class, while I was locked up. Sharee hadn't even touched it before. I was losing my mind when suddenly she asked. "Do you understand?

I stared at her and nodded at her smiling face.

"Well ok Pete let me know if you need any more help with anything."

I nodded again before looking around to see if anyone had peeped what had just went down. And just like before, as I looked around everyone dropped their heads. What the fuck?

When I got to lunch shit even got weirder. Suddenly everyone was shyly saying "Whatsup Pete?"

How did everybody know my damn name? Was there something that I needed to know? Was I gonna get banged up later?

I somehow gathered up enough courage to look down at Duck. I hadn't looked at him at all since I'd been here. I had to know was he looking at me too. Who knows, he might've told everyone to act like they like me so he could have more fun beating my ass unexpectedly. When I looked over to him he was busy taking someone's cake off of their tray. I could tell the person didn't want him doing it by the look of pure disappointment. I quickly shoved my cake in my mouth. Still, I was a little relieved that he wasn't looking at me.

For the next thirty minutes I attempted to use my long lost skill of nosiness to find out why everyone was acting so weird but these mo'fuckers started whispering. I kept catching whole crews of niggas seeming to be talking about me but each time they caught me looking they'd do some nervous little head nod towards me and quickly go back to eating. After a while I just tuned them completely out and continued to think about how much I hated this place.

We went back to class after that for more tutoring. Britney wasn't with me anymore. As usual I didn't listen to anything the teacher was saying. How could I with all this shit weighting down on my brain? I was further away from my Mom than I'd ever been. At least in jail she was in the same town. It wasn't like I could go see her or anything but it just made me feel better. I felt even lonelier than ever now. I knew nobody here and everyone seemed so damn weird. It was like I was in another world all by myself. I never needed my Mom so much in my life.

By the time class was over I was feeling worse than ever and the fact that everyone still continued to stare didn't make it any better. I'ma soldier though so I forced myself to stay calm.

When we got back to the pod it was silent reading and study time. I was the last one to make it to my rack but what I noticed when I got to it baffled me. There was about five books on the bed. I looked around and it seemed as if everyone was staring and nodding their heads up at me. I suspiciously nodded back and sat to read. None of us were allowed to lay back.

DaDa always read when we were on the block so I didn't really mind. It was just a way I could get my mind off of my situations. One of the books on my bed was The Autobiography of Malcolm X. My Mom always talked about him. As usual I never listened to her, so I figured I'd give him a shot. Halfway through reading I was interrupted by a photo of Malcolm. He had red hair. Instantly an image of Duck popped up in my head. I snuck a peek over to him from the corner of my eye. Chills ran down my body as it seemed as though he was looking right at me. I couldn't even get back to the book as my mind pondered on how I would be able to somehow beat his ass. There was no way I could run from him. But I couldn't just get my ass whipped. Why he gotta be so big though? I bet he don't have a single soft spot on his entire body.

Soon an hour had passed and it was time for mail and canteen. I sat on my rack as everyone stood in line to get there new mail and snacks. I know the feeling. With everyday being so monotonous, this part of the day always seemed to feel like Christmas. Unfortunately this time I was the orphan kid who didn't get a damn thing.

When it came down for Rec time I found out I would be forced to remain on the pod, I didn't have enough star points for rec. You had to earn them but I was cool with that. I didn't feel like associating with these hell bound niggas anyway.

That was until I saw who else didn't have enough star points. Yep you guessed it. Duck!

They sent some little bitch ass staff member in the dorm to watch over us. All I could do was shake my head as I watched his Gary Coleman looking ass baby stepping his way over to me. As little as he is I know for damn sure there was no way he could protect me from getting pummeled by Duck, he'd probably just end up kicking both of our asses.

"Whatsup man? What's your name?"

"Lil Jesse."

"Alright whatsup Jesse. I'm Mr. Rodgers," he said looking up to me. "And I'ma tell you how I run shit. I don't give a fuck. Duck'll tell you. You can cuss, go to sleep, fight. Long as you don't kill each other, I could care less. I'ma be ova there takin a nap. You need me. Ask him," he said pointing over to Duck who was laying on his rack most likely contemplating something devious.

I couldn't believe what he just said. I was counting on him to protect me. How could he leave me alone when there was an animal lose. Was he crazy? Did he want dead? I nodded and went over to my rack. It was obvious that I was gonna have to pretend like I was sleep.

Fifteen minutes had passed and my eyes were closed the entire time. Only peeking once in a while to ensure my safety. Everything was going as planned until I suddenly heard footsteps of a mutant slowly approaching. By now Mr. Rogers ass was knocked out, I could hear his snoring from way over here so that only left one other person in the room. Initially I panicked. I had no clue as of what to do so I quickly weighted my options, it didn't take me long to realize that I had none. So I said a quick prayer and decided to open my eyes. There he was.

I sat up, our eyes locked as he towered over me. Lord help me. This was the first time I had ever gotten to look at him up close and personal. Looking at him all I saw was mayhem, I saw horns and smoke. Besides his freakishly big size, nothing resembled an athlete to me. More like a serial killer. A serial killer with bad acne, freckles and red hair. I remember Josh used to always say Red heads had no soul, I never took him serious until now. This nigga was bad news. I couldn't help but wonder what his next move would be as I watched his massive veins bulging out of the sides of his head.

"Your name Lil Jesse?"

"Yeah," I said trying my best to sound tuff. I made sure I continued looking him in the eyes.

"Damn I thought your name was Pete," said Duck seeming confused.

He knew my name too? I didn't know what to say. I was lost but I figured I might as well tell him the truth. DaDa always said the Truth shall set you free. Shit, at least if he wanted to whip my ass we were alone, no one was here to witness it.

159

"Yeah that's me," I said as I slowly clenched my teeth and fist.

The Lord was definitely on my side. He smiled. "Damn whatsup Bro. Everybody been talkin about your ass. Your cousin Sho sent up the word about you dog. You good in this bitch bro. I'm Duck," he said as he held out his fist for a pound as I tried to comprehend what had just happened. "I run this bitch dog. You have any problems holla at me, dog. Well, I know your ass ain't gonna have no problems but if you need somethin I got you. Hold on for a second," said Duck as he jogged over to his rack to retrieve something. "Hea my nigga," he said as he made his way back to my rack tossing me a box of honey buns. "I know you ain't get no canteen yet."

Thanks," I said still not believing what was happening.

"No problem. But I'ma let you get back to your nap. I just had to introduce myself and shit."

"Alright my nigga," I said as he made his way back to his rack.

Whoa, the entire time I'd been locked up I thought Sho had betrayed me. But in actuality, my nigga looked out more than I'd ever imagine. I couldn't believe it. For the first time in months I actually have an at ease feeling. No wonder everyone had been looking at me all weird, I was the new nigga that the Urkel looking guy was talking about.

"Thank God," I whispered to myself! Considering where I was, things were actually looking up. I closed my eyes preparing to take the most peaceful nap I'd taken in a while.

Chapter 7

I floated down the Beaumount hallway with a smile on my face. The smell of misguided teen spirit would now be filling my nostrils for the very last time. My reign as King was over and it was finally time to make my way home. In three years I went from being a naïve 14 year old kid to a 17 year old convict. And not just any ol convict. I was Pete. Around here that's an important name. Still, the streets were going to be a different story. I had become a master at handling myself around gangsters but I had forgotten the art of handling myself in front of everyday people. I had walked around here acting like a *'Don'* for so long that I don't think I even know how to be myself anymore. To be honest I have no clue who the fuck I am. I damn sure ain't that 14 year old kid I came in as. Back then I had big dreams. The world was my oyster, I could've been anything. Nowadays I'm confused as to what a dream actually is. Those innocent childhood fantasies quickly transformed into nightmares of the night Officer McNair died. I know I had to have relived that night at least a thousand times.

It wasn't always like that though. When I was at the jail I hardly ever thought of it. I was too busy worried about the trial, but once I came here and had the respect of all the inmates. I guess karma couldn't allow me to vask in the feeling of acceptance. Everytime my mind would travel away I was forced to relive the night that changed my life. And there was no one I could talk about it too. No one. Being trapped in here plus being trapped in my past, resulted in me hating life. It seemed as if I'd never be happy again. And it most definitely seemed like I'd never go home. But thanks to a little thing God created called time, my day was finally here. I was a free man.

"You're frree to go," said Mr. Thomas, the head of Staff, as a collosal steel gate opened, revealing the world I'd been fantisizing about for all these years.

I placed my feet onto the pavement and devoured the air. After everything I went through I had made it. I felt like a man born blind who had somehow gained his vision. And with my vision I looked out and saw what had to be the most beautiful thing God had ever crafted. Instantly I froze as our eyes connected. I struggled to keep my balance as I made my way to her. After only a few steps I found myself taking to long to reach her and I had no choice but to run, arms spread as wide as the ocean. "Ma!"

"Pete," she screamed back as her purse fell to the ground in leu of running towards me. It had been so long since we'd touched one another without being stared down by C.O.'s and camera's. When we finally merged, her body felt as though it transported life back into me. I held her like I'd been craving to do these last three years. Hours seemed pass as I attempted to make up for all the hugs I'd missed out on. My cheeks soon became drenched with tears as we both whispered *'I love you's'*.

"Oh my God. I've been waiting for this moment for two years, nine months and eleven days," Mom said, squeasing me tighter.

"Me too Ma, me too."

My Mom talked a whole in my head for the entire drive back to Norview. Mostly about shit I could give a fuck about but what could I say. So I just smiled and through in a couple *'I know Ma's'* and *'Yeah you're rights'* every so often.

When we finally passed the sign the read *'Welcome to Norview'* I rolled down my window and took in the air "Ahh." It still had the same smell. I really can't explain it but I just know it when it hits my nose. Up until now I had completely forgot all about it. That dry, dead smell I 'd encountered in the jail must've altered my memory or something.

I asked Mom to drive slow so I could marvel at what I'd missed. Nothing much seemed to have changed. The same shops were around, *'Mr. Blues Barbershop'*, *'Hatties Country Fried Chicken' 'Mabels Dry Cleaning'*.

Everything looked exactly how I'd been picturing it the last three years. People were out walking and riding bikes aound. It appeared to be the same peaceful Norview that I'd always knew and loved, still I avoided any eye contact. I wasn't ready to be making any appearances quite yet. I didn't know how they'd react to me being back. Supposedly the town was still pretty segregated. There hadn't been anymore fights and no one had spray painted anything on my Mom's gate lately but all in all shit was still fucked up. Knowing how Norview operates I know my Mom told one person that I got out today and that was like telling a million, still I wasn't about to go out my way to speak to anybody

"Pete, you know you're gonna have to work twice as hard to show people the real you," my Mom said staring at me as we paused at a red light. "It won't be easy but you have to do it."

"I know Ma. You been tellin me this every week for the past three years," I said.

I wasn't exaggerating she really did. And each time she'd say it, she'd act as though she'd never said before.

"Pete I have to. When you're hurting I'm hurting and I don't' wanna hurt anymore. Times been really tough these last three years."

"I'm sorry Ma," I said.

I really was sorry. Ma already had enough on her mind. I didn't like the fact that I made it worse.

"Pete I'm not asking for an apology. Do you know who Buddha is?"

"I heard of him, aint he the one who had Tina Turner doin all that,--" I closed my eyes and raised my hand in a praying position like all them Munk niggas who be sitting Indian style be doing. "Ali, umba ya, Ali umba ya."

"Something like that," Mom said laughing. "But he was a spiritual teacher and he once said 'What you think, you become."

"Huh?"

My Mom had to be the smartest person I knew. She always knew some shit that they would only ask on Jeopardy or something.

"He means whatever you allow yourself to think about yourself is what will come true."

See. Who looks up this type of shit?

"If you let people convince you that you're a criminal then that's all you'll ever be," Mom said as I nodded my head. I guess I understood what she was saying. "Pete, I love you and I know you can do anything I just want you to know it."

"Thanks Ma. I do know it and I love you too."

Before I knew it we were in front of the crib. My eyes blew up like a rocket as I admired the pleasantly familiar scenary. Besides my Mom's new picket fence everything on the block appeared to be the same as I left it. I saw a couple faces I'd forgotten, sitting on their porches and in their lawns but I still wasn't ready to speak so I acted like I didn't see them.

As I was exiting the whip, the front door swung open and there was Korb. He had gotten big as hell. He was 13 now and already about 5'7. This wasn't my first time seeing him since I had been away. He and my Mom used to come and visit me once a month in Beaumont but I never got to do what I wanted to him. Now was the time. I sprinted towards him and did what had bonded us his entire life. I through him in a headlock.

"Aint nothin change boy. You big but not big enough."

Yeah he might've been 5'7 but I had grown to be a well toned 6ft. He was definitely no match for me. My Mom smiled as she walked past us into the house. I know she missed her two boys playing around.

"Hey my Peta Wida," said Aunt Tina walking out the front door.

167

Immediately I dropped Korb and thrusted myself onto her. She and Aunt Fonda had really held me down during my bid. They never came to see me but atleast three times a month I'd get a new inspiratiional book from one of them and they were always throwing a couple bones in my canteen.

"Hey Aunt Tina," I said.

"I missed you so much," she said admiring my new look, smiling. "Oh my God, you got so big and what is that growing on your face?"

"That's my mustache," I said rubbing it. It wasn't that thick but it still showed up pretty clear.

"Oh my God. Your Aunt Fonda can't wait to see you," she said before grabbing me by the arm, "Come inside."

I stepped into the house in awe. My Mom always kept a nice house but this was extreme. It looked like some artsy type people lived here or something. She had paintings placed alongside the walls, a new bookshelf filled with all types of literature precisely filled to capacity, little African statues standing in the corners of the room, new sofa's and love seats, each wall painted a different fluorescent color. Yet with all that going on everything still seemed to mesh. Looking around I had no choice but to take off my shoes, this was the kind of crib you showed the up most respect to.

"Look who's here," said Aunt Tina as Aunt Fonda hopped off the couch and ran towards me.

"Hey Pete," she said hugging me tightly.

"Hey Aunt Fonda," I said still gawking at my new pad. I looked over to the kitchen entrance and discovered my Grandma walking up with a smile only she could deliver. No one had told me she was here but I should've known by the aroma of immaculately seasoned Soul food. I released Aunt Fonda and rushed over. Even though my Grandma could be crazy I had missed her a lot. "Grandma. I missed you."

"Grandma missed you too baby," she said as we embraced. My Mom and Korbin walked over as everyone joyfully crowded around us. I hadn't been in a room full of love in a minute. It felt great. "Now I want you to stay out of trouble. You hea me," Grandma said pointing her finger in my face? That was the Grandma I remembered.

"Yes Grandma."

"And I made you somethin to eat."

I sniffed into the air. "Is that Collard Greens, candy yams with marshmallows, macaroni and cheese, stuffin and is that fried chicken I smell?"

"Sure is," she said smiling. "Grandma knows you ain't had a good meal in years."

"True indeed. I'm starvin," I said rubbing my stomach, making my way to the kitchen.

"Before you eat anything," said my Mom stopping me in my tracks. "Go upstairs and take a shower. I don't want any of those jail spirits lingering around in here."

My Mom had really gotten into some crazy spiritual, meditation type stuff since I'd been gone, she had all types of new believes and shit. Week after week she sent

169

me letters about it. I never understood it so I didn't really pay it any mind.

"Alright but what I'ma put on?"

I had grown 7 inches since I was gone. It was no way I could fit any of my old clothes but on the other hand maybe I could. Trell had told me that big baggy clothes weren't popping anymore. Tight fitted threads was in style. I didn't believe him till I finally got enough points to watch T.V. and noticed all the rappers dressing like RnB singers. But, hey I kinda liked it. Still my old clothes were played out. Fresh gear was a must.

"I bought you some clothes, there on your bed."

Uh oh this could be bad. My Mom was a fly lady but I didn't want her picking out my get fresh gear. There's no way I can step back on the scene looking like a lame.

"And before you go all crazy, Trell helped me pick out the stuff," she said as I headed up the steps.

"Thank God," I whispered.

Trell was always on top of all that fashion shit so I was happy. I slowly walked up the stairs reveling in everything I had missed these last three years. Like the rest of the crib Mom had upgraded the look of the steps by throwing more painting along the wall but what really made me smile was something as simple as the creaking of the steps and the sweet smell of Febreze. I was reminded of a time when I lived problem free. The good ol days.

I burst into my room and everything was how I left it. Well almost how I left it. I don't remember it being so clean. Ma must've came and tidied up the place. Still

170

everything that was hear before was still around; my posters, Playstation, T.V.. The picture me and Sharee had taken at the zoo was still on the dresser alongside the picture of my Dad. I nodded my head to Pops but of course the picture I couldn't take my eyes off was the one of Sharee and me. How could I? Look at her. Them dimples, that smile, that cute little scar. After a while I found myself drooling and had to literally force myself to turn away. After all these years she still was hypnotizing.

Boy, things had really changed. Sharee never stopped writing but she was no longer my girl. She was Dante's. She told me all about him. He was the starting QB at Norview High. I've gotta admit I was sick when she first told me about the nigga. The thought of her talking to another guy made my soul cry. Initially I vowed to never speak to her again but after a week I realized I was outta my mind. After all I was the one locked up. I couldn't expect her to stop living her life. It was better to be her friend than to have her completely out of my life.

I looked over to my bed to check out my new apparel. There was about four bags thrown across the bed. I charged over to them to begin my inspection. The Hundreds, Obey, Stussy, 10 Deep and Pink Dolphin. I had never heard of not one of those designers, not to mention they looked extremely small but I guess I gotta get used to it. I tossed the clothes back on the bed, took another look around the room and exhaled. I was finally home. No more uniforms, shakedowns, punk ass C.O.'s 2 minute showers. Thank God I was finally home.

I hopped out the shower feeling like a brand new man. I was smelling good and looking even better. I through on a The Hundreds tank top, some Obey shorts and a pair of fresh Nike's I discovered on the floor of my room.

Again I didn't know the name of the shoes but as I took a look in the mirror there was no question I was looking pretty dope. The only thing left to do was brush my waves. There was no way I could forget my babies. I had been taking tender care of them for the past three years and I wasn't gonna stop now. I searched endlessly around the room but couldn't find a brush anywhere.(probably cause I never used to use one). After an intense hunt, I remembered I'd still had one in my duffel bag I'd bought home from Beaumount. I jetted down to my Mom's car to retrieve it. When I got back to my room and busted it open the first thing I saw was a little note DaDa had sent me while I was upstate that I'd been holding on to.

"What's up Lil nigga. I'm home. Don't forget what I told you. Hit me up if you need me 8452338177."

I must've reread that note a million times since I'd gotten it.

"Pete! Someone's at the door," My Mom screamed to me.

Company already? I found my brush and got it in. I looked in the mirror one more time to make sure I looked nice. Who knows, it could be Sharee.

I sprinted downstairs to the door, everyone was in the living room talking. They all smiled as I came down the steps in my new fit.

"Aww look at my baby," said Mom.

"G.Q," said Aunt Tina.

"Sexy, Sexy," said Aunt Fonda as I smiled.

172

"Thanks," I said before looking over to my Mom. "Who is it?"

"Go see," Mom said pointing to the door.

"Alright," I said anxiously.

I walked outside and what do you know, it was my main nigga Trell. He still looked exactly the same except he was now about my height and he had him a mustache too. But what I couldn't believe is the fact that he was sporting a Burger King uniform.

"Bro," we both screamed. This was the first time in all our years of friendship that we hugged.

"I missed you dog," I said as we released one another.

"I missed you too my nigga."

Trell sat back on the rail as I copped a squat on some new wooden rocking chair my Mama had on the porch. "How's it feel to be a free man?"

I looked around and smiled. "I can't even explain it dog. And oh yeah congrats my nigga. Heard you got a little seed lue on the way."

I don't know why we said lue after everything but it became a habit while locked up. I had all types of new lingo I was planning on hitting these niggas with.

"Yeah man," said Trell disappointingly. "April's three months."

173

Trell never really mentioned April in his letters but Sharee told me that they had gotten pretty serious. She's also the one who told me that Trell had gotten her pregnant.

"My Mom spazzed. She's makin me go to the Army after graduation."

"Your pretty ass in the Army? That's funny."

I had forgotten that the military had even existed. No one I was locked up with ever seemed to mention it but I guess it would be a good move. Still I know for damn sure my black ass wont goin. I had been taking orders for the last three years. I won't bout to do that over again. Hell no.

"Shit ain't funny. She even made me get this stupid ass job," Trell said pointing to his uniform. "You know it ain't my style to come home smellin like onions and shit."

I couldn't help but to burst out laughing. "Damn I can't believe you bouta be somebody's Daddy. I hope you ain't tryna catch up to Sho."

Sharee told me Sho had created his own little basketball team since I'd been gone.

"Hell naw, I learned my lesson the day April took the pregnancy test."

"True. True," I said as I paused to take in the scenery once more. "Yo, you seen Sho lately?"

"Oh, yeah I forgot to tell you I just saw him earlier. He said he was gonna stop past."

A burst of joy flew through my body. I hadn't heard from Sho for the entire three years. He was the only one I could even mention my feeling too. Besides I had to thank him for putting that word in for me.

"Yo, I know you gonna take Sharee from that sucka nigga Dantae," said Trell.

Damn just hearing her name gave me the urge to ask Trell about all the details that went on in their relationship. Did Sharee look happy? Did they hold hands? Had he ever seen them kiss in public? Did he think they made a good couple? Did they look like a better match than she and I did? There was so much I wanted to know but I know if I did he'd hit me with the 'I'm a sucker' shit, so I refrained.

"Man me and Sharee just friends," I said trying not only to convince Trell, but also convince myself.

"Are you crazy? You better smash that. You worked too hard to give up now."

I didn't even feel like thinking about Sharee right now. All that was gonna do is make me mad.

"Man forget her, yo you ever talk to Josh?

"Hell naw," Trell spat out.

"At all?"

"Neva," Trell said strongly. "Norview's a whole different place dog," he said shaking his head. "Shit changed round hea. It might look the same but trust me my nigga, it ain't."

We both shook our heads. I didn't know what to say. It sucked knowing that I was partially the reason.

"Yo. Did I tell you Tinka smoke crack now?"

"What?" I shouted. "Crack? Who the hell would dare start to smoke crack in 2011. You gotta be lyin bro. I went to school with her."

"Well now she gettin that higha education," Trell said, laughing at his own joke. "You know she always been a freak. She hooked up with some wanna be pimp ass nigga and the next thang I know she was suckin dick in the woods for ten dollas."

"Suckin dick in the woods? That's crazy," I said still in shock.

"Who you tellin? I still can't believe I lost my virginity to that."

"Damn"

"Yep. Yo, you still comin back to school this year?"

"Hell yeah. I made it back just in time for senior year," I said as Trell pulled his brush from out of his pocket and began brushing. He must've taken a look at my waves spinning all crazy. I smiled. He was used to being the only pretty boy.

176

"Yeah hopefully your virgin ass can finally get you some cheeks," he said before looking at me playfully suspicious. "You still is a virgin ain't you?"

"Fuck you," I said throwing my middle finger up as Trell's playfully demeanor quickly turned serious.

"Ay bro what happened that night?" he asked looking me in the eyes. "That shit's like a Norview mystery or somethin."

No one besides my lawyer had ever asked me that question and I was hoping I'd never be asked. So much for that thought. I couldn't even look Trell in the eyes.

"Your guess is as good as mine." I had to change the subject. "But that's the past man. I just wanna forget about it."

"Yeah, I guess that's probably the best thang to do. Well I gotta be off to work man. I gotta family to take care of now," he said sarcastically.

We both stood up to dap.

"Alright my nigga. Holla at me lata," I said.

"Alright big dog."

It was cool kicking it with Trell but I was ready for some food. I had been dreaming about a home cooked meal for years now. It was time to get loose.

We all sat at the dinner table together. The food was even better than I expected. Between all the laughin and the food, my stomach felt as though it was ready to burst.

"Don't eat so fast. The food ain't going nowhere," said my Grandma.

But I just couldn't help it. I was eating for the rest of the homies behind the G-Wall. Before I knew it I had downed four plates. I sat stuffed listening to my fam talk about everything going on in their world. They even talked about the no good men they'd been meeting and made me promise to never be one. I hate to say it but I was kinda glad they hadn't found a man. I also found out Korb's little ass had a girlfriend, Mercedes. He showed me a pic of her and I have to admit, bro got some taste, I was proud of him.

All in all family time was cool but after a while I was feigning to touch the block. I hadn't even taken my first free walk yet. "See yall lata," I said hoping they would let me slide.

"Whoa, whoa, whoa, whoa. Where do you think you're going Mr.? It's 7:00?" asked Mom.

"I'm just goin to take a walk," I said.

"I don't know if that's a good idea Pete," she said looking over to Grandma as Aunt Tina nodded.

"Why not?" I whined. "You just can't keep me cooped up in this house for the rest of my life. I'm seventeen years old," I said as they all eyeballed me wearing identical poker faces. "Don't yall think I read all the lettas you sent me? And Ma, all those spiritual quotes you told me. Don't you think I listened," I said as they seemed to be warming up? "And wasn't it yall who said to put my life in God's hands?"

"I still don't know Pete. I don't think I'm comfortable yet."

Damn I just knew the God line would work. Time for plan B.

"Come on Ma please, please, please. I been waitin for this for three years now. I need it, I won't be out all night," I said pleading as Mama slowly looked around for approval.

"Ok Pete.But here take this phone," she said pulling out some fancy touch screen phone from her purse. I had been dreaming of getting one of those in my hands for months now, Sharee told me flip phones were for wack dudes. "I was planning on giving it to you tomorrow. I want to always be able to contact you. If ever I call and you don't answer. It's mine."

Oh My God! I got a new phone and I get to go outside. Yes! "No problem. Thanks," I said hugging and kissing everyone. I hauled ass over to the door. "I'll see yall lata. Love ya."

"Love you too," they all repeated.

I stepped outside, it was still beautiful out. The sun was fading away and the air had a slight breeze to it. Everything was seeming to make me smile, from the flowers in Ms. Milly's yard to the cracks in the concrete.

I enjoyed watching the little kids play around. They were so young and innocent. They reminded me of better days. Watching them run around made me feel old, it's crazy how much kids can grow in three years. Shit, look at me.

Ah man, I loved that my street was always so friendly. I was trying to be low-key but all I kept hearing was *"Welcome Back", "Thank God"*, Old Man Johnson even slipped me a 10 spot. *"Go buy you something nice,"* he said. Everyone on the block showed love.

Still I was kinda afraid to keep walking. My street is all black but the next wasn't. I was kinda frightened to see how the whitie's would react to me being back. But fuck them I ain't no punk. I just survived three years behind the G-Wall without a scratch. I'll be damn if I'm scared of some punk ass crackers.

I morphed into G-mode and crossed the street before almost being pummeled by some Blue Impala that came to a screeching halt inches away from me with dark tinted windows.

Detective Fraley, the Detective who had interrogated me hopped out followed by some skinny ass white guy. I wanted to walk away but figured that would cause more shit. So I stayed. I hadn't done anything wrong.

"Welcome Home. How ya doing Pete? Where ya headed?" he asked, leaning on his car staring at me with an unpersuasive smile as they both awaited a response.

"I'm chillin, just takin a walk," I said avoiding eye contact.

"Yeah I bet you are," he said sarcastically while tapping the skinny white man. "Ahh man I'm being rude. I didn't introduce you two, Detective Smalls this is Pete. Pete this is Detective Smalls," he said never taking his eyes off of me.

"What's up Pete," he said staring at me, looking like a Detective Fraley wannabe.

"What's up," I said still never looking over to him.

"Pete's the Norview Cop killer," said Detective Fraley.

He shot his eyes over to me to see how I'd react. I outsmarted him by standing, trying my best to look unbothered. I wasn't going to give him the satisfaction of making me mad.

"Is that right?" said Detective Smalls, acting as though he didn't already know who the fuck I was.

"Yep. He's fresh home from a well needed vacation," he said still never taking his eyes off of me. "But it's cool. I'm gonna make sure he goes on an even longer one this time around." They both stared. This time I stared back. "Well I'm sure you wanna catch up with your homies. I know we'll be seeing you pretty soon. You're excused."

I stormed off. I couldn't believe them. Didn't they have better shit to do with their time. They better be lucky I ain't really no murderer. Cause they'd both be on my damn hit list. I speed walked away from them so fast down the street that I didn't even bother to notice how the white people were reacting. I did notice a familiar voice from behind though.

"Pete. Pete," the voice shouted. I spun around and there was Sharee darting towards me. I stood stuck, unable to move a muscle. "Pete." She continued shouting until she finally reached me, squeezing me tight, blessing me with the most passionate hug I'd ever received. "Oh my God you got so tall. You look good! I missed you so much," she said. I had been waiting three years to hear those words come out of her mouth.

"I missed you too," I repeated as she pushed me away from her.

"Why didn't you call and tell me you were home?" she asked with her hand on her hip reminding me of the Sharee I'd always knew and loved.

"What? I wrote you last month and told you I was comin home today?"

"So. You couldn't pick up a phone and tell me?"

"I swear I was gonna call. I just thought you might've been busy."

And I wasn't lying I was going to call her. I just wanted to play it smart. I knew she had a man. I couldn't be too thirsty.

"Busy? Whatever. Where you headed now?" she asked.

Her teeth were gorgeous. Beyond gorgeous, they actually kinda looked fake. I know they were real but damn I'd never seen anyone's teeth like hers besides movie stars and shit.

"Nowhere. Just takin a walk," I said looking around at the neighborhood. Trying hard not to stare too hard at her vivacious body. Trying really hard. "It's been a while since I been able to do this. A lot of shits changed out hea."

"Tell me about it," she said shaking her head. "You mind walking me home?"

This had to be the dumbest question I'd ever been asked.

"Sure why not?" I answered.

We walked shoulder to shoulder down the street. I wanted to put my arm around her so bad. She looked amazing but I just took what I was given.

"Thanks for all the lettas you wrote. I read them so much I memorized them."

"Whatever," she said.

I made her blush. Let's see if I can do it again.

"I'm serious I don't know if I could've made it without you."

"Aww thanks Pete." Jackpot two in a row. Maybe I was on to something. "You know I'm always here for you," she said still blushing. "Unless you go back in there, because my letter writing days are over," she said seriously.

"Damn. I can understand that."

"I'm just joking but seriously you better not go back."

"I'm not. Trust me," I said as we paused, briefly locking eyes.

"Yeah, you better not," said Sharee breaking the silence. "And can I ask you a question?"

Something told me I already knew what she wanted to know. "Yeah. What's up?"

"You didn't have anything to do with that cop dying did you?"

I knew it.

"Naw Sharee, not at all," I said avoiding eye contact again.

"I knew you didn't. I know you do stupid things but that's just something I know you wouldn't do."

Man I loved this girl. We walked up to Sharee's porch still shoulder to shoulder.

"Yeah. I wish everybody thought like you."

"Yeah but everything's going to be ok Pete," she said as we sat down on her steps. Man I missed these steps. "You're home now and you have a second chance. A lot of people don't get one." She was still perfect.

"Yeah you're right," I said looking up to the sky. It was dusk and the sky gave off a kinda romantic feeling. It seemed as though we had just seen each other yesterday. Trell was right. I had to get my girl back.

"You love that nigga?" I asked out of nowhere.

"Huh?"

"Dantae. Do you love him?"

"We've been through a lot together. He's a great guy," she said before pausing. "So yes."

184

My heart dropped. Why did I even ask that shit?

"But Pete you know you'll always be special to me," she said as we locked eyes once more. I guess I was ok with that for now.

"You're special to me too," I said.

There she was blushing again. I hate all these mixed signals but it's gonna be worth it one day. I just know it. Fuck Dantae.

Suddenly I heard the loud thumping of Gucci Mane music rolling up towards Sharee's crib. Sharee and I both looked in the directions of the music.

"Yo is that Sho?" I asked before hopping up, peering deep inside of the car before noticing that it was. I could tell he noticed us too by the mile long grin plastered on his face. He quickly slid to the side of the street.

"Yep. So I guess that's your Q."

I kinda ignored Sharee. I was too busy watching Sho jump out the car. He looked like a superstar. Gold earrings, gold teeth, gold watch, gold rings, gold bracelet, fitted hat, and an outfit that I'm sure was in style I just didn't know what it was. Not to mention the fresh Jordan's. He looked like Money.

"Pete!" Sho hollered over to me, I wasted no time darting over.

"What's up my nigga," I said as we dapped up. I don't know who I was more happy to see, Sharee or Sho.

Sho stepped back and examined me. "I'm chillin my nigga. You lookin good dog. Got all tall and shit. I was just

185

on my way to your crib," he said looking over to Sharee who was still on the porch. "What's up Sharee?"

"Hey Sho," Sharee said dryly as I stared at Sho, mesmerized.

"I ain't interruptin nothin am I?" Sho asked looking at Sharee.

"Nope. I was just about to go in the house," she said as she stood to her feet. "My room is in desperate need of some cleaning."

"You sure?" I asked finally taking my eyes off of Sho.

"Yeah," said Sharee walking towards Sho and I. "You guys go catch up," she said before hugging me."

I could tell Sharee didn't really want me to go. Not just because she wanted to kick it some more but because she never like Sho. Something inside me told me that she even suspected that Sho was the real killer of Officer McNair. Still I had to go with Sho. We had some top notch shit to converse about.

"Alright. I'ma text you to give you my numba," I said before pulling out my phone.

"Oh shit. The lil nigga got a jack already," Sho joked.

"What's your numba?" I asked Sharee even though I knew it by heart.

"The same as it's been since I was 14. 7148685."

186

"That nigga know he remember that shit by heart," said Sho as I texted Sharee my number.

After a slight giggle Sharee looked at her phone. "OK I got it," she said before hugging me once more before walking away. "Alright. See ya later Pete."

"Alright Sharee,"

"Aww yall so cute," said Sho. "Bye Sharee."

"Bye Sho," she said without turning around.

I stared as she pranced back into the house. I hated for her to leave but boy did I love to see her walk away. That damn sure wasn't the same 14 year old body I remember. This was the shape of a full grown woman. A bomb full grown woman.

"Come take a ride with me," Sho said interrupting all the dirty thoughts running through my head.

"Huh," I said looking over to Sho's car suspiciously. We both knew what happened the last time I hopped in a whip with him.

"It's not stolen. I just wanna chill with you," he said in his most convincing voice. I looked at Sho. Then took a look at everything he was wearing. The jewelry, the clothes, if he had enough money for all that shit than he clearly had enough for a whip. "Trust me Dog."

"Alright," I said walking towards the car.

"That's what's up," he said hopping on his side. I got in and the insides were spotless. Leather seats, T.V.'s, not to mention the bass. Sho was living good. He sparked a cigarette and pulled off. "Motherfuckin Lil Jesse," he said

187

smiling. "Damn three years," he said shaking his head as I admired the car, impressed. "Yo I heard you had shit on smash upstate."

"Yeah man thanks for putting in that word," I said.

"Nigga fuck that, I had to do it. I owe you my fuckin life."

I stared over to him. I guess Sho had been thinking about me. I had wondered about it every day. Now I finally know. I'm satisfied. I can't say it made everything worth it but I'm satisfied.

"It's all good man," I said.

"Naw dog," Sho said shaking his head. "It ain't a lot of niggas who woulda held it down like you did."

I was thrilled that Sho respected me. I sat there nodding my head as he reached into his pants pocket and tossed a large stack of money wrapped in a rubber band into my lap. I stared at the gwop before picking it up. There was a one hundred dollar bill on the top and I saw the tips of several other 50's and 20's. It was clearly over a thousand, maybe even five thousand. Shit maybe, ten thousand. I don't know but it was definitely more than I've ever had before.

"What's this for?" I asked as I cautiously picked up the money, taking in a whiff.

"That's my lil thank you," he said without even looking over to me.

"I can't take this,' I said handing Sho the money back. "You got four kids man."

188

"Nigga I got plenty money," he said looking offended. "My kids straight. Nigga that's yours, you deserve that shit. I been stackin that shit sense you went in that bitch."

I've got to admit I was happy as hell he didn't want the money back. Shit, he was right. I did deserve it. "Alright. Thanks man," I said still staring at the money. I knew it was time to ask Sho a question I could only ask him. "Yo," I said as Sho looked over to me.

"What's up?"

"Yo, you--you eva think about that night?"

"What?" Sho blurted.

"I mean do you eva, like feel bad about what happened," I said looking straight ahead. I had been dying to ask him. "Cause man I can't stop havin these nightmares."

"What?" Sho snapped. "What the fuck you feelin bad for? You ain't even do shit."

I couldn't believe how Sho reacted. Could he really be this cold? I stared in disbelief but still, I was happy that he was saying I ain't do shit. It bought a little peace over me. I had been feeling guilty for so long. "I mean--"

Sho cut cross me. "Man fuck that shit. I'll answer to that shit when I die," Sho said staring over to me. "To tell the truth I ain't really gave the shit too much thought after it happened."

Hadn't gave it too much thought? How can you kill someone and just forget about it? Sho was a strong nigga.

189

"I mean I felt bad about what happened to you but other than that, FUCK IT, I ain't got no love for no fuck ass Policeman, especially a white one." he said.

I was now feeling a little envious of Sho. I hadn't even killed the man and I thought about it every day. I'd love to just forget about it.

We road in silence down a few blocks. The light from the sky was slowly fading away as the stars began popping out from behind the clouds, one by one. I rolled down my window, sucked in some air and through my head up to the sky, in search of a shooting star. I had more than a few things I could wish for right now.

We pulled up to Sho's apartment building. I couldn't help but to think of the last time I was here. I looked around and the neighborhood seemed a little dirtier than before. It appeared more like Tidewater Park than ever.

I glanced over to the left and saw a lady walking over to us in nothing but a dingy pink bathrobe and matching bedroom slippers. Her hair was matted down and all over the place. And I may be wrong but I think I smelled her from here. It was a fishy, musty kinda smell, mixed with dragon breath. When she finally reached us and leaned over to the window I realized exactly who she was.

"Hey baby. What ya got for me?" the lady asked Sho showing all six of her yellow teeth. Sho took in a breath and handed her a small a bag of crack.

"Ma, this the last time. I ain't runnin no damn charity."

"I know, I know baby," she said peering deeper into the car focusing her eyes onto me. "Pete, is that you?"

"Hey Aunt Sheila," I said with a half smile.

I still remember a time when she was beautiful. Ever since I could remember she'd been on drugs but it never seemed to effect her. Those times are long gone. Still I couldn't believe Sho actually served his own Mama. I couldn't imagine doing anything like that. Shit like that really kinda made me feel sorry for Sho. You gotta be a pretty hurt dude to do some shit like that.

"Welcome home baby. You look good," I forced myself to smile. I thought about saying she'd looked nice also but I figured she already knew she didn't.

"Alright Ma. I got shit to do. I'll see you later."

"Alright baby. Bye Bye Pete it was good seeing you baby."

Sho sped off before I could even respond. "I know what you thinkin man," Sho said looking over to me. "But hey, she gonna get it from somebody, might as well be me."

In a way I guess Sho was right. I can't count all the times I heard she was going to rehab. I guess after a while it's just like fuck it. But Sho was wrong, what really was on my mind was what he had given to his mother.

"Bout how much you make a day off that?" I asked.

"Off what?" Sho asked before realizing what I meant. "Cuzzo don't tell me you wanna get on the block?"

191

Sho looked like he was living good. And DaDa always told me that the most important thing in the world was money. I wanted in. Sho was able to just throw me a few thousand dollars and not worry about it. I don't know anybody else who can do some shit like that. And with all the stories I'd heard in jail I knew all the ins and outs, this would be a piece of cake.

"Man I just want some money in my pocket."

Sho smiled as we pulled up to a small crib around the corner from his. There was trash, tricycles and kids toys spread all across the yard and the appearance seemed to coincide perfectly with all the other homes on the block.

"I feel you on that. We can talk bout that lata though," Sho said hopping out the whip. "But right now I got a lil surprise for you. Come on."

"What kinda surprise?" I asked as I stepped out.

There were two thugged out niggas on the porch. What kinda surprise involved niggas like them? Just because I been around niggas like that for the past three years don't mean I wanna be hanging and getting surprises from them and shit. What the hell was this all about?

"You'll see in a minute," Sho said dapping up the guys on the porch. I dapped them too. I started to fist pound them but remembered that I was no longer in a cage. "This my lil cuzzo Pete I been tellin yall bout."

They both said whatsup.

"But yall can get up lata," Sho said walking into the crib. "Follow me."

I went inside the house. The place was a dump. There was clothes and shoes everywhere, the couch and chairs looked as if they were found on some curb, cigarette buds and ashes filled every table. The only decent looking thing in there was a giant flat screen hanging off the wall. But it was impossible to actually hear what was going on, on the TV due to the millions of kids running amuck, hollering to the top of their lungs.

Three of them ran over to Sho. "Daddy, Daddy Daddy," they screamed.

"Hey baby," Sho said hugging them all before pointing over to me. "Yall say what's up to your Cousin Pete.

They all said, "Hey Cousin Pete," in unison.

Sho sure couldn't say he wasn't their Dad. They all were spitting images of him.

"Hey yall," I said back before looking over at the overweight woman laying on the couch, wrapped up in a king sized mattress sheet.

"That's Amy," Sho said.

"Hey Pete," she said as if she'd already knew me. I hoped that this wasn't one of Sho's girls, if so he sure has downgraded. Yuck!

"What's up?" I said.

"This her crib and shit. We just be kickin it in hea. She cool as hell. Most of these bad ass kids hers."

"Shut up mothafucka. My kids ain't bad," she screamed.

It was obvious she was lying as I watched her kids terrorize the entire living room.

"Follow me," said Sho as we made our way down a short hall way, which was equally as trifling as the living room.

"Where we goin?" I asked as we approached a closed door.

"Welcome Home," Sho said as he opened the door.

What a sight! My mouth dropped and saliva oozed out of it as I feasted my eyes on two of the thickest women I'd ever seen laying down on the bed. They had the bodies of porn stars and they were both in nothing, butt ass naked. Sho shoved me into the room before I could even fully take in what was going on.

I had yet to take my eyes off the women as the door slammed. I stood in front of the ladies nervous as a sinner on judgment day. Never in my life had I had one girl and now Sho throws me into a room with two. Usually my dick gets hard at the sight of something as simple as a naked picture. But for some reason my little soldier hadn't moved an inch as I contemplated my next move.

Obviously I was taking too long because before I knew it one of the girls came over, unzipped my pants and the rest was Black history.

Afterwards I went to the bathroom to get myself together. I splashed water on my face and stared into the mirror. I couldn't believe what I had just done. I always thought I'd lose my virginity to Sharee. But shit, I'm pretty sure she'd already lost hers, so fuck it. Besides if I ever do get the chance with her at least I'll know what I'm doing now. After all these years I finally felt like a man. A real man.

"Damn nigga, it don't take that long to wash your dick. Hurry up," screamed Sho from outside the bathroom.

I cut off the water and walked out grinning. "What's the rush?"

"Come with me," Sho said.

This shit must be important. He didn't even ask me about the girls. What the fuck? We walked through the living room where Amy was still on the couch yapping away on the phone while the millions of kids continued terrorizing the house. We made our way to the kitchen that lead to the back door, of course dishes were piled up to the ceiling surrounded by flies.

When we got outside the two guys who were on the porch, some light skinned nigga and two bitches were outside drinking and smoking.

Sho led me to the middle of the grass. Everyone ceased what they were doing and gathered around him. Again I had no idea what the hell was going on.

"Me and the homies wanna have a little talk with you," Sho said as he lit a cigarette. Everyone focused their attention to me. I was feeling nervous. What was this all about? "This my family right hea. Call ourselves The Warriors," followed Sho as he slowly surveyed our surroundings. "No one in this family goes hungry. We work togetha to get this mo'fuckin money," Sho said staring at

195

me along with everyone else. "And when you told me you wanted some money I had no choice but to tell my family."

I looked around at all the faces staring at me still not understanding what was going on.

"Shit changed out here lil cuz. You need to be round some niggas who want the same shit as you. It's all love ova hea baby," he said looking out into the crowd, finally cracking a smile. "You tryna ride on our side or what?"

I was still a little confused. I had to make sure I was hearing him correctly. "What's this like a gang or somethin?" I asked.

"Nigga this is a family. We ain't no gang," Sho said sounding offended. "We bout gettin money by any means necessary," he said before briefly pausing. "This a once in a lifetime opportunity, my nigga. You down?"

No matter what Sho was saying I still knew this was a gang. I mean no matter how well he sugar coated it I knew what it was. I had never in my life imagined myself ever in a gang. I didn't even know gangs existed in Norview. I'd encountered plenty of gangs while I was locked up. Shit, niggas had even tried to recruit me a couple of times but I was never interested. What was the point? But this was different. This gang was led by Sho and as I looked into everyone's eyes I sensed that we all had one thing in common. We all wanted money. There was no question what my answer would be.

"Yeah. I'm down."

"You sure?" asked Sho.

I looked around once more. "Yeah, I'm sure."

"Alright. Let's do it," Sho said, nodding to the other Warriors.

In an instant what felt like fifty men jumped on top of me. I fought for my life but I was no match for these guys. Still, I refused to fall so I put my head down and swung irately. They were connecting with me way more than I connected with them but fuck it after a while I didn't feel anything, my adrenaline had taken over my body.

"Alright that's enough. That's enough," screamed Sho, pulling the men up off me before grabbing a hold of me.

But I wasn't even close to being done so I relentlessly tried my hardest to break free. Everything was moving so fast, I didn't know what the hell was going on as I continued my attempt at wrestling away from Sho.

"Get the fuck off me. Get off me," I screamed. At that point I would've been willing to fight Sho. I'd fight anyone. They just beat my ass for no apparent reason. Who the fuck did they think they were?

"Calm Down," Sho said still holding me back.

"Calm down? Calm down?" I screamed as blood shot out of my mouth. "I'ma kill somebody," I continued as everyone began laughing which made me furious. "Get the fuck off me. Get the fuck off me."

"Calm down. You just shed blood for us. You officially a Warrior now."

I calmed down as everyone approached me with their hand out attempting to show me our handshake. I was

197

officially a Warrior. Suddenly I was proud of that ass whipping.

I got home about eleven that night. I snuck in quietly, which really was a task considering Sho and my new homies had just gotten me fifth grade high. Not to mention I felt as though I'd been hit with a ton of bricks. I needed some ice stupid bad, I carefully crept over to the freezer, retrieved a bag of ice and headed upstairs. It felt good being able to walk freely at night. I slid over to the bathroom to check out the damage. Hopefully I wasn't too bad.

"Damn," I said to myself as I looked into the mirror. My lip was as fat as my face. But at least it was just my lip. It could've been worse.

I took a piss before walking over to my room and just as I was closing the door my Mom walked out of her room in her nightgown. "Goodnight Pete."

"Goodnight Ma," I said attempting to hide my face and shut the door. Thank God I'd dropped some eye drops in my eyes and sprayed some of Sho's cologne on.

"Pete what happened?" Mom said looking worried as she pushed the door forward.

"Oh nothin," I said with my head down. "I was just wrestlin around with Trell and he made a mistake and elbowed me," I said as my Mom walked over to gently touch my lip.

"Aw baby, I wish you boy's would stop playing so rough. Looks like he could've knocked a tooth loose. You have any ice?"

I held up the ice and attempted a smile. "I got it all covered."

"Well… ok. I have some business to take care of in the morning. But when I'm done do you wanna go out for lunch and a movie?"

"Just me and you?"

"Yeah. Just me and you."

I felt like a little kid. Me and Moms was always real tight. She's actually one of the coolest people I know. I knew this date would be fun. "Alright. That's what's up," I said.

"I'm so glad you're home. And remember what we talked about."

"Alright Ma," I said as we hugged.

"Well I'll see you tomorrow. I'm exhausted. I had to force myself not to call you but I couldn't help but to wait up. Love ya," she said before lightly kissing my boo boo.

"Love you too Ma," I said as Mom walked away.

I closed the door and flopped onto the bed. What a day. I had gotten released from a three year bid, ate a home cooked meal, saw my main man Trell, kicked it with the love of my life, hung with Sho, got some money, lost my virginity and even started a career. Besides being stopped by those pussy ass detectives, this was a hell of a way to celebrate my freedom.

199

The thought of being a gang banger still hadn't quite set in with me. I know if my Mom found out it'd break her heart. But I can at least try it out for a while. I had some catching up to do. Wont no lil Burger King job gonna be able to hold all my dreams. Guys at burger king don't drive cars like Sho's. They don't wear that kinda jewelry. They work for eight hours a day and at the end of the week, just have enough money for gas for their little hoop ride. I can't fade it. Shit, my nigga Trell shouldn't be doing that shit either. I knew I had to get him to join the Warriors. My nigga got a baby on the way. Plus it just didn't seem right without him.

Out of nowhere I felt my phone vibrating in my pocket. When I looked on the caller I.D. I was elated.

"Hello," I said in my *'Denzel Mack Daddy'* voice. I turned the phone on speaker, like the good ol days.

"Hey Pete, it's Sharee. You asleep?"

"Naw I'm chillin. What's up?

"Nothing, just got off the phone with Dantae."

Hearing that damn near sent a burst of flaming hot fire through my body. Still, I kept my composure.

"Oh Foreal? How's everything goin?"

"Not too good. I broke up with him."

"What?" I asked. I had to make sure my ears weren't deceiving me. "What happened?"

"I somehow fell back in love with my ex."

200

"Your ex? Who? Me?" I said excitedly stuttering.

"Yeah dummy, who else?"

This couldn't be real, could my best day ever be getting even better? I hopped out of my bed, I couldn't help but to dance. I hadn't been this happy since… since… since I gave her my number on Chantal's porch.

"I know I'm probably stupid for feeling like this. It's ok if you don't feel the same way. I just had to let you know?"

"Are you crazy?" I asked losing all my cool. "I been wantin you eva since I first laid eyes on you." It was time to let it all out. Fuck being composed. "I love you Sharee," I said before flopping back down onto the bed.

"I love you too Pete."

We talked on the phone until the sun came up. Just like that my life was back in order.

The next day me and Moms went to see American RapStar together. It was crazy because it was Rated R, which made me ecstatic. I know to most seven teen year olds that's nothing. Most kids had been seeing rated R movies as long as they could remember. But not me. My Mom was the only Mom I knew who forbid. Even Josh's parents let him watch what he wanted and he was white. They the ones who usually had all the damn rules. Man I swear, it don't get no better than this, me, Mama and a Rated R movie.

When the movie was over we went to the Cheesecake Factory. I don't know what the hell my Mom had, some sorta salady shit. I had something called Chicken n Biscuits and not just some ol KFC meal. This shit was sautéed just right, the chicken was boneless and the biscuit seemed to make love to my tongue. I was in heaven, I craved thirds fuck seconds. Meals like this is what's gonna keep me out of jail.

Of course my Mom talked a hole in my head about being a man and how much work I had to do. I acted as though I was listening but truthfully I was thinking about how I would convince Trell to join the Warriors. Still, I acted as though I was taking in every word. As usual she didn't even notice. I think she just loves to hear herself talk.

Just like Ice Cube, I gotta say, today was a good day. But now it was time to handle business.

I walked up to Trell's job about six, he said that's when he would be on break. Before then I was with my baby indulging in a little make out session. For the first time in my life I got to see her room. It was everything I expected, flawless just like her. Besides kissing I really didn't try to take it far. I was dying to tap but I could wait. Besides I had just gotten some ass yesterday. Actually I got double ass. I was straight.

When I arrived at Burger King, Trell was already on break, eating his complimentary meal. I sat down next to him and explained everything that had happened between me and the Warriors and the first thing he shouted was, "So you want me to join a gang?"

"It's not a gang. It's a business opportunity," I said trying to calm him down and remove the attention from off of us. From Trell's facial expression I could tell my point of view wasn't really sitting well with him.

"Business opportunity?" he shouted again as I signaled for him to quiet down. "Sho my nigga and all but I can't have him tellin me what to do."

This nigga still wasn't understanding. Maybe I should've bought Sho along with me. The way he explained it could persuade anyone.

"Man it's not like that," I said scrambling to find the right words.

"Dog, I neva committed a crime in my life. What the hell I look like being in a gang?" he asked.

I started to lie and say that he still wouldn't have to commit any crimes. But I wasn't too sure about that. "My nigga, I told you it's not a gang. Besides," I said pointing behind the counter to all of his co-workers busting their ass in the back. "Flippin burgers can't properly take care of a family."

"You're right," Trell said shaking his head. I really thought I was getting to him now. "But I definitely can't take care of a family from a cell."

Damn I thought I had him. Still I wasn't gonna give up. "We not goin to jail all we gotta do is play smart."

"Fuck that I'ma play smart in the Army."

"Trell, that's a year from now. Your kid's gonna be hea in six months. Might as well start the college fund early.

"Man--," Trell said shaking his head. I was grabbing a hold of him and I knew exactly what to do to pull him over to my side.

"Sho gave me this yesterday and it didn't even hurt'em," I said pulling out the stack of money. I had counted it and it was exactly five thousand big ones. "Five thousand dollas."

Trell sat in amazement. "Yeah. But how you know we gon be getting that type of money?"

After Trell asked that I knew everything else would be simple. "Just trust me dog. I can't do it without you man."

Trell stared long and hard before hesitantly muttering, "Man, O.K. But if we go to jail I'm shankin your ass." I burst out laughing but Trell was serious as a heart attack. "I ain't jokin."

"My nigga," I said excitedly as we gave each other dap.

Trell's manager, some fat greasy lady shouted from behind the counter. "Montrell! Breaks over. Time to get back to work." I could tell from Trell's facial expression that he was ready to walk out that very second when suddenly a customer on the other side of the room wasted an entire tray of food and drink all over the floor causing food to splatter all over the place. "And I got the perfect job for you," she said looking over to the floor.

"So when exactly we gonna start gettin paid?" asked Trell.

After Trell got off I took him over to Amy's crib. It didn't take much for me to convince Sho to allow Trell to join. In no time Trell was surrounded by the same guys who had surrounded me, only this time I was included.

Initially I didn't want to be involved. Trell was my best friend. I didn't want to beat his ass. But Sho forced me. Lucky for Trell I had already warned him that this would happen. I told him that I'd just pretend to be hitting him with all my mite but in actuality I'd be taking it easy.

Still, with that said, when Sho said *"Go"* this nigga came charging at me like a bat outta hell. If it weren't for my naturally quick reflexes he could've slam, knocked my ass out. I was forced to dodge his blows and commence to beating the shit outta him along with the other homies. It may sound sick but I actually found myself enjoying it. I beat his ass for all the times he had gotten on my nerves. Nothing serious just doing what I had to do.

Chapter 8

Sho had everything down pat, seeing him work was like watching a mad genius in action. I was amazed, everyone was. It seems as if me and Trell had linked up just in time, Sho was still in the process of getting everything in order. Gone were the days of him and his homies just out there doing crimes haphazardly, it was time to do this the right way, if that makes any sense at all. His focus was to make sure he put everyone in a position to get the most money for the Warriors. Everyone had their own little specialties and Sho's job was to exploit them.

The first couple weeks after I'd joined, Sho had us kick it with each other all day every day. He wanted us to become a real family. It was like we were in Training Camp or something.

Sho wont bullshitting, the nigga even taught us lessons and gave out homework. Not gay ass school homework but cool gangster homework. Most of the time he just had us watch some Documentary on famous crimes families and shit. Then he'd quiz us on what they'd done wrong and what they could've done differently to change it.

He taught us life lessons, like *'A man with no loyalty is not a man at all'* or that *'Nothing was more important than the money besides loyalty'* and *'That if there ain't no money involved don't get involved'*. But the most important lesson of all was to *'Stay on your 5 p's.'*

'Proper Planning Prevents Poor Performance.'

Sho taught that anything was possible when applying the 5 p's. I agreed. I wasted no time incorporating it into my daily life.

If I was gonna be a Warrior, Detective Fraley and the rest of his dick head friends were the least of my worries. Sharee and my Mom were the only ones who had me shook. There was no way I could let them find out what I had going on. So with the help of the homies I came up with a sure fire plan to keep everything under wraps. I got a pair of steel toe boots, vest, hard hat and woke up every morning at six. I was now a *'Full time construction worker'*.

And just like that it was time to go to work. Sho assembled our crews and had all types of get money schemes mapped out. Me and Trell were the drivers since we both had our licenses. Trell had gotten his a couple months ago and I got mines in a special program when I was upstate. Sho even found a way to get me and Trell some top notch whips. He said it was only right that Warriors drove in style. So being the evil genius that he is, he found a way for us to get loans from the *Navy Federal Bank*. It turns out since the days of Kevin bucking all that shit from the Navy Exchange, nothing had changed, them military niggas was still dumber than a bitch and Sho made them pay for it.

Since me and Trell weren't 18 Sho got a couple of his baby mama's to apply for Car loans. They'd fill out the app and when it asked for employment they'd make up some fugaze job and put Sho's number as the jobs contact name. Then when they'd call he'd put on his most professional business voice and say that they worked for him, making five hundred dollars a week and worked 40 hours a week. After that it was on, no pay stubs, nothing, we were awarded fifteen thousand dollar checks to cop whips.

Trell got a 2002 Infinity Q45. His whip was only nine thousand so he was able to give five thousand to Sho for some shit he needed to handle with the Warriors and got to pocket the other thousand dollars. I spent my whole check on my whip since I still hadn't even spent all the money Sho had given me when I came home. I went and got a silver 2007 Lincoln ls I don't' really know too much about cars but it looked sweet as hell plus Sho liked it.

And since my Mom was definitely gonna bitch, Sho advised me to park the car around the corner every night. I even put tints on the whip so no one could see who was whipping. Sitting behind those tints I felt like the President. There's no better feeling than pulling up on some whities and slowly rolling down the window revealing that is was my young black ass sitting behind the steering wheel. Boy, if the homies behind the G-Wall could see me now. I was styling on a whole new level.

But styling wasn't my job. I was a transporter. Me and Trell were both responsible for getting shit where it needed to go. Basically we just drove the real niggas around to make money. Sho knew that the cops couldn't check a whip if they had no probable cause and the driver had a license.

The niggas I usually drove around were Randy, Zeus, or Whiteboy. They were our hustlers. Sho had met all of them throughout his various jail and Detention Home stints. Randy was the Dopeman. He came from a long, long linc of hustlers. Ilis Dad sold Dope, Grand Dad, Uncle's, everybody. The nigga had been hustling since he was twelve. Randy was all about money, he never talked about

209

sports, girls, movies, hell, he never even mentioned what he was gonna do with his money. All he talked about was getting it. And judging from his appearance he had to have some big ass stash hidden somewhere cause Randy had to be the bummiest drug dealer walking God's green earth. Yeah I know he can't control the fact that his teeth, face, nose and lips were oversized but he didn't have throw on his old ass super sized Tee-shirts and jeans to match. It's 2011 doesn't he know that fitted clothes were in? I'm no fashion guru but damn! Hopping out the whip next to him was always an embarrassment. I hate driving his ass around.

Now Zeus, that's my nigga, he's about my age. He's the pill man. When I first went up state weed was the drug of choice for most young people. But since I had come home pills had taken over. Of course weed was still the shit but pills were beyond the shit. And since all the young niggas popped them, Zeus was the perfect dealer. His biggest seller were Molly's, some little powdery shit niggas would spread all over there gums or they could pop the pill or crystal version. That's the new shit everybody was on. I never popped any pills but they say Molly was hands down the best, outta this world.

Then you got your ecstasy pills. All I know about them is that they say if you mad you were gonna be madder and if you horny you're even hornier. I was too scared to pop them. Zeus couldn't pop either. Sho didn't allow you to get high on your own supply. But fuck them pills, my nigga Zeus smoked hella weed. He was a weed connoisseur.

On his spare time he even watched video's dedicated to showing exactly how each type of weed was grew and shit. He always tried to tell me something new he'd learned but I always told him that I didn't give a damn about that, just pass me the blunt. And that he did, Zeus smoked more weed than anyone I'd ever encountered.

Especially since Sho had quit. He said bosses had to be clear headed at all times. Thank God me and Zeus weren't bosses. Seems like every time I'd look over to Zeus he was rolling up. Now I know that kinda defeats the purpose of me driving, cause if the police pulled me over they'd have probable cause to check the whip. But fuck it, like Drake says *'You Only Live Once, YOLO!'*

Last but not least you had Whiteboy. He specialized in selling weed, but he was more like a jack of all trades.

See, whiteboy was mixed with black and white. We all knew the black people around town but thanks to whiteboys Mom he also knew all the whitey's and if it's one thing I learned since becoming a Warrior, it's that white people love to do some motherfucking drugs. Crackers who I thought were the whitest of the white were getting high as a bitch on the low. Sho really knew what he was doing when he put Whiteboy down with the squad, he hit the jack pot and he knew it. Sho even gave Whiteboy a pass on the whole "Don't get high on your own supply rule".

I mean he sold them all, everything from adderall and percocet to promethazine and hash. Plus Whiteboy absolutely loved being high too much to ever quit. I'd bet my last dollar that there was never a time when he was awoke that he was completely sober. Never, I don't think he went as far as to smoke crack but I know for a fact that he indulged in each of the other drugs he pumped. I can't help but to wish that he'd at least try the sober life. Don't

211

get me wrong, Whiteboy was cool and all but something about being under the influence had his ass an emotional wreck. The entire time we'd be trappin his ass would consistently bitch about his life. I swear within the 1st 2 hours of ever kicking it I knew his entire life story. Sometimes the nigga would even start crying when telling me some dumbass event from his childhood. I swear he had me contemplating stopping smoking weed. If this the shit drugs can do to you, I don't know if I wanted to be involved. But as soon as I'd get back in the whip with Zeus those thoughts always vanished.

Me and Trell weren't the only drivers. We also had Doodie and Kiera. Me and Doodie were daytime drivers and Trell and Kiera were on the night shift. Which was good cause I could still come in the crib on time and spend quality time with Sharee.

Doodie and Kiera were two of Sho's bitches. They both knew that the both of them were fucking him but I guess it didn't really bother them. Except for the occasional eye rolls they were the best of friends. I guess you can say they were like Sho's 'Warrior Wife's' or something. But don't get it twisted, everyone knew that neither of them could ever really be taken serious by Sho. Sho liked his girls different. Doodie and Kiera weren't exactly that ugly and they both were kind of thick but they never got their hair or nails done, they didn't really dress all that good and they were both my age with two kids a piece. Sho was a boss, ain't no way they could belong to him.

Still, even though none of their kids was his he still let them all call him Daddy and since their Pops wont around to teach them discipline he even beat them like he was actually they Father. Shit, he even beat Doodie and

212

Kiera like he was there's too. Sho always said, *"Bitches gotta learn some respect"*.

I never really agreed with hitting girls. I couldn't even imagine myself cranking a girl as hard as I could. It just wasn't in me. Maybe you gotta be born with traits like that or something. If so Sho definitely was. My nigga Sho was by far the craziest nigga I ever met. I guess that's why he and the Lunatics got along so well. I can't tell you how grateful I am of the fact that they worked the night shift. The Lunatics specialized in anything violent. If any ass needed to be kicked, robbed or anybody owed money The Lunatics were there. They were like mini Sho's or something. They were Zeus's #1 customers. Besides hearing Whiteboy whine they were one of the main reasons I never wanted to pop pills.

I knew the Lunatics since I'd moved to Norview. Back then they were just Lil Rob, Todd, and Omar. The school basketball stars. They were just like me, Josh, and Trell. You never really caught them away from one another. I remember all them niggas ever talked about was going to the NBA. They never even wore regular clothes. Every day they dressed like they were prepared for a pickup game at any time. Even when we first started smoking weed they were totally against it. *"Naw man we're athletes."*

So when Sho bought them to Amy's crib I was shocked. I knew the faces but these damn sure weren't the athletes I knew, sagging pants, smoking cigarettes.

It turns out freshman year they met Mary J. And not no damn Mary J. Blige. I'm talking about the original, Mary Jane. After their encounter their life's were never the same. Soon they began skipping school and everything was

213

downhill from there. They were quickly thrust into the real world and in the real world there's something that's real important, *'Money'*. You can't buy drugs without money. So eventually they came up with an idea to get some. At night they broke into any car they could find with a nice radio or anything else they could sell and sold them in the morning for whatever they could get. They had a nice little operation going on until they slipped up and broke into the wrong nigga shit and tried to sell his stereo system to his homeboy.

So of course upon inspection of the merchandise the guy called his homie and within minutes the guy was running up on them like some tough guy, thinking that they were just some little punk ass kids. Mind you these were former athletes.

Man, I heard they beat the living dog shit outta those men. It's said that, that was the spark that lit the fire and after a few years of doing shit like that on the regular, Sho had no choice but to recruit them. But they weren't going to be doing any more break ins, they were our goons and once Sho introduced them to the wonderful world of pills, it was a wrap, they turned into straight up Lunatics, hence the name.

Their little break-in business did in fact inspire Sho to recruit the Tyson Brothers, Lil Tyson and Big Tyson. Them niggas been getting in trouble around Norview for years. They just can't seem to do the right thing. Big Tyson was my age and Lil Tyson was like a year or two younger. Neither one of their names were Tyson, they just both looked like mini versions of Mike Tyson. They kinda fought like em too. I was upstate with Lil Tyson for a while. He was one of Duck's main niggas, he was a ass beating machine.

214

But anyway there specialty was stealing cars. For years they'd been going to other nearby towns and cities and wrecking shop before coming back to Norview to stunt, switch plates and wait out. They were doing that for fun so naturally when Sho came up with a plan for them to get some money, they were all for it.

Sho knew a chop shop in Richmond so at night he'd get Trell or Kiera to drive them around for hours searching for whips to get. Sometimes Sho would even send the Lunatics out to car jack niggas with sweet ass cars.

Before long shit was going exactly how Sho said it was. We was getting money. Sho payed everybody weekly. Usually I'd bring in anywhere from three hundred to seven hundred dollars a week. By now, School was less than a month away and I couldn't wait. I was gonna show up like a brand new man. Shit, I was a brand new man. I had a new confidence. Not to mention money and respect, Sho even told me that one day I would be one of the leaders. So that meant Power. He said all of us would. We were the originals, the O.G.'s. Soon we were going to take over the state, maybe even the country. I now felt like I had a purpose in life. It felt great being happy again. You know your life is good when you can honestly say that you love your life and the people in it.

Chapter 9

"Bae guess who you're looking at?" asked Sharee as she sat in the passenger seat of my newly detailed whip, fresh off of cheerleading practice.

Like always she was in a great mood, I think she loved the fact that I picked her up every day in the *'Stinkin Lincoln'*. None of the other girls had boyfriends with wheels like this. And that's exactly how it's supposed to be, she got a reputation to uphold.

"Sharee," I said sarcastically.

"Ha Ha, very funny. Actually you're looking at Norview High School's new cheer captain," she said grinning, playfully throwing her hands in the air, raising the roof.

"Ayyye," I screamed, raising the roof along with her, trying to share in her excitement.

"Bae. I'm so psyched. Everybody just knew Ms. Williams was gonna choose Takita. Ha!"

"Ah man. You know Takita gonna be hatin."

"What? Gonna be? The trick already is. Soon as Ms. Williams announced the winner her bald headed tail went and made some little status on Facebook. *'I guess kissing ass gets you far in life. Too bad my Mom didn't raise me like that',"* said Sharee in a mocking tone. "So me being the Diva that I am, I commented back. I said *'Yes, with exclamation marks. Girl you are so right. But what I'm really happy about is that my Mom taught me not to be a hater,"* Sharee said as her eyes shot up to her forehead.

"Pete you should've seen her face when she read it. She looked right over to me. Priceless."

I smiled at Sharee. Times like this there was nothing else really to say. Just sit back and let her go.

"Oh my God. I'm so freakin happy. Pete you know I been wanting to be captain of the cheerleading squad since I was like six."

"Yeah I know. Ever since you saw--"

"Kelly Kapowski," we both said in unison.

"Yes God. I used to love 'Saved By The Bell'. Why can't they have more shows like that now? All these damn reality shows and talent competitions. How many singers am I gonna have to listen to? How many celebrity do I have to watch throw their life down the drain?" Sharee said disappointedly.

"Hell yeah. Where the hell are the Wayans Bros., Fresh Prince, Family Mattas?" I said as my mind drifted off to my careless younger days.

"Boy Meets World, Different World, Hangin With Mr. Cooper," Sharee continued, seeming to be visiting the same world I was occupying.

"Where the hell is the damn Martin's?" I screamed.

"Yes bae. Oh my God that was my show. *'Jerome in the house, Jerome in the house'*," Sharee said imitating Jerome from Martin.

"You crazy bae," I said as I burst into laughter.

217

"But you love it though," said Sharee, batting her eyes.

She was right about that. "You know it," I said as we pulled up to her crib.

We began kissing. She had the softest lips ever. I could kiss her forever and she knew it, that's probably why she was always the first one to let up.

"I'm so tired I'm about to take a nap. You coming over later?" she asked.

"Yeah bae."

"Ok. You need to go home and get some rest too. How was work?" Sharee asked as she placed one foot out the door to exit.

"Same ol same ol," I said looking in the opposite direction of her.

Glee filled Sharee's face. "Aw. My bae gotta job, I'm so proud of you."

"Stop it," I said forcing a smile, hoping she really did stop.

"I'm serious, me and my Mom were talking about you last night."

Sharee's Mom was weird, she never really acted like she liked me but then again she never acted as though she didn't like me, of course she'd throw me a standard 'Hello' and 'Bye' but other than that, nothing.

"Talkin bout what?" I asked curiously.

"Nothing bad, we were just saying how good it was that you found a job so quick, a lot of guys get out of jail and act like the world owes them something, you went out and took what you wanted. I never told you this but my Mom hated the fact that I broke up with Dante for you.

"What?" I blurted. Like I said I figured she didn't really care for me but just hearing that sucka's name pissed me off.

"Chill baby, you see it didn't affect me. I know the type of person you are. That's all that matters. Plus, she see's you doing the right thing so she's coming around. You just better not disappoint us."

"I'm not," I said praying to God that neither of them ever found out about the Warriors.

"I know you're not but bye baby, I'm pooped."

We kissed again than it was off to the crib.

"Whattup nigga," I said plopping down on the couch. Korb was already kicking it there, watching T.V.

"Nothin man."

"Where's Mom at?"

Ma usually got home about three thirty. And by six Aunt Tina and Fonda were over, gossiping.

"In South Carolina," he said nonchalantly with his eyes glued to some low budget movie. I can tell it was low budget because Master P was in it. He's the king of low budget.

"South Carolina?"

219

"Yeah. Her, Aunt Fond and Tina. She told you the otha day."

"Oh that was today?"

"Yeah she said she called you three times today. You must've been working or somethin."

"Oh damn."

I'd seen that she'd called me but I was with Zeus today and I was too damn high to be talking to her. She's always calling me to tell me something irrelevant, I assumed her calls today would be no different.

"Yeah. She wants you to call her ASAP," he said still focused on the flick.

By now I had recognized what movie he was watching. 'Lockdown', from the title alone you can tell why I had to leave the room. I don't need no more reminders of that shit.

"Ok." I headed up to my room. "Hold on." I paused. "If Mom gone, what the hell you still doin hea?"

"You're watchin me," he said smiling, finally taking his eyes off the T.V.

"What? Hell naw."

This couldn't be true. The Mom I knew would never leave her babies home alone with no supervision. I mean, this is Mary Turner we're talking about.

"I'm serious. Grandma went to some women's retreat with the Church. That's why Mom was blowin you up."

"What?"

Still not believing him, I jetted upstairs to put my phone on the charger. It had went dead and I had to hear my Mom say this outta her mouth. This was too good to be true. When the hell did I earn all this trust?

I called her on speaker phone as I brushed my hair in the mirror. "Hey Ma."

"Hey Baby. I been calling you all day?"

"My bad Ma. I was workin real hard today, they had me diggin some ditches and stuff."

"Oh ok. Hope you been drinking plenty of water?"

"Yes Ma."

"Good. Well, I left you a huge responsibility. I need you to take care of your brother this weekend. I started not to go on my trip at all. The thought of leaving my boys all alone had me going crazy but I realized that if I want to raise responsible men I have to give you guys responsibility. So I'm giving you guys a shot. Plus with you coming home and being so mature. I think you can handle it."

"Thanks Ma. I can."

"Well ok. I left some money for food on my dresser."

"Naw Ma. I got paid today. I got it."

221

"Aww baby. You're so sweet. But I'm going under a tunnel I'll call you later. Love you."

"Love you to Ma," I said before hanging up the phone.

Shit had happened so fast, I didn't even know what to do. I'd never had my own crib before. I tried to think of all the things I could do but nothing was coming to mind. So I figured I'd spend a little time with Korb. I hadn't really been paying him a lot of attention since I got home. We still laughed and joked and shit but it's time for me to treat him like Sho treated me. I decided to take him to Amy's to kick it. I knew Sho was probably there. Korb was his cousin too, I know he'd be the perfect nigga to school Korb to the game of life. I can't let him take it too far though, there was no way I'd ever let Korb join the Warriors. He's too much of a Mama's boy, he couldn't handle that kinda life.

I headed downstairs and saw that Korb's friend Rell was now in the living room. Fuck it, I knew him forever, he was like my little bro too so I decided to take them both. They was about to feel how it felt to be in the presence of some real niggas. It would be a shame if I had access to all this knowledge and didn't share it.

We walked over to my whip. It was the 1st time either of them had seen it. I had never told Korb about it. I wasn't sure if he'd tell my Mom. Before I went away I remember he was a little snitch. But I figured even if he was still a snitch, after kicking it with Sho for a day he'd never be the same.

When we approached the whip both of them went ape shit.

222

"Bro. This shit is sweet as hell."

"Hell yeah," followed Rell.

It's funny . I had never heard Korb curse, for some reason I was really feeling good about it. I loved my brother but maybe I was going to like him too.

We drove over to Amy's crib, bumping some Young Crazy as Korb and Rell rapped along to every word. And not just rapping. They were partying like they were at a concert or something. I felt like a proud father. My smile was as wide as the ocean, I damn near shedded tears of joy. I couldn't wait for everyone to witness my cool ass little bro.

We pulled up and Sho's car was parked outside. We hopped out and burst into the crib, as usual I walked into a smoke filled room, plagued with kids running rampant while Amy layed down down on the couch watching T.V.

"Whadup. Whadup," I said.

"Hey Pete," said Amy, looking over to us.

"Whatsup. This my lil bro and his homeboy Rell."

"Hey. Aw they so cute," she said smiling before looking over to the kids. "Nigga put that shit down before I come over there and fuck yo lil ugly ass up," she barked, never leaving her spot on the couch. The kids didn't even seem bothered as she turned back to us. "Excuse me but you gotta treat these lil mo'fuckers like grown folk. Yall can gon head and sit down," she said pointing over to the vacant couch across from her. "Make yallself at home. Shit, everybody else ass do."

Korb and Rell, scooted all the toys and newspaper advertisement off the couch and took a seat. The energy they had while in the car was now gone. I could tell that they were a little out of their element.

"Yo. Where everybody at?" I said as I kicked back against the wall.

"I guess they out there handlin business but Sho in the room with Baby Mama #3."

"Oh true. What you been doin all day?"

I don't even know why I asked that shit. She do the same shit day after day. The only time she really left the crib was on the 1st of the month to go grocery shopping with her food stamps and every weekend to hit the club. Oh yeah I can't forget her occasional appearance at the mall when the newest Jordan's came out. Amy always made sure her kids got every pair of Jordan's even though they ass ain't never go nowhere.

"I ain't been doin shit, just lookin at this damn first 48 marathon. It's some snitchin mothafucka's in this world. They baby mama's even snitchin. I hate every last one of my baby daddy's but I still would neva in a million years tell on 'em. That's what the white man want us to do. Divide and fuckin conquer."

Suddenly we heard what sounded like someone getting slammed through a bed. Rell and Korb looked puzzled at one another as the kids, Amy and I carried on like nothing was going on

"I hate you," screamed Babymama #3 as Sho stormed out the room with her in a choke hold. "I can't breathe," she said struggling to speak.

"Shut up bitch if you couldn't breathe you couldn't talk, dumbass," Sho said before opening the front door, tossing her out. "Stupid bitch", he yelled as he slammed the door."Oh shit," Sho said as he looked back. "Damn. Where my daughter?"

"Oh shit I don't know what the hell they ass gettin into," said Amy hopping up to retrieve them. "Where the hell yall little bad asses at?" she screamed.

We all sat silent as Sho paced around the room as BM# 3 banged and screamed like a psychopathic heroin fiend at the door. "Gimme my fuckin daughter, you bitch."

"What the fuck? I'ma kill this bitch," Sho said, enraged. He grabbed the door handle to open the door.

At the same time Amy came sprinting in with Sho's daughter in hand. She hopped in front of Sho and thrusted the baby over to BM# 3.

"Hea Girl," said Amy, seemingly saving the day.

"Stupid bitch," Sho yelled, as Amy stood in the middle of him and BM #3. "Your ratchet ass lucky you got my daughter in your hand or I'da beat the shit out your ass. Dumb hoe."

"Fuck you," she screamed before Sho shocked us all by sucking up everything he had in him and spitting dead in her face. He then pulled Amy inside as he slammed the door shut. "Bitch better watch who the fuck she talking too."

Shockingly, he turned around cheesing, looking over to Korb and Rell. "Damn my bad lil niggas. But if a bitch get out of line you gotta let'em know who's boss. Fuck them bitches. Bitches think just cause you gotta baby with em you owe em somethin. Fuck that." Sho walked out the room. We all looked around soundless until he shot back in. "And don't think you gotta like your damn kids. Fuck that. You just gotta love them mo'fuckas. And don't get me wrong. I usually like all my kids but not her ass. I knew I won't gon like her ass when her Mama named her Sho'ona. What the fuck? Ain't nobody tell her dumbass to name the baby afta me. That shit ugly as hell. Soon as she told me that shit I already knew I won't gon like her. I'll do anything in the world for her but I just don't like her ass. She just got a bad vibe to her. Foreal yo. All my kids look like me, except her. She look just like her trickin ass Mama yo."

Sho paused, briefly locking eyes with us all. "Neva knock up a bitch you meet at the strip club. Them hoes ain't nothin but trouble. Straight up," he said as he plopped down on the couch depressed with his head down. "But they got some good ass pussy," he said raising his head, smiling.

We all burst out laughing.

"Boy you a fool," said Amy. She was now plopped back down on the couch sitting next to Sho.

"I'm dead ass serious. Ask Pete," everyone looked over to me as I smiled and nodded my head.

"They do," I said.

Sho looked over to Korb and Rell who were laughing but still noticeably uncomfortable.

"What's yo name lil nigga?" asked Sho, looking over to Rell.

"Rell."

"Yall two niggas get yall some ass yet?"

The both of them nodded their heads as Me, Amy and Sho looked at one another, unconvinced.

"I knew yall was gon lie. It's alright we all virgins at one point in our lives. Some of us longa than othas," Sho said looking at me with a smirk. "Yall lil niggas probably ain't even smoke your 1st blunt yet."

"Shit, I have," said Rell.

"Hell naw," I said.

"Foreal Bruh. My big cousin Al smoked with me like three weeks ago. I was high as Cooley Brown."

We all couldn't help but to laugh. Rell talked with his tongue forcing everything he said to sound funny as hell.

Sho turned his attention over to Korb. "What about you, cuzzo?"

Korb shook his head as Sho looked over to me. "It's your call big bro. You wanna do the honors?

I thought for a second. I was only a year older than Korb when I first smoked and it's pretty much a fact that he was gonna smoke one day anyway. Might as well be with me.

"Who gotta blunt?" I asked.

"Rich," said Sho.

"Rich?"

"Yeah Rich out in Richmond. We need to go pick something up from him anyway."

Rich was Sho's drug connect. Whenever we went over there we Re'd-Up. Technically I was off the clock but Sho must've needed it so I agreed. I didn't really want Korb in a unknown drug house but Rich was cool. He didn't keep too many niggas at his crib. His Babymama and kids lived with him.

We all loaded up in the whip. We had to take one of Amy kids with us, whenever Sho scored Coke he made sure he bought a baby along to stash it in the baby diaper. With me whipping and the drugs stashed away we were always good. Damn, Sho was smart.

Shit was funny as hell driving over to Rich's crib, Sho was in rare form, he was hilarious. I was really glad Korb got to witness that shit. I know he's gonna remember this day for the rest of his life.

We arrived at Rich's crib and he was chilling on the porch smoking a blunt. He lived in a pretty decent neighborhood so he never had to worry about the Cops harassing him for it.

"Break out the Kush. I'm tryna get high," said Sho as he dapped up Rich.

"What? Nigga your ass don't smoke no more."

"True. But my Lil cousin ain't neva blew it down before. It's only right big cuz participates."

228

Rich looked over to us. "Right, right, I understand. Whadup Pete."

"Whatsup Rich."

"So by looking at yall heads I'm assumin that's yo lil bro," said Rich looking over to Korb.

"Yeah dog. That's Korb and that's his homeboy Rell."

"Whatsup lil niggas."

"Whatsup," they both replied, looking nervous again.

"Yall think yall ready to smoke with the big dogs," said Rich leaning back in his lawn chair, inhaling the smoke and blowing out little O's.

"I already smoked before," said Rell.

"Oh so you already a big dog?" Rich replied.

"Yeah he said he smoked with his cousin a few weeks back," I said.

"True. True. But I don't think yall smoked none of this." Rich raised his blunt in the air. "This some Afghani Kush," he said as he took another hit. "Yall niggas got some blunts?"

"Damn. We forgot that shit," I said looking over to Sho.

"We can go to the store around the corna. This nigga been beggin for some candy anyway," Sho said looking at Amy's son who was playing over by some big tree Rich had in his yard. For a two year old this nigga was crazy, you can't take his ass nowhere without him showing the world that he was from the hood.

"Yeah. And don't forget them lil niggas bouta have the munchies, they needa rack up on some snacks," said Rich.

When we got to the corner store me and Sho couldn't help but notice two bad ass young tenderonies, who Korb and Rell both noticeably avoided. When we hopped back in the whip and pulled off we realized that it was the perfect time to teach Korb and Rell the art of bagging girls.

"Yo. Do yall lil niggas got any game yet?" asked Sho.

"Hell yeah," they both said.

"I got two girlfriends" replied Rell.

"That sound real good dog. But 2 girlfriends is never a good thing."

"Yeah dog you don't supposed to cheat on your girl," said Korb as me and Sho looked at one another and smiled.

"Naw nigga I ain't say nothin bout not cheatin. I'm just sayin you don't need two girlfriends. But I know exactly where you got that ol faithful shit from so I can't even be mad at you," added Sho as he glanced over to me. "All I'm saying is that you only needa have one girlfriend. You can have as many side hoes as you want. But two girlfriends is too many damn problems. And as a black man out hea you don't neva need to botha yourself with extra

230

headaches," said Sho as he lifted his head to the sky as if he was thinking hard. "Matter fact I take that back. One girlfriend is too much. Fuck that love shit. Just fuck these hoes and leav'em. Bitches respect niggas like that more than them sucka faithful ass niggas anyways," he continued before looking over to me. "No offense Pete."

"None taken."

Sho was right about everything he was saying but like I always said, Sharee was different. I didn't have to worry about shit like that.

"Did yall see them girls in the store?" asked Sho.

"Yeah," said Rell. "That's Stacy and Leisa."

"What? They from Norview? Why yall ain't say shit to them?"

"Man they the most popular girls in school. They only talk to high school niggas," said Rell.

"See that's where yall wrong at," said Sho.

"Yeah, Rell's right them girls is stuck up," added Korb

"Yeah if you ain't got all the latest Jordan's and shit. You don't have a chance," added Rell.

"I understand. I understand, I once though like that myself. But it's a secret to gettin all the girls. And it ain't money or clothes. I mean when you get a lil olda that'll be the key but at yall age it's simple. Yall know what it is?"

We all stared at Sho attentively. I even wanted to know this. Sho must've forgot to school me on this one. It wasn't like I was gonna take the advice, I had already reached the age that money and clothes mattered. I just wanted to have the extended knowledge. Maybe one day I'd have to give this game to my son or something.

"What is it?" asked Korb.

"It's simple. It's your attitude."

"Huh?" asked Rell.

"All you gotta do is walk around like you the shit and the bitches will flock."

"I already think I'm the shit and I still can't get girls like Stacy and Leisa."

"See that's where you fuckin up. You can't THINK you the shit. You gotta KNOW you the shit. Once you really start believin it, everybody else will too. Kids yall age really don't have a mind of their own so once you convince them good enough they'll believe anything that's told to'em. Trust me dog. I'm tellin you some real shit. Ask Pete. I won't steer you wrong."

They looked over to me, I nodded.

"So when yall get back to school put that shit to work and I guarantee--."

Sho was immediately halted by something that came as a complete shock to us all. Something I hope I never see again. Rich's house was surrounded by Police. The shit was a circus, squad cars and K-9's everywhere. Sho and I sat silent, desperately trying to figure out what had just occurred.

232

"Damn what's goin on out hea?" asked Rell.

"Pull over there," Sho said pointing down the street to a spot free of Pigs.

I followed the orders. Sho and I slowly exited the whip. We stood outside as the cops bought Rich and his Babymama out of the house in cuffs. Watching his Babymama scream and holler as another officer escorted her kids away reminded me of my own Mother.

Out of nowhere I felt a pair of eyes beaming on me. Wasting no time I looked over. Shit! It was Detective Fraley. What the fuck were they doing here? This ain't even their jurisdiction, we in Richmond for God's sake. We were more than 50 ft. away but that didn't stop us from locking eyes. I'm not one hundred percent positive but from here it looked like he mouthed the words "You're next." I ain't even gonna lie my heart started racing as I quickly turned my attention over to Sho.

He was looking at Fraley too. "Let's get the fuck outta here," said Sho. We both hopped back in the whip. I didn't really know what to say but I knew Sho would. "Man what the fuck?" Sho screamed. "What the fuck? That was my only plug. What the fuck I'ma do now? Ah man. I'm bouta call The Lunatics, we robbin any nigga I see dog," Sho said seeming to be losing his cool. "Fuck that. What the fuck I'ma do?"

Sho wasn't really talking to me. He was more so just talking out loud so I just looked straight ahead. I ain't want him to take a bad look at me and decide I was the person he needed to let his anger out on.

233

Driving back we rode past the jail. Usually I'd look away. But today with Sho to my right still talking to himself about Rich, I forgot. And it was a damn good thing I did. The second I saw that building a light bulb popped in my head-- DaDa! He told me that if I ever was tryna get some money to holla at him and what better time than now. I started to tell Sho about my idea but opted out. I know it'd be smarter to tell him after I talked to DaDa. Don't wanna jinx it. This could be a chance of a lifetime.

"Yo just take me back to the spot," Sho said before looking back at Korb and Rell. "My bad yall. I"ma have to smoke with yall anotha time."

"It's alright. Me and Korb got a little tag team mission anyway," said Rell, trying to fight back his super sized grin.

"Yeah these two girls just text us and told us to come chill," followed Korb, grinning equally as hard, if not harder.

"That's what's up," Sho said attempting to sound excited."

"Yeah. You can let us out at Amy's crib. They live close by," said Korb.

"My niggas gotta couple hood girls, I see," I said looking back to Korb and Rell as they continued smiling, showing off their age.

When we got to Amy's crib Sho hopped out without saying a word. Korb and Rell got out too.

"Yo, if Mom call's tell her I went to sleep," said Korb.

"Ok," I said.

"Oh yeah. You got any condoms bro?"

There are no words to express the happiness that completely took over my body after hearing my 13 year old bro asking for condoms. He impressed me more and more by the minute. I know my Fathers looking down here as proud as can be. I reached under my seat, I had a secret stash down there that I couldn't let Sharee know about and handed them two apiece.

"Thanks dog," said Rell.

"Yeah thanks bro. Don't wait up," he said walking away before pausing. "Well actually do wait up cause we might needa ride. But you know what I mean."

I laughed as I pulled off. "Aight. Yall niggas have fun."

It was about seven when I got back to the crib. It's kinda late but Sharee usually takes long ass naps so I figured I'd go take one as well. By the time I woke up her ass would probably still be asleep anyway.

Before getting in bed I found a lost stash of weed in one of my drawers. This was perfect. High sleeps are synonymous with getting a full body massage from Nicki Minaj.

I got rocket high and ate a bowl of cereal right in my room, completely enjoying my first time smoking in the crib. This was the life. Mom definitely need to go outta town more often. Shit was so peaceful. I do some of my best thinking when I'm high and right now there was only one thing I could think of. After trying repeatedly to ignore it, I finally decided that it was now or never. I had to call DaDa. Not just for myself but for the Warriors. They needed me. I paced the room for about 20 minutes, strategizing exactly what I would say. After what seemed like hours with no progress I just said fuck it. I picked up the phone and dialed. Yeah, I memorized it.

After two rings he answered. Nervous, I started to hang up but I couldn't, "DaDa?"

"Yeah. Who this?" he asked sounding exactly the same as I remembered.

"Lil Jesse," I said as I prayed he'd remember me.

"Motherfuckin Jesse!" He sounded more excited than I'd ever heard him before. This bought an assuasive comfort over me. "When the fuck you get out?"

"Like two months ago."

"You straight? You need somethin?"

I paused and said, "Yeah, actually I need your help."

He cut me off and said for me to come to Richmond ASAP and we could talk. I took down his info and hung up.

When I got off the phone I was way too pumped to go to sleep. I had to smoke again to calm my nerves. I was in Heaven. Before I knew it I was knocked the fuck out.

I was awaken to what sounded like the Police banging on the front door. I jumped out of bed and crept

down the stairs as quiet as a church mouse. I don't know
what the fuck their here for but they sure wont gonna know
I was here.

They continued banging as I peeked through the
blinds. It was dark out and I was still half asleep but as I
focused my eyes I realized it was Sharee and tears were
gushing from her eyes. What the fuck, I thought as I rushed
over to open the door.

"He's gone. He's gone," Sharee screamed as water
continued streaming down her face.

"Who?" I asked. "Who?"

I ain't even gonna lie, Dante's face kept popping up
in my head. Who else could she be talking about? And shit,
I've gotta be honest I really didn't like the fact that she
could be crying over some other nigga. I understand the
nigga might be dead and all but fuck him.

"He's gone Pete. He's gone," Sharee said as she
dropped all of her weight onto me.

"Bae. Who?" I repeated as I hugged her tightly.

"He's gone. He's gone and I didn't even get to tell
him I loved him. I never visited him. I never wrote, I let
him rot. I acted as though he didn't even exist. I acted as if
he were dead and now he really is and I'll never have a Dad
again."

This may sound fucked up but hearing that it was
her Dad who died did make things a tad bit better. But still,
I didn't know what to say. Sharee's Dad was the one
subject we had never touched on. I always kinda figured he
was in jail. Just the way Sharee always preached to me

about not going let me know. But since I didn't really know about the man I had no idea what to say.

So I just pulled her inside, slowly walking her over to the couch. For about ten straight minutes she laid tucked into my arms sobbing. It was only a matter of time when tears started to slowly fall down my face as well.

Finally Sharee lifted her head up. "Pete. I know I never told you about my Dad or the reason I moved here. It was just too personal," Sharee spoke in a whisper, her head hung down in a way that I'd never seen her before. "You remember that book *'Coldest Winter Ever'* that I sent you?" she asked, raising her head in effort of gaining her composure.

"Yeah. I read that shit about 18 times. I loved it."

"Well I was Winter Santiago in Memphis. I was the girl with the powerful Father. I was the one who had it all. We had it all. All the latest everything. We went on vacations, we had huge cookouts. Everyone loved us. Everyone loved us until it all hit the fan," Sharee said without pausing for air. She spoke as if she'd been holding all of this in for so long and she finally couldn't hold it any longer. I listened attentively. I had to let her know that I understood. "Until my Dad and all my Uncles got arrested. All of a sudden we were flat broke. The Feds took everything. My Mom didn't have any family there. And all my Dad's family turned on us because he snitched. We were all alone, I was so used to seeing my Mother so strong. So vibrant. Now she was weak. Absolutely weak. My Dad always paid the bills. He might not have always lived with us but he always payed the bills. My Mom never worked a day in her life so when he went away we were lost, stranded. Pete, we literally had nothing, my Mom and

I were forced to live in a shelter for a year before they finally found us a place. So off we were to the projects. It was cool to have a new spot, but everyone hated us because of my Dad. Then someone started a rumor that he had left us some money and that we had it stashed away in the house. I don't know why anyone thought that? We were living in the same mess they were in. But one night while my Mom was at work. She worked the night shift at WalMart. I woke up to a gun to my face and three guys standing on top of me. *'Bitch where the fucking Money at?' they screamed.'* I was in such shock. I couldn't speak. Next thing I remember I'm waking up in a pool full of blood. I guess they hit me with the gun and knocked me out. That's how I got the scar. Our house was torn to pieces. That was the worst night of my life," Sharee said.

I could feel the pain in her voice as she spoke.

"After that my Mom swallowed her pride and called her sister. No one in my Mom's family ever wanted her to be with my Dad anyway. So they got her a job and a place and here we are. I hadn't spoke to or seen my Dad since he got locked up. I tried to forget he existed. And I think he did the same because we never heard from him," Sharee said before taking a large breath. "I never wanted a guy like him. Sho always reminded me so much of him. But you, you were different. You had some sorta inner glow. It's like when I saw you ,God told me your were the one. That's why I stuck with you when you went to jail. I know you couldn't have done what they said you did. I grew up with a killer and when I look into your eyes I know you're not. Pete, all the love I had for my father I passed it on to you," Sharee said as more tears sprouted from her eyes. "I just hope you don't break my heart like he did. Ya know, even though I disowned him, I can't explain how it feels for him to have gotten killed in that place. I know you understand me. That's why I had to tell you. I feel incomplete. But Pete, I swear you sitting right here is making everything so much better. It's like I have so many mixed emotions right now, I'm confused. My mind is everywhere," she said before wiping her tears from her eyes. "But one thing I do know is that I need you," she said as she grabbed the both of my hands, staring at me in a way she'd never done before.

It's like her eyeballs turned into hearts, all I saw was love. Then it happened, she kissed me and before I could even fully realize what was going on we were one and as our bodies connected we became love personified. The wait was far worth it. This was beautiful.

The next day I told Sho about DaDa. "You know DaDa?" he shouted. Sho said he'd heard stories about DaDa all his life. "That nigga's full up. He got all the money. I was tryna figure out how we could rob them niggas but if he a connect, I'm with it."

With Sho's approval I made arrangements with DaDa to meet up with him at his barbershop the next day.

When we got to the spot *'Spotlight Barbershop'* it looked like your everyday barber shop. Barbers, hair on the floor, niggas arguing about pointless shit, nothing special. But when one of the barbers escorted us to DaDa's office I knew right then and there DaDa was a different type of nigga.

First off, he was fresh from head to toe. His Gucci shoes were kicked up on top of his luxurious dust free desk.

The entire room smelled like exotic weed . The hardwood floor was sparkling, matching DaDa's teeth. The mini bar was full with every top shelf liquor imaginable. I looked over to Sho and I could tell he had never seen some shit like this either. His eyes bulged as he gazed over to a giant fish tank mounted into the wall housing some of the most flamboyant fish I'd ever seen.

Sho and I sat down on some pillow soft seats in front of DaDa's desk in amazement. This nigga DaDa was really an official business man. I thought Sho was doing it big, but this nigga took the cake. Sho's jewelry came from the middle of the mall, the most he ever paid for anything was about two G's. DaDa had the real deal shit. I kept looking over to Sho's watch and comparing the two. If I was Sho I would've been kinda embarrassed. He should've never even wore that shit. DaDa straight stunted on him. I could precisely see every single diamond on the watch shining at different times. No funny shit.

After sitting down we small talked a bit. DaDa seemed to be a little looser as a free man. I guess cause this was his environment.

Before long we got down to business. I let Sho do most of the conversing. I really ain't understand all the numbers they were talking. I never did, I was just a driver. I was happy with the money Sho had been giving me. Actually I hadn't really even thought of getting more money. Shit, I was balling in my book. I was straight. I pretty much had everything I wanted. Me and Sharee even went out to eat at least two times a week and I always made sure I bought her an outfit any chance I could. What more could a nigga ask for?

241

By the end of our meeting DaDa was really feeling everything Sho was kicking. And since Sho was the one who taught me everything I knew DaDa felt comfortable with Sho. With little hesitation, DaDa had come to a conclusion.

"I'ma fuck with yall lil niggas cause somethin tells me yall got heart. Well I already know my nigga right hea got heart," DaDa said as he gave me a little head nod. "No question. But to tell the truth, when Jesse told me who he was bringin up hea I had my people do a lil research. Found out you one of the realest niggas in the whole Norview," said DaDa as he and Sho seemed to be engaging in a friendly staring competition. "So this what I'ma do for yall niggas, I'ma hook yall up with everything you need. But everything you score gotta be picked up by my nigga Lil Jesse. This a dog eat dog world and to be honest I don't trust you dog. Nothin personal but if my lil nigga don't eat ain't nobody gonna eat," said DaDa finally condensing the staring contest.

He now focused his attention on the both of us as he rubbed his hands together slowly. Me and Sho both looked over to each other before nodding. It was weird seeing Sho not in control, for the first time we were both in the same shoes.

"Lets get this money, fellas," DaDa said as he extended his arm for a hand shake.

Chapter 10

Eyes shot to the ceiling as I strolled hand in hand with the undoubtedly baddest bitch in the building. Despite the fact that my jewelry could certainly damage a few eye sights, all eyes were on me. The reason being could be that my Polo shirt, True Religion jeans and Lebron James kicks were blended perfectly together but I'm smart enough to know otherwise. Still as I latched eyes with each and every pair that I spotted studying my every move, I couldn't have been happier. I was back. And this time, I had every ingredient to ensure the perfect school year. Last time I was here, I was worried about fitting in. This time niggas better be worried about fitting in with me. It's a new Sherriff in town and he's rocking gold teeth. Honestly it wouldn't be right any other way. I mean lets be real, none of these niggas been through half as much shit as me, Sho said it was only right they follow my lead. He even gave me a special mission. Shit had been going so good that he wanted to recruit all the lil niggas in school that went hard.

Everything had really started to pick up ever since we'd hooked up with DaDa. We had access to the best of everything. Pills, weed, coke, guns, anything. Compared to Rich, DaDa's prices were dumb cheap. We had been making a killing. Nobody could compete. And the people who tried were quickly halted by The Lunatics. Either you got down or laid down. Needless to say, most got down. Only a fool wouldn't.

With all the new recruits Sho was in position to give out more jobs. Gone were the days of riding niggas around. I now had the best job ever. '*The Plug*'. Sho said that since I was the connect to all of this shit all I had to do was sit back and collect. So far Sho had been paying me at least $1000 a week, I was a certified baller.

Trell even moved up. He was now Sho's apprentice, his right hand man. Ever since he joined he'd been on top of things. It didn't really surpise me, Trell always wanted to be the best in everything he did, whether it was basketball or skipping rocks, it didn't matter, Trell was gonna be the best. Intially Sho had tried to make me his apprentice but drugs really weren't my forte, Sho hated that shit, he said every man should know his craft. I guess I understood what he meant but every time he started talking all those numbers; eighths, quarters, half's and shit, that shit went in one ear and out the other. It was clear to see that I was just better off being *'The Plug'*. That was definitely a job I could handle.

Well that and recruiting these lil niggas. Since business started booming and niggas been getting down, Sho been wanting to paint the town black. Black was the Warriors new color. Sho had given us all black bandanna's. He said we could wear it how we pleased. We didn't have to wear it all the time but, we were required to always have it on our person. Sho said it was like our I.D., it let people know who we were. I only rocked mine when I was in another city. I already had enough attention here. Of course, no one would really knew what the hell it meant anyway. Still, rocking that flag kinda made me feel invincible. With it I was bullet proof, I had all the confidence in the world. I felt like I was representing my family. That's part of the reason none of these stares were bothering me. With my flag neatly tucked away in my right back pocket. I felt like my family was right here. Not to mention I was with Sharee. She always made me feel like I could make it through anything. Too bad she couldn't be with me all day.

Sharee and I stopped in front of her class. She looked up to me smiling.

"You ready?" she asked.

"For what? This ain't shit."

"I'm serious Pete." Sharee's smile disappeared and she switched over to *'Mom Mode'*. "I know you saw the way everyone's been looking at you. You know everybody been talking about how they let you back in school. They don't want you here and you already know they gonna do whatever it takes to make you leave."

"Come on Sharee, I survived being locked in a cage for three years, I know I can survive this shit," I said still looking around at all the eyes clocking me as Sharee did the same.

"Be safe, I love you."

"Love you too, I said leaning forward for our first senior kiss.

And I was off. This time alone. The stares weren't the same as before. Now, people were undeniably frightened. Maybe earlier they felt that Sharee could somehow tame me. But now shit was weird. My presence had the entire school stumbling, fumbling and bumping into one another trying to make sure they wouldn't accidentally bump into a murderer. They were terrified. I loved it.

Chapter 11

Just when I thought life could get no better and that I was at my peak, I found out that I couldn't have been more wrong if I tried. Every week shit just seemed to be getting better and better. I was now receiving five stacks a week. Five fucking thousand dollars a week! Money was comin in on some other shit. With all the new recruits Sho was able to run our family like a fortune 500 company. We had niggas in Norfolk, Petersburg, Richmond, Va. Beach, everywhere and Sho had generals set up in each location. The Warriors were making DaDa's empire even better than he probably ever imagined and he loved us for it. And with his love came crazy advantages, including some of his old jewelry. I was stunting, I might've been the only 17 year old in the whole state with a Presidential Rolex.

But that wasn't even the best part, DaDa knew everyone and in turn he introduced us to everyone. We were in every club throughout Va. for free, Bottle service, V.I.P,. kicking it with celebrity's. I even got to get on stage and rocked out with Gucci Mane when he came to town. You couldn't tell me shit that night. I had a ball and we got high as a son bitch afterwards with him and his entourage. The entire time I had the urge to tell him how much I loved his music but I didn't wanna seem like a clown so I chilled. By the end of the night, sadly I hadn't said one word to him.

But hey, at least Sho did, he always had a way with Gangsters. Still, even though I didn't get a chance to share any words with him, doesn't mean I didn't get a chance to share something even better,-- Groupies.

Yep the Warriors had groupies. Who would've thought? Of course I was always low-key but whenever me and the homies went out with our new whips and jewelry, bitches flocked. They did anything for us. Anything. Bitches acted like just because we had money, they did too. I mean some of the homies did kick off to them but not me. I just fucked them. I already had a girl I ain't need no more. All I needed was the pussy, who ever said ain't no pussy like new pussy wont lying. Fucking round with the Warriors I done fucked all types of bitches, black, white, Puerto Rican, Asian, smart bitches, dumb bitches, I even got so drunk one night that I fucked a fat bitch. I was ashamed at first but Sho said he'd done it before too so fuck it.

Now, I gotta admit, at first I was feeling real bad about cheating. I never wanted to hurt Sharee. But Sho told me that's what God wanted us to do. He kicked me some story from the Bible about Solomon and his many wife's and if the Bible says it's ok, who am I not to oblige. Plus Sho said black men were meant to have a lot of women. He said before the slave masters came over and kid napped us we were kings with all types of hoes. After he schooled me on all that, I never felt guilty again.

Besides I bought Sharee everything she wanted and took her places most seventeen year old girls could only dream of. Shit, the way I look at it, I deserved to be able to do what the hell I wanted to. It ain't like I was cheating with Norview girls. Hell naw, to Norview girls I was still Pete the Murderer. Sho made sure we kept a low profile in Norview, anyway. He didn't wanna draw too much attention to ourselves. All them Gangsta documentaries he had us watch really came in handy, we knew exactly how to stay under the radar. We made perfectly sure no one who mattered knew we had any money. It wasn't too hard since it won't really shit going on in Norview anyway. And we all know Sho ain't have to stunt for bitches in Norview, he had already fucked damn near all of them.

Despite the fact that me Sho and the rest of the O.G. Warriors were low-key, don't think for a second the Lil Homies were. Oh hell naw. *'Warriors'* was spray painted in black damn near everywhere around town. You couldn't so much as walk down to the corner without seeing our logo, well that and *'Warview'*. That's what the little homies were calling Norview now. I loved that shit, I feel like it gave the town some swag.

I guess it's kinda crazy how I always call the new Warriors *'lil homies'* when we're all practically the same age. It's just that I don't feel like them. They didn't go to clubs, rock expensive jewelry or fuck bad bitches. I was different, I was a young Boss nigga, shit, I was the plug. Plus them lil niggas was too wild for my blood. Them lil niggas were training under the Lunatics supervision so you already know how they were. They did anything under the sun to earn respect.

Mainly because Sho didn't let the lil homies hustle yet. He wanted them to show that they were really down for the Warriors. And boy did they, with the conditions the town was already in plus all the racial tension them niggas still took it up a couple notches. Who am I kidding, probably a little more than a couple. They turned Norview into a Warzone. School was already segregated on some 1950's shit. Whiteys stuck with the whiteys, niggas with the niggas and any other people had to sorta pick sides. But now there was nothing but pure hate in the air.

It all started when the lil homies started beating whitey ass like they had stole something. In school, outside of school, it didn't matter. At first it was just school age kids but pretty soon it was any whitey. Lil homies were spitting in their faces, snatching purses, anything to get a name. Niggas was even killing shit. Naw not people; dogs. And we all know how white people feel about their pets.

Niggas was beaming baseballs at them, pissing on them, straight torture.

This, along with all the other shit had whitey's in a frenzy. They won't taking this shit from no niggers. Fuck that, they felt that Norview was there town, shit this was their world. They won't gonna have no niggers taking over. So just like that, they retaliated. Warriors wore our black rags around their faces when shit was going down.

Now the whites were wearing white rags around their faces on some new school KKK shit. They called themselves 'The Supreme'.

They were no match to the Warriors but the ones who did join were spray painting in red over our Warview signs, sticking confederate flags in our yards and whipping any nigger ass they found alone. Little by little you started to see more and more white boys shaving their heads. Shit was getting crazier by the second. You couldn't go a day without some sorta altercation.

After a while it got so bad Norview High had to get involved. Anyone caught with a black or white bandana would automatically receive 10 days suspended.

On the outside lil homies were getting locked up and going to the detention home left and right. Word around town was that it was crazy in there. Especially for

251

the whites, who were always out numbered. In all honesty, I kinda liked all this shit, them white motherfuckers hated me anyway. They had spray painted my Mom's gate, threatened me, through neuses at me. Fuck them, I was glad my homies was whipping they ass. Shit, and I dared one of them to fuck with me. Jumping the little homies in had improved my fighting skills and with all the anger I had built up inside me I knew I'd whip some ass.

They ain't never fuck with me though. I guess they felt my O.G. aura or something.

Still, there was one person who never seemed the least bit frightened-- Josh. I'll never forget the day I walked into the hallway and saw him staring at me with a soul chilling smile as his bald head seemed to take up the entire hallway.

I had been seeing him the entire school year. Usually he just acted as though he didn't see me but I guess since he's down with The Supreme, shits different now. Damn. For a while I still had hopes of us overcoming all the bullshit and getting back to the way we used to be. But after seeing that, I knew it was over. It hurt me, but I had to move on. Our relationship was fully out of my hands. I know I said it before but I really know it's over now. Yep, sad but true.

Chapter 12

"Get up. It's time for school," shouted Mom as she banged on my bedroom door. No matter how big I got in the Warriors, Mom always reminded me that I wasn't quite grown yet. She got on my nerves treating me like I was five sometimes but fuck it, she missed out on three years of telling me what to do. She deserved this. That's the main reason I hadn't quit school yet, I saw her cry so much I just wanted to see her smile.

Thank God, it was only three more months of school left. I couldn't wait for this shit to be over. As graduation approached it seemed to be harder and harder to walk through those double doors each morning. To this day, I can still see the disgust in the teachers eyes as they stared through me. But I been dealing with shit like that for years now so I'm pretty much immune to it.

Beaumounts classes were ten times harder than the rinky dink shit they call lessons, so it really wasn't the work that I was tired of. What irked me each and every day was the Rules. Here I am one of the Leaders in the biggest Family's to ever touch American soil and I have to ask permission to use the bathroom. What kinda sense does that make? Why am I respecting rules from mo'fuckers I'm 100% positive that I'm smarter than. These niggas say their trying to set me up for a bright future and shit but little do they know, my futures my present, I'm already living my dream. Maybe I should be the one teaching them a thing or two. On days I was really pissed off I always had the urge to just whip out a wad of cash and make it rain on a teacher while screaming, *"Dance bitch dance."* I don't know why but that just seem like some real player shit to do, show them who's really boss. But since I know I'd never have the balls to do anything like that, I just knock the days out one by one. School and jail, one and the same.

Before class every morning I'd walk down the block to my whip. I was still hiding it from my Mom like I did everything. She's been real cool lately though. She'd heard about the Warriors around town and she never even suspected that I was a member. In fact she told me that maybe I should talk to some of the members in my school and let them know that their headed on the wrong path. I didn't want to prolong the conversation so I just said, "OK."

And since the summer was over, she knew I wasn't working construction anymore so she'd do little things like slip me twenty or thirty dollars and tell me, *"God is good."* She'd look so happy when she did it, that shit was funny as hell. Still, I wish she was cool like Trell's Mom. As long as he was bringing in some gwop, she didn't care what the hell he did. Trell was even able to buy his Mom a new Nissan Altima. But, hey fuck it, DaDa always said you gotta play with the hand you're dealt. Hiding shit was still a million times better than being locked up.

I walked towards my whip admiring myself in the reflection of cars when I heard a vehicle creeping up from behind me. Without looking I already knew who it was; Detective Fraley and bitch ass Smalls. They did this at least twice a week. Ride past staring and shit. Never said nothing, just stared. At first I was nervous, now I just stare back, fuck them.

Like always they sped off once they past me but this time, about thirty seconds later I heard another car creeping up. They had never came back twice so I was a little

255

apprehensive about turning around. I was only a few feet away from my car and I didn't want to lose anytime turning around and it be some bald headed cracker. But as they crept closer and closer the suspense was killing me. I counted to three and quickly turned my head.

It was Trell, in his 83 Caprice Classic. Usually I would know it was him because he'd have his music blasting, he must be tryna scare me, it worked.

Trell rolled his window down before speaking, "Nigga when you gon stop hidin this car from your Mama?"

"When I get a new Mama," I said sarcastically.

"Damn," Trell said laughing. I could tell he wasn't just laughing about my joke. I always knew when he was in a real good mood, he always grinned and bopped his head up and down like he was listening to some music that only he could hear. His ass must've just came home from some strippers crib or something. He didn't bother coming back to school this year so he could always stay out as late as he wanted. "Well I'll see you lata dog. I'm on my way to the hospital. My seed on his way hea."

"Foreal?" I said excitedly. I was the baby's God father. A lil boy, I couldn't wait to spoil him. Or at least try to spoil him. I know Trell ass gon already buy the nigga everything imaginable. "Congrats my nigga," I said walking over to his whip. I'ma be up there lata."

Alright bro," Trell said dapping me up. "I'm bouta be a Daddy," he shouted still bopping.

I drove down the street bumpin some Lil Boosie. He always got my mind right before I went to school. He had this one song called *'Give up'* that always put me where I needed to be. Sharee hated him. She said his voice was annoying, I know soon as she hops in the car she's gonna try to turn to some RnB bullshit. I wish I could tell her about the Warriors so I could just cop her a whip so she can stop touching shit in mines.

I pulled up to her crib, reclined my seat back and blew the horn, I knew she was gonna take forever, it never fails. As the minutes flew by I grew more and more impatient. She's usually late but not this late. No question, her ass is definitely gonna be late to her own damn funeral. After even more minutes tick tocked away, I was going insane. I'd like to consider myself a patient nigga but this shit is uncalled for. I called her three times and even blew the horn a few more times and still no Sharee. Finally, enraged I stormed over to her door. Her Mom was at work so I proceeded to bang like the Police. This was the last time she was gonna pull a stunt like this. Hadn't she heard, time is money!

After a minute of banging I finally heard the sound of the door being unlocked. I was prepared to cuss her ass out but as soon as she opened the door she shot straight back to the bathroom, not saying a word.

"Baby, You alright?" I asked calmly, forgetting how angry I was. I followed behind her as she fell to the floor vomiting into the toilet. "Damn bae what you eat last night?" I asked, dropping to the floor beside her.

Sharee got up, forgetting to acknowledge me once again and walked straight to her bedroom.

"Sharee. What the hell goin on?" I said as I continued following behind.

257

Sharee then reached onto her top dresser drawer and held up what I thought was some funny looking pen until I took a closer look and realized it was a pregnancy test. A positive pregnancy test.

"What I'ma do?" Sharee whined.

"Baby don't even worry about that. We can do this," I said.

I didn't understand the problem. By the time the baby would be born we'd both be 18. She was tripping.

"We can do this? What the fuck? I just got accepted to Howard. What the fuck am I gonna do. My Mom's gonna kill me. I'm so fucking stupid," she said dropping to the floor crying uncontrollably.

"Baby chill out," I said dropping next to her. "Everybody got kids round hea it's cool," I said attempting to comfort her.

"It's cool? It's cool?" she asked looking me in the eyes as she fought back tears "What? Are you gonna take care of our baby with your little drug dealer money? Huh?"

"Huh?" I asked.

I was shocked, Sharee had never acknowledged how I got money. She knew the construction job was over but I always tried to make it seem like someone in my family had given me some money every time we went out or something. I knew how she felt about dirty money and I tried my best to hide it. I thought it had been working. Guess not.

"What?" she screamed "You think I don't know about the Warriors Pete?"

I guess she knew everything. I hope she ain't know bout the bitches.

"You're so dumb. No fuck that. I'm dumb. I should've went with my instincts and left you alone. I'm stupid," she said banging her head with her fist. I tried to restrain her but she violently pushed me away. "Don't you know you're going back to jail?"

I looked away. I can't lie the thought of jail had crossed my mind a few times, but we were too smart for that, we were professionals. Still, knowing Sharee, she wouldn't be tryna hear that shit so I remained silent.

"Is that what you want for your child? To grow up without a Dad just like you. Just like me?" I stood silent as she stared at me with her right hand on her hip and left foot out. "Oh my God I'm so stupid. I always said I wouldn't but look at me. I'm so stupid, stupid, stupid," she said finally breaking down, screaming and crying.

Yet again I couldn't control myself and sprinkles of tears began dropping from the corners of my eyes as I failed to find a way to comfort her. "You needa make a decision," she said finally gaining her strength. "Us or the streets."

We stared at each other. I couldn't believe what she was saying. My mind went blank. I need to talk to Sho.

Sharee didn't say one word to me the entire ride to school. No good bye kiss, nothing. At lunch we usually sat together at the front of the cafeteria with all the cool kids but today, she sat in the back with the teachers. This wasn't that unusual, she was real cool with all of them but she never even looked my way and I was too scared to walk over to them. This the kinda shit that'll make a young nigga get high blood pressure.

By last period. I was a wreck. I kept replaying in my mind the last thing she'd said to me *'Us or the streets'* Why the fuck did she have to say that? Life been so good? I know she scared that the same thing that happened to her Dad might happen to me but it wouldn't-- I think. Man I don't know, all I know is that I couldn't wait till the bell rung for dismissal. I wasn't in the mood for all this learning and shit.

"I want everyone to write a Eulogy," said Mr. Johnson the twelfth grade English teacher. He was my only black male teacher but he didn't really act like it. This whole school year I can't remember him using any incorrect grammar or even a simple slang word, something was real strange about this nigga.

"Eulogy?" said Amy the class dumbass.

"Yes. I want you to write from the future as if you've died, from the point of view of someone close to you," he said looking around the room. "I want you to write as if you had lived a great life. I need to know how you want to be remembered. Graduation is approaching and you guys are about to experience the real world," he said as the bell rung. "It's due tomorrow. Everyone will present in front of the class. Good luck," he said as everyone packed up their belongings.

Forget what that nigga was talking about, I'll just do that shit at lunch. At that moment my heart was so heavy, I couldn't even find enough strength to get out of my seat, resulting in me being the last nigga left in class. This only meant trouble.

"Come here man," said Mr. Johnson who was standing at his desk. I slowly walked over. I should've known he would do some shit like this. "You ok?" he asked sounding concerned. "You been kinda quiet today."

"Yeah I'm good," I said.

This nigga was always trying to be nice to me. He was cool and all but I'd rather he be like the other teachers and treat me like I didn't exist. At least I always knew what to expect. Sho told me when a nigga was too nice he was up to something.

"Ok. You been thinking about college?"

College? This nigga must ain't no how much cash I had. I got fifty thousand dollars stashed away. College can kiss my ass.

"Naw. I don't really think I got the right credentials for all that," I said.

"Sure you do," he said. "Just start off at a community college. That's what I did."

"Alright I'ma keep that in mind," I said hoping that would shut him up.

"OK. If you ever have any questions call me. My numbers on your syllabus.

"Alright Mr. Johnson," I said as we shook hands. I rushed out of class, I had to get away from his crazy ass.

When I finally arrived at the hospital Lil Trell had already made his appearances and he was now laying asleep in some germ proof room along with about ten or fifteen other babies as Sho, Trell and a few other parents watched from a huge glass window. It felt good to see Lil Trell but there was no way I could fully focus on him.

"Look, he got your long ass head," Sho said playfully.

"Fuck you," said Trell.

"Sharee's pregnant," I said staring at the baby. I couldn't hold it any longer.

"What?" shouted Trell in disbelief.

"Bout time. What took yall so damn long?" asked Sho. The way he stared at me I couldn't tell if the question was rhetorical or not.

"Congrats my nigga. Ain't no betta feelin in the world," said Trell looking back over to his son.

"Yo how April feel about the Warriors?" I asked.

I still couldn't manage to take my eyes from Trell's son. To think, in a matter of months that would be my seed laying there.

"She cool with it as long as I keep puttin that money in her hands," Trell said.

262

I already knew the answer. I don't even know why I asked that shit. My Mom and Sharee were the only two cornballs in Norview who had so called *'Morals'* and shit.

"I ain't even gon ask bout your Babymama's," I said looking over to Sho.

"Nigga my Babymama's wanna be Warriors," he said smiling. "You gotta start wearin the big drawers. Wheneva she start talkin that bull shit, put a blunt in her mouth. That'll calm her down. Shit, that's what I do."

That sounded nice but Sharee hates smoke, I gotta spray cologne on and pop visine's whenever I'm high around her.

"Sharee don't even smoke. Plus she pregnant, she can't smoke weed," I said.

"What?" he exclaimed. His reaction made me feel as though I had said the dumbest shit known to man or something. "Boy, all my Babymama's smoked durin they pregnancy. Weed ain't neva hurt nobody. That shit's from the earth. Nigga you crazy as hell," said Sho as he and Trell slapped five.

In a way I kinda agreed with Sho too. All his kids were super smart. Hell, those niggas knew all the latest songs word for word. They even knew about sex. I'll never forget the time his three year old son Lil Sho had seen me with a banging ass broad over at Amy's and when she got up to take a piss he looked over to me and said, *"You gon hit that ass tonight?"* Yo, that had to be the funniest thing I ever heard. I swear that nigga gonna be gifted or something. How he know to ask some shit like that at three years old. Crazy.

263

"Anyway," I said changing the subject. "Sharee told me it's eitha her and the baby or the Warriors."

"What?" Sho shouted causing the other parents and the receptionist who sat at her desk behind us to look over. "She fuckin trippin," he said in a low stern voice. "You needa start smackin that bitch," he said pointing to me aggressively.

Sho had told me plenty of times that you gotta discipline females like kids or they'll act up. Sure that was cool for him but Sharee was a whole other type of girl. Sharee wanted to be a counselor, she had real goals. Sho's girls ain't have no goals. Yeah, a couple of them wanted to be nurses but every hood bitch wanted to be a nurse. Knowing goodness well they ass probably never even finished high school. They never thought about life ten years from now, shit, I never really did either. I mean, I said I'd be doing this but to be honest I never gave it to much thought up until now. I guess I was just living for the moment.

"So yall tellin me yall think we can do this foreva?" I asked.

"Hell yeah! Why not? Long as we keep shit organized and niggas happy, we good foreva."

"Yeah Pete. We good," followed Trell.

For the first time in my life it hit me that I'd listened to Sho for so long that I didn't know how to think for myself. I was lost. All I knew was that I had to be in my child's life. I always felt incomplete without a Dad and there's no way I could allow my child to grow up like that. But I vowed to Sho, I'd be a Warrior for life. I could never betray him. Plus I don't know how to do shit. I don't got

264

any special talents or hobbies. How could I take care of a child without the Warriors?

When I got home that night I stayed up weighting my options. Sharee wasn't answering any of my calls. She never did this before. I knew she was serious. Still, I wondered if I could be able to hide the Warriors from her. It didn't take long to realize that would be damn near impossible. She was too smart for that. And even if I could, it was only so long I could hide it. After a while I even tried to think of positive ways I could take care of a child. Maybe Mr. Johnson was right. Maybe I could go to a Community College of something. I could still work with the Warriors on the side. Sharee would never figure that out. But what if she did? I couldn't risk not seeing my child. It was then, when it was the furthest thing from my mind I found the inspiration for Mr. Johnsons eulogy. I grabbed a pen and pad and thoughts poured onto the paper. I still didn't know how I'd handle things but I knew I had to be in my child's life.

After another day of being completely ignored by Sharee, I was back inside Mr. Johnson's class, front and center. I hated reading in front of the class but Mr. Johnson insisted.

I cleared my throat and read, *"Samuel Turna aka Pete was a lot of different thangs, he was a friend, a husband, a son, a millionaire...But most importantly he was my dad. I was born when my dad was only 18. He was just a kid himself. He neva had a dad of his own so he really had no idea what he was doin. But you'd neva guess it. He was my football, basketball, and baseball coach. He was neva really too good at sports so we neva really won any games... But I wouldn't trade those memories for the world.*

265

I still rememba when he took me fishin, it was both of our first time. He always liked to act like he knew what he was doin but it was clear he didn't... We were out there for bout 3 hours and we didn't catch nothin. I could tell he was gettin mad til he saw a fish jump up for air. Next thang I know he's jumpin in the water after it. He neva got the fish but at least he learned how to swim that day. My Dad taught me how to be a man. And to me that's amazin cause I don't know who taught him. But I do know that the Lord might've taken my Dad earlier than I might've wanted him too. But no one can eva take the memories he left with me. I love you dad."

I finished and realized tears were flowing down my eyes as every black student in class stood to their feet. I received a standing ovation as the bell rung. That was shocking enough but what really got me was the fact that I had actually cried in front of people. Sho would definitely not approve of that.

I darted out of class and immediately bumped into Sharee. Of course she pretended she didn't see me and continued to walk away but I wouldn't let her leave my site. I couldn't take her ignoring me any longer.

"You needa ride home?" I asked smiling attempting to break the awkwardness. "I'm not leaving," she said, still not looking at me. But shit, I was just glad she was actually speaking. I missed her voice. "I have to teach the J.V. cheerleaders some cheers for next year."

"You sure it's a good idea to be jumpin around in your condition," I said grabbing her arm to stop her from walking.

266

"I'm pregnant Pete, not crippled," she said sounding annoyed. "And I'm telling my Mom about our little situation tonight when she gets off. Be there," she said before continuing to walk.

Oh snap maybe she was bullshitting about me choosing between the Warriors and her. Either way I wasn't going to mention it. But I'd damn sure be there. "Alright," I said.

"Then we're going to your house to tell your Mom."

Sharee had me so worked up about choosing between her and the Warriors that I had completely forgot about telling my Mom. I know she was gonna spazz. She had never talked about sex with me but I knew her well enough to know this wasn't a good thing.

"What?" I asked. "Damn. Do we have to?"

"Yep," answered Sharee looking straight into my eyes while walking even faster.

I speeded up alongside of her. "No kiss?" I asked puckering up playfully.

"Nope," she said looking straight ahead.

"Damn."

Just looking at her walk away made me realize why I couldn't let her leave. I gawked at Sharee's video vixen physique getting smaller and smaller until worrisome ass Mr. Johnson walked up on me.

"Hey Pete," he said smiling. Man this nigga will not leave me alone. "You did an excellent job on your eulogy."

"Thanks Mr. Johnson," I said still trying to figure out his angle. No teacher had ever told me I had done well on anything. I gotta admit it felt pretty damn good.

"You busy right now?" he asked. I really wanted to lie and say yeah but shit he was the first teacher to ever give me a compliment so I guess he kinda deserved a pass.

"Naw. What up?"

"You mind taking a ride with me? I wanna show you something?"

Ah man, I knew I should've lied. Shit! What could he possibly want to show me. "Yeah why not," I answered regretfully.

"Cool. My cars around back," he said motioning for me to follow him.

When we got to his car, he had a Mercedes S550. I had seen the car in the parking lot before and always wondered who it was. I assumed it was the Principals or something, I'd never thought a teacher would be pushing something like this. I mean damn, where the hell was his minivan? I looked around before I got into the car. Even though the whip was bangin I ain't want anyone to see me with him. Cruising around with a teacher was almost as bad as cruising around with the police.

When we drove off. This nigga was playing some Biggie, "Ready 2 Die." We both looked at each other when it came on. He damn sure didn't look like a Biggie type of nigga. More like a Will Smith, MC Hammer type. We drove for about forty five minutes. During that time we somehow got on the topic of new age rappers versus old school. I told him that rappers now a days are ten times better than his old school dinosaur rappers. He started talking about Big L, Nas, OutKast, Jay-Z. I had heard of all of them and they were cool and all but they jams was weak compared to Nipsey Hussle, Gucci, Boosie and Kendrick Lamar. After an intense argument we both agreed to disagree. But I was in awe that he was an actual cool dude. He was cursing and everything. I guess the sayings right, you really can't judge a book by its cover. Before I knew it we were in Richmond. I had been talking for so long that I had forgotten to even ask where the hell we were going.

"This is the B-Lo. This is where I was born and raised," he said pointing out the window. The neighborhood looked like some shit off the Wire. There were people everywhere. No, not regular people, ghetto people, trash was everywhere, houses were boarded up. This was the kinda place The Warriors could make a killing at. But shit, what do I know, Sho probably already getting money out here.

I couldn't believe this was where he grew up. How the hell did something like this create someone like him?

"Man I used to get into all types of shit out here," he said smiling, reminiscing as we pulled up further to an old boarded up home. "Until I met Mr. James. He lived right there. He was the only person I knew who owned his own home," he said as he looked as if he could still see Mr. James sitting on the porch. "I don't know what drew me to him but I used to go sit with him on his porch all the time. His wisdom probably saved my life," he said still staring at the home.

"Where's he at now?' I asked curiously. I really wanted to know. Mr. Johnson made him seem so interesting.

269

"He died a few years back," he said shaking his head before pausing. He continued staring at the house as if he was about to start bawling any second. "Hey I need to stop past my crib. It's on the way back to school. I forgot my work out gear. You mind?" he asked quickly changing up the entire vibe in the car."

"That's cool," I said.

We talked on the way to his house about how he always thought he wanted to be a rapper growing up until he finally realized he couldn't rap. He said he always had these stories in his head and he assumed rap was the only way to get them out until Mr. James told him he should write books. After that he started studying anything that had to do with the art of storytelling. That's what led him to becoming an English teacher. He never forgot what Mr. James had told him though and within the last ten years he's published four books. 'Last of a Team', 'Raw', 'Laser', and 'Pocket' under the pen name Jonathan James. And what was crazy was the fact that 'Raw' was one of my favorite books when I was locked up. When I asked why he'd never told any of us about his books he said he liked it that way. He only taught because he loved helping students. And once I saw his crib I knew he wasn't lying. He lived in East Point. Everybody in Norview knew about East Point, it was the only neighborhood in Norview that you had to know a password to get in the gate. That damn Teachers salary couldn't even pay for the utility bills in these cribs.

"This your crib?" I asked admiring his house along with the other beautiful homes around it? His spot was huge. I didn't even know they let black people live in hoods-- excuse me, *Neighborhoods* like this.

270

The crib was all brick but the bricks didn't really look like bricks, they were a tanish color and he had big wooden double doors that matched with the huge windows spreaded out around. The grass was like some sorta florescent green and every piece seemed to be the exact same length as the others. There was no trash in the gutters, not even a stray leaf, his driveway didn't even have any old oil stains. And the craziest thing about the crib was that it was probably the least expensive on the whole block.

"Yep this is my house," he said as he called his Wife and asked her to bring out his gym bag.

"Damn," I said still staring at the crib before some tall, exotic, model looking chick stepped out, forcing me to glance over to Mr. Johnson. He was an ugly dude. He really must got some long money to pull something like that. I tried not to stare too hard as she glided over.

"Hey baby," she said kissing him on the cheek and handing over his Nike gym bag.

"Hey babe," he said looking over to me. "This is the kid Pete I'm always telling you about. We were just hanging out a bit."

"Hey Pete," she said smiling.

"Hey. How are you doing?" I asked tryna figure out what he could possibly have told her about me.

"Great," she said smiling, somehow growing even more beautiful.

"Well I'm about to drop him off. I know he doesn't want to hang out with an old man all day."

"Ok bye honey. Nice meeting you Pete."

"Nice meeting you too," I said as Mr. Johnson drove off.

We pulled up to the school. Mr. Johnson already knew which car was mine. "Remember Pete you can be anything you want to be in life. But you gotta look deep inside and tell yourself that I don't wanna be just another nigga," he said as I nodded. "Just because you were dealt a bad hand doesn't mean you can't win in the end," he said making sure he looked me in the eyes.

"Thanks Mr. Johnson. Foreal man thanks." We shook hands and I jumped out and hopped in my whip. I had a brand new respect for the man.

I pulled up to my daily parking spot. A lot of shit was weighing down on me, my head could no longer take it as it collapsed in my lap.

BOW POW BANG were the sounds that rang in my ear as glass shattered around me. Making sure not to waste a second ,I ducked my head down further. I was being shot at. My body trembled as I struggled frantically to discover my next move. I remembered that Sho had put a gun in my glove compartment but I was too scared to lift my head and reach over to get it. Besides Sho had never even showed me how to use the thing. I always said that if something like this ever happened I'd just say a prayer so that if I died I'd still go to heaven. That was obviously before I'd ever been in a situation like this, the thought of Prayer never even crossed my mind.

After what seemed like forever, I heard the car skirt off. I instantly felt all over my body, I hadn't been hit "Thank God," I shouted.

I hopped out the car and examined my whip. It was fucked. Bullet holes everywhere. Every window was gone and both drivers side tires were flat. This didn't feel real. It couldn't be. Again I felt my body for gunshots wounds. How hadn't I been hit?

Soon neighbors rushed out from everywhere. *"You good? You OK? Do you want me to call the police,"* they said.

Fuck them, I ignored everyone before maneuvering my way through the crowd. I sprinted down the street, Forest Gump style. If this wont a sign then I don't know what a sign is. I felt like the biggest fool on earth, how could I ever even consider the Warriors over my son. Was I crazy?

I ran up to Sharee's door and banged. When she opened I hugged her tighter than I'd ever done before. Everything was so clear. I was beginning my new journey in life.

Chapter 13

I convinced Sharee that we should set up a meeting with the both of our parents. I figured it would be a lot easier to kill 2 birds with one stone.

They both were visibly upset about the pregnancy. But surprisingly neither of them fussed. It might've been the fact that we made it so that we looked like two sad puppies when we told them. I don't know, but they still had a long talk about how we had to grow up now and that we weren't little kids anymore. Neither of us said anything. We both just listened, well I pretended to listen. I recently learned that as long as you make sure parents feel there in full control they don't talk as much.

After the talk Sharee worked with the counselors at school and got accepted to Norview State. It damn sure wasn't Howard but at least she could stay home and still go to school. Everything worked out perfectly.

I was even working with Mr. Johnson on getting into some type of college. I still ain't know what the hell I wanted to be but he said it didn't matter. *"College would be the time I could figure it all out."*

I even found my first job. I was now a part time cook, slash flunky at the world famous Burger King. From the day I first stepped my feet in that sauna they call a kitchen, I hated it. The smell, the people, the shit stains left in the toilet that I was forced to clean, everything. I couldn't stand it. Never in a million years I'd imagine I'd be working like a slave for $5.75. The homies couldn't believe what I had done. Left all that gwop I was bringing in for this shit. But what can I say, I ain't have no choice.

Once you're a father you're a man and a man's gotta do what a man's gotta do.

After I got the gig, I convinced DaDa to let Sho pickup the packages, he agreed. It wasn't too hard to get him to do it. He and Sho had become cool as a bitch these last months. Plus DaDa said he thought it was dope that I was doing something positive. He said he'd do it too but he's too far gone, he'd grown to be addicted.

Sho on the other hand called me every name in the book, but as long as he had the connect, I knew he really ain't give a damn.

And I didn't completely give everything up. Mama ain't raise no fool. I still had that fifty g's stashed away. I was gonna make that shit stretch for as long as humanly possible.

It would be easy for me to be upset about the way my life's drastically changed but despite all the hurdles I'd been faced with lately I still gotta say everything was going great for me.

I wish I could say the same for others. Before leaving the Warriors I had made the crucial mistake of telling Sho about my car getting hit up. He went bizerk. He felt the Warriors didn't have enough respect. So he made the lil homies turn it up a notch. Whiteys wont just getting fucked up no more. They were now getting beat to a bloody pulp. And that was just the beginning. I'll never forget the day I turned on the news and saw that Detective Fraley had been found slump, dead in his whip. I can't lie I hated the man but I never wished death. Needless to say I didn't even have to ask who did it. I already knew. Surprisingly I was kinda sad. Deep inside I knew that I had somehow found myself involved in yet another murder. Still, that was far from the worse.

The night me and Trell sat in his whip staring at the school marquee that read *'R.I.P. Josh You Will Be Missed'* will undoubtedly haunt me eternally. We both sat next to each other sobbing as the entire town met up in the school football field. Blacks and whites alike consoled each other as they held candles to the sky in his honor. Seems like people had really had enough of this black on white shit. It was time for a change. This was by far the saddest shit I'd seen since seeing Pops die.

Sho had really went overboard this time. Even though Josh and me were probably never gonna be cool again I still felt like I'd lost a part of me and I know for a fact that Trell felt the same way, he knew Josh his entire life. That night me and Trell both came to the conclusion that it was time to part all ties with Sho. It would be hard but we had to do it. He killed our brother.

After that Trell even signed up to get his G.E.D. He decided that the Military was where he needed to be. Josh's death was definitely an awakening.

Chapter 14

Just when things seemed like they couldn't possibly get any worse, God blessed me. The moment that had seemed so far away for as long as I can remember had finally arrived-- Graduation. Not only was I graduating but it was also my 18th birthday. After everything it took to get here, who would've ever believed I'd actually make it. I looked up into the stands of the hundreds of people in attendance and saw my family with balloons all dressed up for me, I felt accomplished. After a quick assessment I realized that right now, graduating was the only real accomplishment I'd ever made. And to think, a year ago I was just getting out of jail unsure of what I'd be doing. Today I was in a cap and gown graduating alongside the most beautiful girl in the world who was also carrying my baby. I had a job and plans for the future. This was only the beginning. I couldn't wait to live life and feel like this a million more times. Like my Mom would say. *'God was good.'* I had defied the statistics and I was on my way to being a real man. Nothing could ruin this day.

After graduation my Mom threw a huge graduation slash birthday cookout for me at the Norview Park. Music was bumpin, food banging, black people, and even a few white people were out mingling peacefully amongst each other, it was perfect, and everyone was having a ball. Everyone besides Sho. I had still been ignoring him and I prayed he didn't show up. I had been avoiding him at all costs. In a way I felt bad but I knew this is what I had to do.

Me, Sharee and Ciara were standing by the food tables kicking it when Mrs. Red walked up. She looked exactly the same as I remembered her from Wellington

Oaks when I was a child, only prettier. She hadn't lost any weight or anything but I don't remember her having those hazel eyes and long thick hair. I couldn't help but to search her face for bruises. I don't think she could tell though "Hey Pete," she said hugging me tight.

"Hey Mrs. Red," I said.

I ain't seen you in years, she said stepping back. "I'm so proud of you."

"Thanks Mrs. Red" I said as she looked over to Sharee.

"I see you got you a pretty one. Make sure you treat her right."

"No doubt," I said looking over to Sharee as she blushed.

"Ok I'ma talk to yall later," she said looking over to the table full of food. "I gotta go make me a plate before it's all gone," she said cheerfully smiling. "I'm so proud of you Pete," she said again before walking away, with her huge booty swaying left and right damn near knocking people over

Trell walked over accompanied by April and his son. They looked like they were about to enter some Ebony family of the year contest of something. This wasn't unusual, neither Trell or April would even think to step out the house looking average. I always told Trell he'd found his soul mate. There aren't too many people who care as much about themselves as Trell but April was damn sure one of them. Both of their three favorite words were Me, Myself and I. I can only imagine how Lil Trell will turn out.

278

"You did it Bruh," he said dapping me up.

"Damn right," I said happily as Sharee looked over to the baby.

"Oh my God. He is too cute. I can't wait till I have my little bundle," she said rubbing her protruding belly.

"Girl you better have patience cause once you have him, sleep will be a thing of the past," said April looking deeply into Lil Trell's eyes. "But it's worth it."

My Mom walked over from behind and tickled the baby. "Hey Precious," she said smiling.

"Hey Ms. Turner," April said in a baby voice as everyone smiled.

"Aww he's so cute, said Ma before turning her attention over to me. "Pete come out here and dance with your Mama, this is my song," she said as she grabbed my hand pulling me to the little basketball court we were using as a dance floor.

Some old school song was playing that I'd never heard of. Obviously my Mom had, she was singing along to every word. The happiness she was feeling right now had subtracted about ten years from her face. I hated dancing but seeing her like this, I was left with no choice. So I did a little two step and let her hold my arms as she got busy.

"Pete, I'm so proud of you and the man you've become. I'm upset about the whole pregnancy thing but I see you making positive strives and that's all I can ask for," she said as tears rolled down her face.

"Ma, what's wrong?"

279

"I just look at you and I see your Father. He had so many dreams. I still remember the first time he held you. He said *'This boy don't look like a Samuel, he looks just like this genius kid named Pete from High School,"* she said attempting to sound like a man.

"Ma, I know you told me a million times," I said. She really did tell me a million times. I knew she had to be reminiscing any time she bought that up.

"He always knew you'd be somebody special, baby. He'd be so proud of you. I love you Pete," she said with tears still pouring down her face.

"I love you too, Ma."

'Before I let go' by Frankie Beverly and Maze came blasting through the speakers and my Mom along with all the other old folks went wild. You would've thought Frankie Beverly and Maze had made a special appearance at the cookout of something.

"Boy this was me and your Daddy's song," she said grabbing both my arms. From the way she looked at me I bet she felt that she was actually dancing with my Father. I had no choice but to play along. I mean she is the only Mother I had. So I danced. I'd never danced in public before in my life but today I danced and honestly I liked it. I wished I could've bottled the moment up and saved it forever.

Especially considering what happened next. Police units pulled up from every direction with sirens blaring. All eyes focused on the vehicles. What the hell were they doing here? No one knew what was going on. Did they think Sho was here? What was going on? Then in what seemed surreal all attention turned to me as Policeman rushed over with guns drawn.

"No!" screamed my Mom.

The look on her face as the cops ordered me to get down on the ground mixed with Sharee dropping to her knees in sorrow, broke me down, I couldn't take anymore, I fainted.

Chapter 15

I sat in the jail visitation room in my jumper, sitting across from my lawyer Daniel Jolley as some Mexican C.O. stood in the corner. I was the only inmate in the room.

"They don't have anything on you," he said holding the phone to his ear.

"So why the fuck I'm still in this bitch?" I asked with force.

"They got it out for you man. They think you killed a cop. Remember?" he said.

"Man fuck that. My son was born last week. I gotta get outta hea."

"And I'm gonna get you outta here. Don't forget, I'm the one who got you off a capital murder case. Trials in three months. You're going home."

Man fuck what he was talking about. I slammed the phone down and looked over to the C.O. "I'm ready," I commanded.

He escorted me to my cell. The feds had indicted me on thirty three charges. Everything from the distribution of drugs to murder. They arrested Sho, Trell and some other Warriors too. Our faces were plastered all over the news. They had been watching us for months.

The C.O. opened the entrance to my one man cell. All I had inside was a toddler size mat that I laid on the floor, a sink and a toilet. They say they put me in a one man for my own safety. But I think they just wanted me to go crazy and start snitching. But I was cool. It gave me a lot of time to think. I hated being caged in like an animal but I had faith I was getting out. I had too. I already missed out on my son being born. There was no way I was missing out on anything else. I was getting out and that's all it is to it.

They didn't allow us to talk to any of our codefendants but Sho had taught all of us not to say anything and that's exactly what I did. It worked for me last time. I just had to be patient. Patience was the key.

I had to learn to block myself out from what was happening in the real world. It was driving me crazy. I found myself alone crying nightly. This bid seemed even tougher than the last one. This time I actually had a life on the outside. A good one. I only open mailed with my sons picture in it and I refused visits from everyone besides my lawyer. I finally understood why Sharee's Dad had stopped communicating with them. I was ashamed of myself. Besides, there was no use in me talking to anyone. I had a family out there and I couldn't even help them. Fuck that. Fuck everything. Fuck the world.

After what had seem like an eternity. It was finally court day. I sported a gray three piece suit, Steve Madden loafers and my waves were on 360. I was feeling good for the first time in months. My entire family including Mr. Johnson was there to support me.

Best of all I saw my son for the first time in person. Pictures didn't do him justice. He looked identical to me. He even had the family head. I was itching to hold him, I couldn't help but to keep turning around and gazing at him. Every time I did, Sharee would mouth the words *'I love you'*. It was good to see she understood the reason I was unable to keep in contact with them. This bought a sorta peace over me. This may be a good sign. Plus everything was going just how my lawyer said it would. They had nothing on me. Nothing. He was eating them alive. For fifty thousand dollars he better I spent my entire life savings on him. But freedom would be worth it.

He was like a boxer out there. I was just waiting for him to knock 'em dead. But he was playing it smooth. I could tell by the way he winked at me after giving his statement. That was definitely a good thing.

As he sat down this white skinny chicken looking prosecutor, Ms. Jones stood up. She was the same prosecutor from the Officer McNair trial. We had a mutual understanding-- we both hated each other's guts.

"Your honor. We would like to bring a surprise witness," she said.

Surprise witness?

"Granted," said the judge as the bailiff opened the door.

I wanted to hop up out of my seat as I saw a man who looked like Sho trot in. But it couldn't be. But indeed it was. He slowly walked in looking as though he hadn't showered or shaved in decades, wearing shackles on his hands and feet, head hanging low not once looking over.

This must've been some sorta master plan he'd been scheming up while he was locked. I may not like everything he does but I can't lie the nigga is definitely smart as hell. He probably figured a way to get all of this bullshit out the way.

Sho approached the bench and sat down. Ms. Jones paced back and forth silently before questioning Sho.

"What's your name sir?" she asked.

"Shomar Galloway," he said emotionless, still not looking at anyone but Ms Jones.

The courtroom was dead silent.

"And what's your relation to Mr. Turner?"

"He my first cousin."

"First cousin huh? And would you say you two were close?"

"Yeah we were like brothers."

Damn we were like brothers and I just stopped talking to him with no explanation. What kinda brother was I?

"And Mr. Galloway. What are the Warriors?"

"A gang."

"A gang that participates in illegal activity?" she asked still never turning to face the crowd. It was as if her and Sho were the only ones in the room.

"Yes."

"And are you a part of the Warriors street gang Mr. Galloway?"

"Yes I am."

285

"And what is your rank in the gang?"

"Second in command."

"Is Mr. Turner a part of the Warriors street gang, Mr. Galloway?"

"Yes Ma'am."

Whoa what the hell is going on? Sho was losing me. I didn't know what was going on.

"And what's his rank?"

"First in command."

Everyone in court gasped as I peered deep into Sho's soulless eyes. I knew he could feel me. What the hell was he doing? I thought the number one rule a man should live by was never snitch. But this wasn't even snitching. He was lying. I wasn't first in command. I mean yeah I was *'The Plug'* but we both know I ain't know shit about nothing. What the fuck?

For the next fifteen minutes Sho spilled out gallons of bullshit to the prosecutor. He told her that I was the one who introduced him to DaDa. I set up the murders after my car got shot up. He even had other Warriors testify against me in written statements. I felt like death. I grew up thinking Sho was the true definition of what a man was. Didn't he realize that I could tell about Officer McNair? Did he care that at any given time I would've died for him and here he was killing me with no mask? I always thought he had all the answers. Turns out the blind was leading the blind. My entire life had been a lie.

When it came time for deliberating my lawyer and I walked to the backroom. I have no idea how I actually made it back though, I couldn't feel a single bone in my body. My world seemed completely ruined. How could he do this? This couldn't be real. The only thing I could think to mutter as me and Daniel sat down was "Yo. What the fuck is this?"

"Don't worry the Jury will never listen to a convicted felon. Relax," he said trying to convince himself. I wasn't convinced. I fell onto the floor. I wasn't unconscious, I just simply couldn't move.

By the time I managed to stand to my feet it was ShowTime.

I couldn't bear to look at my family. I walked right past them, depressed, I was fed up with myself.

For the second time in my young existence, my life was in the hands of someone else. I knew if I got some time this won't just gonna effect me. This would affect my entire family.

Korbin, besides smoking a few blunts with him from time to time I had been completely ignoring him. Now what man is he gonna look up too? Is he gonna follow my path?

I turned around to take a look at my son. I could only look for a second because the sight of Sharee and the rest of my family was killing me. Still they were the least of my worries.

My son. Who would be there for him? Who would be there to protect him from niggas like Sho? I know

287

Sharee's gonna be the perfect Mother but can a Woman teach a boy how to be a man?

I fell into a dizzy daze as Judge Manley banged his gavel.

"Will the defendant and his representatives please rise."

I gathered every bit of strength left in me and stood, locked eyes with the judge and prayed to God for Mercy.

"The Jury had deliberated and has come to a decision," he said staring back at me. "The Jury has found Samuel Turner Jr. guilty on all charges. And he faces the minimum, of 181 years in a federal corrections unit with no eligibility of parole.

The sounds of horror lit up the room. I distinctively heard Sharee and my Mom call out. My mind was blown. I couldn't comprehend what he had said. I slowly looked back at my screaming family. I told myself I had to be strong. I have to be. I'm a man.

Out of nowhere my knees buckled as my body dropped like a sack of potatoes to the ground. Fuck being a man. I was dead. I had never even held my child. Never took him to a football game. Never seen him walk, give him a spanking, talk to him about sex. Teach him to tie a shoe, talk to a girl. I never got to buy him his first condoms. Go on any family trips. No family pictures. I never got to buy us a house, cut the grass in the house. Marry Sharee. Watch her graduate, go on our honeymoon. Watch my son go to the prom. I'd never go the gas station, go to the movies, make love, take a walk around the block. Talk on a cell phone. Eat my Grandma's cooking. I was never doing shit again. I really was dead.

"You got me 181 years," I shouted, picking myself up before conjuring up all the strength I could to punch my lawyer square in the face. "I'ma kill you," I said as I continued colliding my fist with his face.

The courtroom went into a frenzy as three sheriffs darted over to me like vultures on their prey, ferociously dragging me to the ground.

Time ceased. I looked over to my son, he was already staring at me.

Part 2: 'American Maniac' out now!

If you enjoyed American Boy make sure you spread the word.

If you purchased on Amazon or Kindle please leave a review.

If you're incarcerated please request to get this book and my other novels 'American Rap Star', 'American Maniac, 'Us Vs. Them', and my latest, 'American Dream', in the building!

Thank you for the support. If you need to contact me:
Phone: 757-708-4890
Facebook: Kevin Brown
Instagram: __KevinBrown
Website:KevinBrownBooks.com